The Programmed Man

by the same author

THE HELIX FILE

THE PROGRAMMED MAN

MAN

WILLIAM D. BLANKENSHIP

WALKER AND COMPANY
New York

First published in the United States of America in 1973 by the Walker Publishing Company, Inc.

Published simultaneously in Canada by Fitzhenry & Whiteside, Limited, Toronto.

ISBN: 0-8027-5279-9

Library of Congress Catalog Card Number: 72-96502

Printed in the United States of America

10 9 8 7 6 5 4 3 2 1

For all the kids:
Lisa,
Doug,
Kristen,
Adam,
and
Beth

CHAPTER 1

THE ADDRESS I had been given turned out to be an old two-story pink stucco building on Century Boulevard out near the Hollywood Park race track. The first floor, once a retail store, had been converted to office space. Drapes covered the showroom windows on the inside. They were the kind you rent from an office furnishings company, rather tattered from being taken down, carried around in trucks, and put back up again. I found it difficult to believe that a couple of million dollars in stolen industrial secrets might be hidden behind those dismal beige rags.

There was no lettering on the windows, though a small piece of white paper was taped to the front door at eye level. I sat in my car a couple of minutes watching the office and listening to the jet planes howl in for their landings a couple of miles down the boulevard at L.A. International, then got out and crossed the street.

The small, hand-lettered sign announced very modestly that this was the Computer Specialties Company. I went in. The door closed behind me with a whoosh of pneumatic air and I found myself standing on a dusty square of beige carpeting that matched the drapes. On one side of the room stood two scratched old chairs that must have decorated barber shops for fifty years before ending up here. Between them, the inevitable end table that should have been supporting a pile of old magazines. The bulk of the office had been partitioned off behind a cheap painted plywood wall, so that I was standing in what served as an outer office.

A shadow moved behind the single curtained doorway between the outer and inner offices. Then the curtain parted with a slight rustle and a man slipped through quickly, as if trying to keep visitors from peeking past the folds of the swaying beige material.

"What can I do for you?" he asked, looking first at me and then slightly past me to make sure I was alone.

"My name is Michael Saxon. I'm a salesman for Data Peripherals." I extended my hand with the unctuous cordiality of an eager salesman. "I noticed that you've just opened your office and I decided to stop in and say hello. I might be of service to you. We manufacture quite a complete line of peripheral computer products, you know."

He didn't want to shake my hand. But when I'd been smiling and holding it out for ten seconds he came forward another five feet to acknowledge the introduction. He was about thirty, with close-clipped wiry brown hair. A very big man. Taller than me by five inches, and I measure a couple of inches over six feet. The hand that closed around mine had the casual strength of an Alaskan brown bear. He was wearing an expensive but very sober grey suit and the heels of his shoes made that brisk clapping sound produced only by expensive British

2

wingtips. He had an executive-suite face, wide and square and big-boned, with tiny dark eyes. I'd seen that face on the sports pages some years ago, but I couldn't recall the name that went with it.

"What kind of data processing work does your company do, Mr. . . . ?"

He sighed. "Franklin. Adam Franklin. We're a service bureau. We'll be handling data processing jobs for small businessmen who need only a few hours of computer time a month."

His slightly bluish lips stayed tight and thin even as he spoke. I was reminded of the prissy, cold mouths I've seen on clergymen who think they have exclusive communications with God. His name was familiar, too.

"Perhaps you'd be interested in talking about a lease on one of our computers," I went on. "We have a new two hundred and fifty-six K model that leases for only three hundred dollars a month."

"Sounds good. We might be interested."

His hand touched my elbow gently, a little hint that I could be on my way now. Body talk. Very subtle and nicely done. But a computer with a two hundred and fifty-six K core memory would cost several thousand dollars a month to lease, and why didn't he know that?

"When can we talk about it?"

"Next week some time."

"Tuesday?"

"Sure. Tuesday's fine."

"About noon? I'd like to take you to lunch."

"Lunch would be great. I'll look forward to it."

Obviously he planned to be gone by Tuesday. The whole setup had been put together just to have a

3

place where Franklin could set up a computer terminal. He was using the terminal's long distance teleprocessing connection to reach into a computer complex four hundred miles to the north in Palo Alto, California, where my client, the InterComp Corporation, was located. I wanted very badly to take a look at their back room. I was wondering how to manage that when a terminal suddenly started clacking away in the rear and Adam Franklin's semifriendly expression fell off to a chilly stare.

From behind the partition, a girl's voice called to Franklin: "It's coming through. We're getting the last of it." The voice was flat, revealing no pleasure in the announcement. The kind of voice you hear on recorded messages.

Franklin turned on his heel and went back through the curtain.

"Shut up!" I heard him say quietly, though not quietly enough. "There's someone out there."

"Who is it?" A little touch of anguish and worry in the voice now.

"No one. A salesman. I'll get rid of him."

When he came back through the curtain I strained and caught just a glimpse of a young girl, red hair and brown dress, head down over a computer terminal, staring at the printout paper churning through the machine at the noisy rate of several hundred lines per minute.

"You'll have to come back," he said. This time it was a command. "We're busy as hell right now."

"Then I might as well tell you I'm not a salesman." I took out one of my cards and held it out to him. "My name is Michael Saxon. Saxon Security Systems. I'm in the business of industrial security,

4

Franklin, and I've been hired by the InterComp Corporation to look into the use you're making of that computer terminal back there."

He didn't accept the card so I slipped it back in my pocket. The little dark eyes had shrunk to the size of raisins.

"I see." He hissed the words like a Gestapo colonel in a movie. "Well, there's nothing for you to investigate. We've broken no laws. Get out of here right now and tell your people at InterComp they'll be hearing from my attorney." The raisin eyes were widening like a shutter opening in a camera. "This isn't the first time a big corporation has tried to stifle a growing empire." His voice was rising, too, and he started moving toward me in a hunched, catlike way. I had sense enough to see this wasn't an act; he was working himself up into a genuine fury. "I've been pushed around by big companies before, but this time things will be different," he continued. "This time I'm going to *win!*"

"Win what? All you have here is a new way to steal. You sit down at a computer terminal and snatch a few million dollars' worth of information out of another computer four hundred miles away. Long distance larceny. Don't try to tell me you're an honest businessman being frozen out by a bigger company. You're a thief, Franklin."

I tried to move sideways as his big forearm came at me, but I didn't make it. He caught me across the neck with a wrist as hard as an iron bar and I went spinning against the plywood wall. The girl screamed and ran out through the curtain, yelling, "What's happening? Stop!" Franklin put one of those expensive English wingtips against her stomach and pushed her back into the rear office. By the time I got to my feet he was facing me, grinning, those blue lips even tighter. I couldn't understand why he hadn't followed up his attack while he had me on the floor, but as I straightened and faced him he slipped his big right hand into an unusually bulky leather glove. I'd seen gloves like that before, when I was on the L.A. police force. Some of the rougher cops carry them. They're called knuckle sap gloves. They aren't too different from regular gloves, except that the fingers are weighted with lead. A small man can take your head off with one punch using a knuckle sap glove. There's no telling how much damage a big man like Franklin could do. He came toward me in a shuffle, his left shoulder in front of him and his right gloved fist swinging loosely at his waist. When they move like that you have only one choice: stay low and ignore the left hand. Wait for the blockbuster right to come for you and try to get out of its way or get far enough inside to go for the man's jewels with your knee.

He threw a few exploratory jabs with his left, which I slapped away with the palm of my hand. Then I took a chance and shot a lucky right foot into his left kneecap. Franklin yelled and let his left hand drop to his knee for support and at the same time I lunged at him, trying to get inside. But I'd taken too much time recovering from throwing that kick, and before I reached him he brought his right hand in tight with a very short punch that caught me in the right shoulder. The gloved hand seemed to tear clear through my shoulder. I grunted like a bull and fell. Another arcing right hand came down at me and I rolled and struggled upward. His fist tore

6

along the surface of the floor, erupting big chunks of tile and wood. When he came at me this time I couldn't raise my right arm and so he chopped me once in the face with his left and then once more with that deadly right fist going cleanly into my stomach. The air came up out of my diaphragm with a booming sound and the world turned black.

Some time later I tried to sit up and found that my gut was twisted into knots the size of baseballs and my right arm was numb from the collarbone down. I sat on the floor a long time waiting for the pain to ease. Trying to draw a normal breath. And wondering why I'd let myself be drawn into this disaster.

The disaster had begun a couple of hours earlier, at about nine-thirty, when I answered my office phone. A voice boomed: "Michael Saxon? This is George Francis Hogan at the InterComp Corporation! I want you to pay close attention to me. I'm calling long distance and I don't intend to repeat myself."

Hogan's hot, demanding voice had been trembling slightly. Before I could ask his consent to tape record the call, he plunged on. "About thirty minutes ago someone managed to bypass the security codes on our computer system and dial into the computer by long distance phone from Los Angeles. The number they called from is . . . Are you getting this, Saxon?"

"I am, Mr. Hogan. But I'd appreciate it if you'd slow down a little. I'll want to ask questions as you go along."

He paused. I heard him take a few deeply measured breaths. I could almost see him struggling to

7

regain control of himself. "You're right, Saxon. I have a big problem and I can't afford to panic."

"Where are you calling from?"

"The InterComp corporate headquarters in Palo Alto. You probably know our company. We make small computer systems. My problem is this: our central computer here in Palo Alto is connected by telephone lines to branch offices around the country, but someone other than one of the branch offices just dialed into our computer using a teleprocessing terminal. They're stealing valuable information right out of the computer. That's not supposed to be possible! There are security codes you have to know in order to gain access to our computer."

"Obviously someone's stolen your codes. What kind of information are they after?"

"The designs for a new product we're about to market. It's a mini-computer that can take the place of cash registers in supermarkets and department stores. We call it System/Sell." His voice began quavering again. "We've spent *millions* developing this product. There are *hundreds* of jobs at stake here."

"You have the number they called from?"

"Yes. It's not listed, of course." I heard a paper rattle and a second later Hogan gave me a phone number with a 213 area code, which could have been anywhere in the greater Los Angeles area from Santa Monica to Pasadena.

I wrote it down and asked Hogan, "Who discovered the theft?"

"Mickey Iwasaka. He's manager of our internal systems department. He happened to be monitoring the long distance lines this morning because he suspected one of our computer operators was calling

8

his girl friend in Denver on the company phone."

"Was he?"

"I don't know. What difference would it make?"

"None. I was just curious. We'll run down this phone number right away and find out who's gotten into your computer. If I can, I'll recover whatever information they've taken. Meanwhile, I'd suggest you put a programmer to work changing your security codes."

"I'll do it myself," Hogan answered brusquely.

At that moment I recalled seeing a story on Inter-Comp in the *Wall Street Journal* about two weeks ago. InterComp was announcing System/Sell, and it was mentioned that Hogan had just assumed the presidency of the company following the sudden death of InterComp's founder, Arthur Avery.

"Another question, Hogan. How did your company's former president, Arthur Avery, die?"

"He was killed in a hit-and-run accident just a few weeks ago. A tragic thing. So useless. I was vice-president in charge of marketing and the board of directors appointed me to fill his shoes. Believe me, he's a tough man to follow." Hogan sounded genuinely sad, but as the point of my question became apparent his voice quickened. "Why are you asking that? What are you implying?"

We both knew what I was implying, but neither of us wanted to talk about it. Could this theft of information be linked in any way with the sudden death of Arthur Avery? It was too early to bring the possibility out in the open.

"I'm not implying anything. Just asking a question. I'll put one of my best men on your problem and by this afternoon . . ."

9

"I thought you understood," Hogan interrupted. "I don't want one of your men working on my case. I want you to handle it personally."

"Sorry. I seldom do the legwork on a case myself. But I assure you the man I plan to assign is highly qualified in this type of . . ."

"I don't care how qualified he is. I want *you*, Saxon. The article in *Fortune* magazine said you like to get out from behind your desk to run important cases yourself. That's why I called you."

I groaned inwardly. Six months ago *Fortune* ran a piece on me that brought in a hell of a lot of business. But one paragraph in the story left the unfortunate impression that I personally handle many of the jobs that come into my shop. It gave the profile a nice touch, but what the writer implied wasn't strictly true:

Within three years Michael Saxon, a thirty-year-old iconoclastic former Los Angeles policeman who earned a master's degree in business at the University of Southern California, has transformed his one-man private detective agency into a multimillion dollar corporation. Saxon Security Systems now employs twelve hundred security guards in a dozen western cities and provides uniformed guards and other security services for many of the blue chip companies in the west. But despite his new image as a corporate whiz, Saxon still likes to get out of his office and run important cases himself.

I cleared my throat and launched into the pitch I've developed to change a client's mind about demanding that I work on his case personally.

"When I direct a case personally, Mr. Hogan, I get

five thousand dollars a day with a minimum guarantee of five days' work. You'd have to guarantee me twenty-five thousand dollars. And it might run to more than that, depending on the complexity of the case."

"Twenty-five K!" Hogan sputtered. The letter K stands for the figure one thousand in the hexadecimal computer world. "That's a hell of a fee for a private investigator."

"I agree. The going rate for one of my staff investigators is only two hundred dollars a day, with no guarantees involved. Why don't you let me turn the case over to my staff."

To my surprise, Hogan said, "No. There are millions of dollars at stake in System/Sell. I want the best help I can buy. You're hired, Saxon. Get to work on it."

"Right away," was the only answer I could give him. "I'll be back to you this afternoon. Will you be in your office?"

"Yes. I'll talk to you then."

I was about to put down the phone when Hogan said, "Just a minute. I'm wondering why a sharp graduate of a top business school like USC is running a glorified private detective agency."

"Haven't you heard, Mr. Hogan? Crime is a growth business."

I said goodbye, put my finger on the telephone cradle, and lifted it immediately to get a dial tone. I called an old friend at the telephone company, Roger Max, chief of security for the Southern California district.

"Roger Max."

"Good morning, Roger. This is Mike Saxon. I have

11

an unlisted phone number here and I need the name and address of the person or company it belongs to."

Roger groaned. "You know I can't give you that kind of information. You're a private investigator, not the police."

"Come on, Roger. Bend a rule. It'll make your day."

"I can't, Mike."

"You owe me a favor."

"We both have rules we have to live by," Roger said patiently.

"Loose interpretation. That's the secret."

"No, Mike. That's final."

"I could still find the blueprints to that little black box if I had to."

"You son of a bitch. I'll be doing favors for you the rest of my life. What's the number?" I gave it to him and he said, "Hang on. I'm putting you on hold."

The receiver clicked into a neutral nonsound and I waited. The "black box'" was a device that a smart engineer in Hollywood invented a couple of years ago. You could plug it into any pay telephone and make all the long distance calls you wanted for nothing. Before my agency caught up with him for the phone company he'd sold more than fifty of them around Los Angeles at a thousand dollars a copy.

Roger came back on the line and told me, "The number belongs to a company called Computer Specialties. They're located out near Los Angeles International Airport at 5545 Century Boulevard. Is that sufficient, master?"

"You have done well, my son. The gods are pleased."

"Go screw yourself, Mike."

"So long, Roger."

I put down the phone and wrote out the name and address of Computer Specialties in my notebook, then asked my secretary to call Joe Bacon and Lou Hemphill into my office. I also asked her to clear my calendar for the rest of the week.

I had time before Joe and Lou came in to make one more call. This one went to my stockbroker, Harry Sharp, a man of such low and devious character that just talking to him makes me feel more respectable—which is the main reason I do business with him.

He answered with his usual bluff good nature and I said as quickly as I could, "Harry, this is Mike Saxon. I don't want to buy or sell any stock today. I just need some . . ."

"I'm delighted you called," Harry said smoothly. He went on to ignore my opening remark. "I know you must be unhappy with that convenience food stock I put you into last month, but how was I to know they were buying diseased chickens from Paraguay? Anyway, you have to average out your losses and I've found a nice little utility in New Jersey that . . ."

"Harry. Shut up about chickens and utilities. I need information about the InterComp Corporation."

"InterComp? Good company. Had a rough time last year but it looks like this year might be a winner for them."

"Because of System/Sell?"

"Right. If they meet their market projections with that new product they could earn a dollar a share this year."

"What if System/Sell falls through for them? For instance, suppose a competitor jumps into the marketplace with an identical product."

Harry snorted. "Then goodbye InterComp." He lowered his voice to the intimate level he uses when he's pitching a stock. "Cash flow is their big problem. The banks are carrying almost eighty million dollars of commercial paper on InterComp. Four months ago InterComp had to sell its corporate headquarters building and plant in Palo Alto to an insurance company on a lease-back deal to get cash for current operations. They also laid off three hundred people. Their stock is selling at a multiple of fifteen, which could go up to twenty-five if they do good business with System/Sell. But if System/Sell bombs, three things will happen: InterComp's stock will drop. They won't get another cent in financing from the banks. And instead of being able to hire back those three hundred employees, they'll probably have to lay off another thousand people."

"But System/Sell could solve their problems?"

"You bet. They're really at a critical point. It's make it or break it time for InterComp."

"Thanks for the information, Harry."

"Why don't you let me pick up a hundred shares of InterComp for you, Mike."

"Not today."

"Fifty shares . . . ?"

"No."

Harry was silent only briefly. "Then let me say just two words that could mean a small fortune to you: Coconut oil! Do you have any idea how many ways coconut oil is being used today? I can buy you coconut oil futures for only . . ."

14

"Goodbye, Harry."

Joe and Lou were already settled in chairs in front of me. "I've just agreed to take on a case personally," I told them. "The InterComp Corporation is the client. I might be gone a good part of this week. Is there anything we should talk about?"

I made a show of locking my desk to give Joe and Lou a chance to exchange disapproving glances. They don't like me to take on cases myself, no matter what the fee is. Joe is a former military policeman who runs the force of twelve hundred uniformed guards we employ. Lou manages our branch offices and the staff investigators, about three hundred people. He and I broke in together as rookies at the old University station on Jefferson Boulevard.

"We're negotiating a new contract for plant guards at Wallenback Chemicals tomorrow," Joe said. "Wallenback expects you to attend the meeting."

"Tell him I'm on a case."

"He won't like that, Mike. He's the kind who expects to negotiate with the top man."

"Use your famous diplomatic touch, Joe." His face reddened straight up to his crew cut. Joe has no diplomatic talent and knows it.

"I'll do that," he said.

"Lou? No words from you?"

"You know I'm against the idea of you handling cases personally. Mike, you're the figurehead for this company. Suppose you go out on this InterComp job and it blows up in your face. The bad publicity could cost us a lot of business we can't afford to lose. We've expanded awfully fast in the last fiscal year.

15

Maybe too fast. Any revenue we lose now comes right out of the bottom line."

I smiled at Lou's little speech. "When you and I were busting stick-up artists and dope pushers over on Sunset a few years ago, I never thought we'd be talking about *expansion* and *bottom lines* and *fiscal years*. Don't worry, Lou. I like the good life, too. I won't take any chances that could hurt our business."

Joe Bacon stood up. "I've got an appointment, Mike. Good luck to you."

"Good luck with Wallenback."

"I might need one of our men in the Bay area," I said to Lou. "Someone is using InterComp's computer security codes to rob their own computer. I'd like to put a man into their plant to find out how those codes got into the wrong hands."

"It's an inside job," Lou said flatly. "You'll need someone with electronic experience." He pulled out a fat notebook that he uses to keep track of every one of our three hundred plainclothes investigators day by day. He thumbed through it and said, "There's not a man free in the San Francisco office."

"How come? We wrapped up the case at that Berkeley stock and bond house on Friday."

"Yeah. But this morning the five biggest department store chains in San Francisco dropped a nice piece of business in our laps. It seems there's a new shoplifting ring in town that's costing them a fortune. They think the operation is run from Argentina, no less."

"So who do I use in Palo Alto?"

Lou stopped and frowned at one of the pages in his notebook. "Paul Avilla is on vacation up north.
16

He's staying with a cousin or an uncle on a fruit ranch in the Santa Clara Valley. Here's the number where he can be reached." He passed the notebook to me and I wrote the number down.

"Paul would be a good man for this job."

"I suppose so," Lou agreed sourly. Paul Avilla is not one of Lou's favorite people.

"I'm on my way then."

"Be careful," Lou cautioned. "Try to watch your ass and our goddam image at the same time."

Sitting there on the floor in the empty offices of the Computer Specialties Company, I was painfully aware that I'd done a rotten job of following Lou's advice. Both my ass and image were suffering, but I was more concerned about number one than I was about number two. I'm a little too big and rumpled and shaggy in the hair to fit the image of the typical corporate executive anyway. Besides that I have a big welt of a scar that meanders like a lazy river from the corner of my mouth up toward my right ear and makes bankers reluctant to loan me money.

I tried moving again. It was better this time. My legs were still like rubber but my arm and stomach were no longer paralyzed with pain. I stood up. Things went in and out of focus for a few seconds. Franklin and the girl were gone, of course. The terminal in the back room was silent. It was another ten minutes before I felt well enough to go outside. When I did, the late morning sun and the sharp little breezes from the ocean made me feel almost human. I looked at my watch and discovered I'd been out of action less than thirty minutes.

Down the street from Computer Specialties some

17

red and yellow pennants were flying and a quick squirrel of a man in a green sports shirt and baseball cap was waving his arms at the passing traffic. The pennants were attached to a sign that said: JOCKEY JOE. BEST PICKS AT HOLLY-PARK. BUY YOUR WINNERS HERE. I walked slowly down to him and stopped at a big bulletin board set up on an easel. Dozens of colored envelopes were pinned to the board labeled *Third Race* or *Sixth Race* or *Daily Double* or whatever combination of races you might want to win.

"Two bucks a race, dude." Jockey Joe went up on his little toes. "You buy three races and I throw in the Daily Double, which is usually four bucks alone."

"Sure things?"

He was very amused at that. But he didn't let on. Instead he answered the question as seriously as I had asked it. "Absolutely. In my time I rode forty-two winners at this track, and I know just what every nag can do. I got the winners, dude. Don't you worry."

"I'm not worried. I don't play the horses."

Jockey Joe shrugged lightly. "Then move along and make room, dude. I don't need conversation. I need customers."

"I didn't say I wasn't buying. I just said I don't play the ponies."

The jockey stretched himself to his full four and a half feet. His face withered into the twisted grin of a malicious child. "So what do you want to buy?" A tiny finger flicked a ladybug off the sleeve of his sports shirt.

"Are you at this stand every day?"

"Most of the season. I move around a lot in my

business."

"I'd like to know who you've seen going into the first floor office in that building." I pointed toward the office where Adam Franklin had clobbered me.

"Ahhh." Jockey Joe grinned up at me. "I get it. You're a private cop on a divorce case."

"What makes you think that?"

"You said something about buying . . ."

"Sure. I'll take all eight races."

Jockey Joe's fingers flew over the bulletin board. He handed me eight envelopes and I gave him a twenty-dollar bill.

"Now. The big guy and the broad. They're the only ones going in and out of that place."

"A businessman type? A girl with light red hair?"

"That's them. The office was empty till three or four days ago. Then I noticed a truck unload some stuff, and pretty soon the big guy and the broad turned up."

"When do they come and go? Do they keep regular business hours?"

"Nah. I figure they're makin' it together in there. Wait a minute." A dusty Pontiac pulled up to the curb and Jockey Joe rushed to it, standing on his toes to lean inside and talk to the driver. He gestured forcefully as he spoke. I could catch a few words: "sure thing . . . a bundle today . . . rode forty-two winners here . . ." After a couple of minutes of that he gave the man behind the wheel three envelopes and accepted six dollars. The driver beamed over the deal he'd made and sped away. The car had Iowa license plates.

"A tourist," Jockey Joe said with happy contempt. "My best customers. Let's see. I was gonna tell you about the broad and the big guy. They show up about nine in the morning. In a cab. Leave around noon. I think they come in on one of the morning planes from San Francisco and go back north again in the afternoon."

"Why do you think that?"

"Yesterday she was carrying one of those big flat loaves of San Francisco sourdough bread. You've seen them. They sell the bread in the airport up there in those red and blue packages."

"Yes. I've seen them." What the jockey guessed made sense. This girl and Franklin must certainly have connections with InterComp in northern California.

"What about the man?"

"You said it already. A corporation type. A very cold piece, too. One of those guys who doesn't like anybody to have more fun than he does. That's all I know about him except that today he was pretty sore."

"How do you know that?"

"A half hour ago the broad came tearing out by herself and caught a cab. Right after you went in. Looked like she was headed for the airport. Then a couple of minutes later the big guy charged out, too. Grabbed a cab for himself. Went the same direction. I figured they'd been using that dumpy office to do a little balling and her husband hired you to catch 'em at it. That's why they took off so fast. Am I right?"

"You're close, Joe. Thanks for your help. And I'll take my four dollars change now."

The little jock winced. "Cheap bastard," he grumbled. He handed over the four dollars and turned away abruptly, raising his arms again and waving at the oncoming traffic.

I went to my car and slid gingerly behind the wheel. I was feeling dizzy but the sharp pains in my shoulder and stomach had been replaced by steadily throbbing muscle contractions that were easier to live with. I found a tin of aspirin in the glove compartment and swallowed four of them. With my car pointed toward L.A. International, I tried to piece together what had happened. I thought it likely the girl had become scared and run out on Franklin. Since Franklin went after her as soon as he had finished with me, perhaps she'd taken that pile of computer printout with her. If so, I still had a good chance of recovering at least part of the plans for System/Sell.

I pulled into the airport parking lot closest to the Pacific Airlines terminal. Pacific flies to San Francisco from Los Angeles every hour and it's the carrier almost everyone uses to go up and down the coast. I gambled that Franklin and the girl used it, too. From the trunk of my Mercedes I took the small pigskin overnight case that I carry in the car for quick emergency trips. It's always packed with three complete changes of shirts, underwear, socks, and a portable cassette tape recorder with the insides ripped out to hold my Walther PPK automatic and two loaded ammunition clips. It's against the law these days to carry firearms aboard a passenger flight, so I keep the gun inside the tape recorder in case I have to go past one of the magnetometers that searches out metallic objects in hand luggage. When a ticket agent looks in my luggage he's easily satisfied that the tape recorder made the alarm flash and I can then walk on through. I don't like to do that, but

21

when I have someone under surveillance I can't very well call attention to myself by checking my handgun in with the pilot. Lou Hemphill gets gas pains when he hears I've been doing that.

I hurried to the ticket desk at Pacific Airlines and discovered I'd just missed a flight to San Francisco. New headline for *Fortune*: SAXON NAPS WHILE KNAVES NIP OFF. I retired to a bar to think and nurse my bruises. I ordered Wild Turkey and water in a small lounge behind the baggage claim area, a dark place where bored passengers pass the time between flights and scared ones fortify themselves for certain death.

As I was wondering how I would ever catch up to Franklin and the girl, my eyes were becoming accustomed to the dark. Soon I could pick out faces and details like the patterns of peoples' clothes and the labels on the bottles behind the bar. I tried not to look startled when I noticed the red-haired girl in the dark dress tucked away in the very last booth in the bar. She was the girl from the back room at Computer Specialties. Franklin wasn't with her, and she looked glad of it. She sat there nursing a beer, tearing little pieces off the napkin under the glass. Her eyes darted toward the door occasionally, as if she feared Franklin would walk in on her. Apparently she hadn't gotten a good enough look at me to recognize me now. You just can't underestimate the importance of luck in this business.

I put my back to the girl and studied her in the mirror. She was one of the street people. Her clothes consisted of a long loose granny dress made out of cheap material on someone's home sewing machine, with her hair tied back and held together by one of

22

those combination barrettes and pencil holders waitresses often use. Very round face. Large dark eyes with grey circles underneath. Clean delicate features that reminded me of the stark white face on the red cameo necklace my grandmother used to wear. Little inconsistencies here and there suggested the girl had only recently gone to the Raggedy Ann look. Her makeup was simple but carefully done. Nails manicured. Dinner ring with little diamonds flashing on the fourth finger of her right hand. A canvas tote bag full of computer printout paper was lying on the table by the beer.

Twenty minutes before the next San Francisco flight was due to leave she stood up abruptly and went to the door of the lounge, paused, peered outside, walked brusquely toward the boarding areas. I followed at a good distance, losing her once when I stopped to buy a ticket for San Francisco.

When I got to the boarding gate I found her already in line. I fell in two places behind her. She kept shooting those big dark eyes all over the terminal looking for Franklin. I'd figured out how she lost him. Fairly smart for a scared girl. Instead of running for the first flight to San Francisco, she hid in the bar and let the last flight go without her. Franklin probably looked for her and decided she'd taken another airline to San Francisco to lose him. And so he took off for the other terminals to find her. He was probably still looking.

The agent was checking tickets routinely, calling each person's name as we went through the gate. He paused when he saw the girl's name on the ticket envelope.

"Miss Lane? There was a gentleman looking for

23

you when the last San Francisco flight left. Did he find you?"

"Yes. It's all right." The agent was all smiles. A happy passenger is a return passenger. She went past him into the long uteruslike connection from the terminal to the airplane with me close behind her. Once in the plane, she took an aisle seat about halfway down the cabin.

I caught a better look at her as I went down the aisle past her. Her eyes were moist. Permanently moist, I suspected. Like a dog's. They were eyes that had been on the verge of tears for a long time. I found an aisle seat six rows behind her and wondered if I would find out today what was making this girl so unhappy.

As soon as the big jet lifted off over the ocean and climbed to about twenty thousand feet the stewardesses began circulating through the cabin. They collect your tickets on the plane on the commuter flights. I like to fly Pacific Airlines when I go north because they parallel the coastline most of the way up and you can see all that white sand on the beaches below and an occasional freighter working its way along the coast and even the kelp beds floating close to the shore. Oh yes. Pacific Airlines also has the best-looking stewardesses in the world. Tall, long-legged girls in boots and bright yellow mini-skirt uniforms.

I still had my eye on the red-haired girl when I handed one of the stewardesses my ticket.

"I'm sorry, sir. Your ticket isn't valid for this flight. I'm afraid you'll have to leave the aircraft."

"Leave the plane? We're at twenty thousand feet and going . . . Sandy! How the hell are you? God,

24

you look terrific. I was thinking about you just this morning."

"Sure you were." Sandy Rawlings tore the pink stub off my ticket and handed it back a little more aggressively than usual. "I haven't seen or heard from you for six months, but *this morning* you were thinking about me. Uh huh."

She moved to the next row of seats and continued collecting the tickets, looking back over her shoulder to rake me once more with a half angry, half sardonic stare. Her swirls of blonde hair were stacked high under the little pillbox stewardess hat and she moved with an efficiency produced by a perfect symmetry of strong thighs, arms muscled just enough to ripple pleasurably with every movement, and shoulders that would have been too wide for a girl without Sandy's bustline. Her breasts tended to make the rest of her look positively petite. I'd run into Sandy on this same flight about a year ago, and was so zapped by her that I asked her to go out with me that evening. She answered rather coolly that she never went out with passengers, so I simply settled down in my seat and decided to spend the rest of the day on the plane trying to convince her to change that rule. We went from Los Angeles to San Francisco and back to Los Angeles and then down to San Diego and then to Orange County with a load of passengers for Disneyland and up to Oakland and San José and back to Los Angeles and finally to San Diego, where Sandy lives. Toward the end of the day, whenever we stopped at an airport a bunch of other stewardesses would run on the plane to look at me and giggle and beg Sandy to bend her rule just this once. Even the pilots began making comparisons between me and *The Man Without a Country.*

When I threatened to repeat the performance the next day, Sandy grudgingly agreed to have dinner with me. I rented a car and took her to a Mexican restaurant and then to a jaialai game. By that time she'd thawed out enough to invite me back to her apartment for a nightcap. The nightcap turned out to be one of the highlights of my life. I lived on the memory of it for weeks, even after receiving an American Express bill for $542.38 for the flights, the rented car, and the dinner. We saw each other pretty regularly for six months, until I went to Colorado to find a particularly clever embezzler in a Denver bank. Somehow I'd never taken the opportunity to call Sandy after coming back from Denver. First these had been that Avis girl on Wilshire Boulevard who really did try harder and then . . .

While I was flipping through my mental memory book I almost missed seeing my redhead filling out a reservation card for a rental car. You can order your car right in the air these days, and the pilot will radio your reservation ahead. I unbuckled my seat belt, struggled out of the tiny enclosure, and walked to the rear of the cabin where Sandy and another stewardess were filling trays with cups of coffee, punch, and tea.

"How are you, Sandy? I tried to call you the other night, but you must have been on a flight."

"Liar. I moved from San Diego up to the Bay area three months ago. Redwood City. If you'd *really* tried to call me you would have known that." I stepped back a pace. She looked as if she might let one of those cups of hot coffee fly at me.

"Okay. I didn't call and I'm sorry. But I've been all over the country during the past six months, and

I didn't realize we'd formed any mutual obligations."

Her glare softened a little. "We haven't. I was just disappointed that you stopped coming around, Mike. We had some good times." She hoisted the tray on one of those beautifully tanned arms and started up the aisle.

"Are you too sore to do me a favor?"

"What kind of favor? If you want an introduction to one of the other stewardesses, forget it. I'm forgiving, but I'm not stupid."

"That red-haired girl in seat 12C just filled out a car rental form that she's going to give to you. I'd like to see it before you pass it up to the pilot."

Sandy looked suspicious.

"This is business," I assured her. "You might save her a lot of grief by showing me that card. She's in big trouble."

"She was trying not to cry when she got on," Sandy admitted. "Are you sure you want to keep that kid *out* of trouble?"

"Yes."

Sandy thought about it for a minute. Bit her lip. Let the passengers' coffee get a little too cool. She's a good-hearted girl and she knows what business I'm in. "Okay, I'll do it."

"Thanks, Sandy."

I went back to my seat and watched Sandy and the other two girls on the flight do their strenuous work, passing out coffee and Bloody Marys and smiles and just a little bit of sex to the male passengers.

They also collected a few car rental forms and when Sandy accepted one from the redhead she came back my way and passed it to me under a

27

napkin along with a cup of coffee. After a few moments I took it out and looked at the name on it. Ann Lane. A Palo Alto address. Even the phone number. I wrote them down in my notebook and passed the form back to Sandy with my empty cup.

The flight from Los Angeles to San Francisco takes just fifty-five minutes, and we were soon descending over the southern end of the bay, passing over the San Mateo bridge with the peninsula mountains on our left. I was still watching the redhead. Ann Lane. I don't know what I expected to learn, but sometimes a little movement or facial expression will tell you a lot about a person. And I did learn something about Ann Lane. As the wheels of the jet touched the runway she reached impulsively for the card you always find in the seat pocket in front of you. The one that tells you how to use the emergency doors and what to do if the oxygen mask drops down in front of you and how to use the bottom seat for flotation in case of a crash at sea. Of course, it was too late for that kind of information to be useful on this flight. But she read it as if we were just about to take off on an eight-hour trip over the polar ice cap. I realized then that she was the kind of girl who always takes precautions too late; the kind who puts her seat belt on as she pulls into the driveway or takes an aspirin when a headache is just fading away. I had an inkling now of how Ann Lane had gotten into this mess.

CHAPTER
2

As I LEFT the jet and stepped into the terminal I winked goodbye to Sandy and got a tongue stuck out at me in return. I beat Ann Lane to the rental car booth and had the keys to a new Ford in my hand before she arrived. I went out of the terminal and across to the lot where the rental cars are parked. I found mine in space number eleven and got in and waited. Ann Lane came out a minute later and climbed into a Dodge in space number fourteen.

She drove out of the airport complex and turned south on the Bayshore Freeway with me about six car lengths behind. Now I've read all the manuals about following people, but I've never been very good at it. I once lost a man I was tailing from San Antonio to Corpus Christi on a straight ribbon of lightly traveled road that goes for 150 miles with no big intersections. But I was lucky this time. She turned out to be a steady driver who moved to the right lane and stayed there for thirty minutes, until she turned west on University Avenue in Palo Alto.

After going three blocks on University she turned left onto a side street. I dropped farther back and continued following. She finally turned into the driveway of a small red house. I pulled up under a pepper tree several houses down and watched her go to the door, lugging the heavy tote bag full of computer printout with her. A girl opened the door and as Ann Lane entered I caught a glimpse of the other girl's swinging black hair.

I wrote down in my notebook the license number of an old classic black MG sitting in the carport at the end of the driveway and the number of the house. One forty-five Emerald Way. Drapes were drawn across the one window at the front of the house. I decided to take a chance on being seen to find out who lived there. I went up the street and walked up the driveway. A few years ago the state of California abolished a law requiring everyone to display their car registration in holders that were usually snapped to sun visors or steering wheel columns. Displaying the registration slips like that made it easier for cops like me to give tickets. Some of the older cars still have display holders and the MG was one of them. It felt very natural to crane my neck to look at it. The car was registered to Constance Morgan, 145 Emerald Way, Palo Alto. I wanted to give the car a parking ticket. Old habits die hard.

Instead I stepped quietly to the front door. The name on the mailbox was Mrs. William Morgan. There was something sad about the nameplate on the box. The printing had been done in the elaborate typeface you find on wedding announcements. In fact, the mailbox card had been cut down from one of those announcements to fit the name slot. Then sometime fairly recently the *Mrs.* had been lined out with a pencil. I was willing to bet a small amount that Constance Morgan was a recent divorcée, living in the small home she had once thought would be the stepping-stone to a series of larger and more comfortable homes. Its pleasantly seedy appearance and proximity to Stanford University gave me vibrations that her ex-husband was connected with the University.

I went back to my car and sat there awhile. It was almost two o'clock now. I wanted to reach George Hogan and find out if he knew Ann Lane, Constance Morgan, or Adam Franklin. But I didn't want to lose touch with that tote bag full of printout. It could be the last part they needed to be able to build their own version of System/Sell and put Hogan's company in the red.

A few minutes later both women came out. Ann Lane got into her rented car and Constance Morgan climbed behind the wheel of her MG after giving it a pat of affection. She was the kind of girl you often see riding horses in California. Lots of dark hair falling loosely behind her, man's shirt tucked into a pair of Levi's, brown suede cowboy boots, a nice figure honed to perfection by all those hours of grasping a horse solidly with the knees. Her face, too, had an outdoors cheerfulness. I wondered just what the common denominator between her and Ann Lane could be.

They drove west toward the University, but not following each other. Constance Morgan whipped the MG past a light that was just turning red and Ann Lane stopped, with me right behind her. I wasn't taking a chance on losing her now, whether she spotted me or not. But she didn't notice me. She drove to the Southern Pacific station in downtown Palo Alto and met the Morgan woman in the parking lot. They went inside the station and I got in

31

another door just in time to see them put Ann Lane's tote bag in one of the lockers. Ann Lane put a quarter in the slot, turned the key, pulled the key out. They seemed to breathe a sigh of relief in unison, as if they had completed an important pact. Ann Lane gave the key to her friend, who put it in the pocket of her Levi's.

When they left the station they split up. I followed the Lane girl to her apartment house, where she went into a second-floor apartment and pulled the drapes. Then I doubled back to the house on Emerald Drive. The MG was in the driveway. It was time to talk to George Hogan, so I returned to the train station and found a phone within view of the locker where the printout had been stashed. When I gave my name to Hogan's secretary he came on the line very quickly.

"Saxon? What have you got? Where are you?"

"I'm here in Palo Alto at the SP station."

"Palo Alto! What the hell for?"

"The people who robbed your computer brought some of your property up here. I followed one of them on the plane. Your material is in a locker at this station. I'd better stick with it until you can get someone down here with authority to open the locker and reclaim it."

After a deep silence, Hogan said, "I'll have my lawyer get a court order immediately. If he can't do it inside an hour he's fired. His name is Karl Yoder. Stay right there until he arrives, then come up here and we'll talk. InterComp is in the Stanford Industrial Park." He paused. "Sounds like you've done all right so far, Saxon. But we aren't out of the woods yet, so don't get the idea I'm going to give you a check for twenty-five thousand dollars and send you

32

back to L.A." He hung up.

I found the number Lou had given me for Paul Avilla and dialed it. A soft, giggly feminine voice with a Latin accent answered. "Hello? What do you want?"

"I want to talk with Paul Avilla."

"There's no Paul Avilla here." The giggle was gone. "Papa. Come here. Someone wants a Paul Avilla."

"Who is this? Speak or I go! Make no mistake!" The receiver trembled in my hand and I wondered if the man speaking could possibly be as big as his voice.

"My name is Michael Saxon. Paul works for me. I mean him no harm, believe me. I just want to talk to him for a minute."

"Doan give me that talk, mister. You think I'm a fool? Hell no I ain't no fool! I doan see you but I know I crack your skull with this fist! And I doan know no Paul Avilla!"

"Okay. But if you should see him in the next half hour ask him to call Mike Saxon." I gave him the number I was at as fast as I could talk and added, "Got that?"

"No I doan got that! Go away! Fall down dead! And doan call back or I kill you with my hands!" The phone slammed down. I put a finger in my left ear to clear the buzzing sound that lingered there. Paul's relatives are very protective toward him. The last time I tried to reach him away from the office I made the mistake of showing up unannounced in the middle of the night at his cousin's farm outside Fresno. There's still a small indentation on the side of my neck from the point of the knife Paul's cousin put to my throat on his doorstep. The phone rang

33

and I picked it up immediately.

"Paul?"

"Hey boss. Good to hear from you."

"Really? That's not the impression I got from the jolly green giant I just talked to."

"One of my cousins. Francisco. And he's no giant. He's only five foot three but he was born with an enlarged voice box. He's never lost an argument in his life."

"I can see why. I'm sorry about barging into your vacation, Paul. But I need you for a couple of days. I'm in Palo Alto and I want to put you inside a company here to check out a few leads on a case."

Paul groaned. "The apricots are coming in, Mike. They are so sweet that the bees are committing suicide by flying into them at full force. I'm eating one right now. Why don't you forget your case and come down here with me. I have a wonderful girl for you. A cousin of mine. Very beautiful. Only twenty-two and a widow. Her husband died trying to satisfy her sexually. Even when his corpse went to rigor mortis his prong would not stiffen, so completely had she used him up. How about it?"

"I'd like to, Paul. But I can't walk away from this case. And I need you."

Paul sighed. Not your ordinary sigh. A great long Latino sigh full of pain and understanding and sacrifice and lost love and noble friendship. "All right, Mike. Where shall I meet you?"

"The parking lot at the InterComp Corporation in about one hour. The company is located in the industrial park in the hills behind Stanford. If I'm late, just hang loose and stay tucked out of sight."

"All right. I'll bring you some cots."

"Fine. I'll see you then."

I hung up wondering what Paul's cousin looked like. Paul has worked for me for about a year. He isn't licensed by the state as a private investigator. We carry him on our personnel records as a file clerk, but he does mostly undercover work for us. Paul became an expert at building false identities long before I met him. The reason we can't get a license for Paul is that the state would want his fingerprints and his complete history. That wouldn't do because Paul has been AWOL from the army for the past eleven years. He was drafted at the age of nineteen, a shy and almost illiterate Chicano from Moab, Utah. He was sent to Fort Lewis, Washington, for his basic training and he went willingly. But when his platoon sergeant called him a "shit head" for the hundredth time because he couldn't quite understand what people were saying, Paul decided to get out. Fort Lewis is an open post, which means you don't have to pass through any guard gates going in and out. So one night Paul simply put on his civilian clothes and packed his few personal items in a canvas bag and walked off the post. I guess that's why the army calls all small suitcases "AWOL bags."

Since then Paul has had a thousand jobs under as many different names. He once spent three months on a little island off the California coast photographing sea otters for a university research team. He drove trucks from Kansas City to Denver. Worked in the uranium mines in New Mexico. Dealt blackjack in Carson City. Sold real estate in Florida. Tuned pianos in Seattle. Inspected helicopter parts in a manufacturing plant in Dayton, Ohio. The

35

army would have forgotten about Paul years ago if it weren't for his irrepressible sense of humor. Every year on the anniversary of the day he went AWOL Paul sends a telegram to the Secretary of the Army. It always says the same thing:

PAUL AVILLA LIVES STOP PAUL AVILLA IS FREE STOP KINDEST REGARDS PVT PAUL AVILLA US 56-287-465 STOP.

I decided to place one more call before Karl Yoder arrived. To Roger Max at the phone company in Los Angeles. I called collect. I could hear the operator reach Roger and ask if he'd accept the charges from me. He did so reluctantly. When he came on the line he sounded mad.

"It's bad enough when you pressure me for information you shouldn't have, Saxon. But when you call the phone company collect to do it, you go just too damned far! Go away and don't bother me. Ever!"

"You mean you aren't interested in stopping thieves from using your precious phone lines for grand theft? Fine. I'll tell that to the newspapers when they get ahold of this story. It'll be messy for you, but I'm glad Ma Bell is too cool to care."

Roger sighed. "All right, Mike. It's been a tough day and maybe I jumped on you too fast. What have you got? Is this related to your call this morning?"

"Yes. It looks like Computer Specialties has been using your leased teleprocessing lines to get into the big daddy computer at InterComp Corporation up here in Palo Alto. That's where I am now. They've been stealing industrial secrets from InterComp. I don't have a handle on how big this is, but the value of what's been stolen probably goes up into

36

the millions."

I heard air blowing out between Roger's teeth. "I got curious about Computer Specialties after you called so I did a little checking. Nothing on them at Dun and Bradstreet. Absolute zero. On our books, they've leased teleprocessing lines six times in the past month. Each time in a different location. Stockton. Fresno. San José. San Diego. San Francisco. Los Angeles. Each time they canceled their service after less than a week. Late this morning, following your call, they canceled the service to their office on Century Boulevard. The bill was paid each time with a cashier's check."

"They work smart, Roger. They've been taking what they want in little grabs. If they'd tried to steal all the data in one or two big bites, they would have been caught right off the bat. Fortunately, I think I've stopped them from putting their hands on the last batch of information they wanted. That doesn't mean they won't try for it again. They probably will."

Roger's voice dropped to a conspiratorial level. "Can you keep the phone company out of this, Mike? It would be worth a lot to us."

"I have a client already. I can't look out for two interests at once."

"I understand." Roger was practically cooing. "But anything you could do for us while you're working for your client would be appreciated. We'd show our appreciation in the future."

Roger was telling me he'd throw more work my way if I could protect the phone company. It's a nice ethical point. I wouldn't actually be working for two clients at the same time that way.

"I can't promise much, Roger. Everything depends on how fast this case can be wrapped up, and whether my client will want to prosecute."

"Just keep me informed. That's all I ask. In return, I'll give you whatever backup you need from us."

"Fair enough. I'll call you tomorrow."

When I stepped out of the booth I still had at least half an hour to wait. Longer if Hogan's lawyer couldn't get a court order right away. The train station was quite busy now as the mid-afternoon commuter trains began dropping passengers from San Francisco. I didn't want to be too conspicuous so I went outside and moved my car to a parking place near the side entrance to the station. I could see the locker from there through the doorway.

While I waited I wondered why I ever went into this business. I'm very poor at waiting. Given the choice, I prefer any kind of action to waiting. When I first set up shop as a P.I. I used to carry a paperback book in my hip pocket to relieve the monotony of all the waiting you do in this job. But one day I became so absorbed in a book that I didn't see the guy I was supposed to be watching leave his office. How do you explain to an important client that the adventures of Sebastian Dangerfield in *The Ginger Man* became more important to you than the job you were on?

A few parking spaces away a boy of about five had been left alone in a car while his father took a package into the station. The boy was enjoying his freedom by twisting, pulling, or pushing every button he could put his hands on. The windshield wipers were swinging wildly. The headlights flashing on and off.

38

Horn blasting intermittently. Jets of water squirting across the windshield. Brake lights signaling erratically. When the boy's father returned to the car I expected him to give the kid a good crack. But he didn't. He just laughed and pushed his fingers through his son's hair. Somehow that made me feel even lonelier and more useless.

I got out of my car and walked around the station. The wide green lawn in front of the building had just been watered and a pair of sparrows were fighting over a little sump of water that had filled a shallow depression in the lawn. They flapped their wings and pecked their beaks at each other and set off a clamorous twitter. Finally one of them gave up and flew away. The winner dipped his wings in the water and strutted around it in triumph. This little parable invigorated me as much as the father's loving reaction to his son's mischief had deflated me. The world is full of predators and I was not being useless by sitting around this railroad station. I was helping to stop one of the predators.

About ten minutes later Karl Yoder arrived. He was an elderly looking middle-aged man with little tufts of white hair all over his head and great grey pouches under his eyes. I supposed that working for Hogan did that to you. With him were Mickey Iwasaka, a young Nisei with a computer symbols template sticking out of the pocket of his sports coat, and Lieutenant Joseph Pride of the Palo Alto police department.

"Saxon?" Yoder extended a frail hand. "I could not get a court order in the short amount of time George Hogan gave me." His words had a caustic flavor. I got the impression Hogan was always asking him to do the impossible. "However, Lieutenant Pride has agreed to impound the material in the locker if it can be identified as InterComp property to his satisfaction. Is that correct, lieutenant?"

"Correct," Pride said tersely. He looked at me with bored distaste. Palo Alto is a very sophisticated community, full of professors and engineers and artists and businessmen who work for high technology companies. A private investigator with a three-inch scar across his face is not particularly welcome. Even when he's temporarily associated with one of those high technology companies.

"I'll get the station master to open the locker," Pride said. We went inside together and Pride found the station master and took him aside. The station master listened to what Pride told him with an expression of awe. Pride was the kind of man who generates that reaction. He was only about five and a half feet tall, but almost that wide. No fat. Just bone and gristle. A face made up mostly of eyebrows and eyes. A mouth speaking very precisely. Expressive hands jumping constantly, as if to orchestrate his words.

He came back to us. "The station master will open the locker." His eyes flicked between us. "You should understand that if the property in that locker doesn't belong to InterComp you may each be open to civil action for infringing on the privacy of the person who rented this locker."

"I understand," Yoder answered immediately. "We accept that."

Pride nodded and we followed the station master to the lockers. He opened number fourteen and Pride reached in and took out the tote bag. Mickey

Iwasaka, who had been standing diffidently to the rear, stepped forward when he saw the printout.

"I'd like to examine that," he told Pride.

"Certainly." Pride gave him the bag and watched very intently as Iwasaka carried it over to one of the benches and laid the heavy sheets of paper down in order to handle them more easily. I found myself appreciating Pride. He was smart enough to realize he wouldn't recognize InterComp's computer printout from pumpkin seeds, so he was depending on Iwasaka's reaction to tell him whether the property belonged to InterComp.

Iwasaka certainly reacted. As soon as he began leafing through the heavy pages his already narrow eyes thinned even more. He began muttering Japanese obscenities in a low voice. After a few moments he looked to Karl Yoder. "This is our stuff, Karl. The full set of engineering changes for . . . the new product." He had avoided using the phrase System/Sell when Yoder flashed a quick negative shake of his head at him. Pride and I both noticed that.

"You can see here," Iwasaka went on, standing and balancing the heavy wad of computer paper in his arms. "The heading on several of the pages has InterComp's name on it."

Pride leafed through some of the pages while Iwasaka held the paper for him. He grunted each time he saw InterComp's name and finally nodded and said, "All right. I'm willing to accept the evidence that points to the probability this property was stolen from InterComp. I'm going to impound the printout as evidence of a crime." He helped Iwasaka stuff the material back into the tote bag and then he took charge of the bag himself.

"Charley, come on over here." The station master, who had been watching us from behind his counter, hurried to Pride. "I'm going to ask you to seal that locker, Charley." He turned to Yoder again. "Am I right in assuming this property has a value in excess of two hundred dollars?"

"Very much so," Yoder answered dryly.

"Then I'm classifying this as grand theft and I'll put a man here at the station. He'll take into custody whoever tries to open this locker. That's all, Charley. Go on about your business and try not to ogle the locker all the time."

Pride looked directly at me and said, "Now the question is, who put that material in the locker?" Yoder and Iwasaka stared at me with equal curiosity.

"It was put there by a girl named Ann Lane." I gave him the address of her apartment. "But the man behind this is named Adam Franklin. At least, that's the name he gave me." I'm not sure why I didn't give Constance Morgan's name to Pride, except that I wasn't sure just what part she had played in stealing the System/Sell plans.

"Where can we find this Adam Franklin? What's he look like?"

"He's a big man. Six foot five at least. I vaguely remember his name from the sports pages, but I can't remember what sport he played."

"I remember him," Iwasaka said. "He played basketball for the University of California about ten years ago. A rough player. He was too dirty for the Pacific Coast Conference, in fact. I remember that he had a way of getting an elbow into a man's ribs that was hard for a referee to spot. He put one man
42

from Oregon in the hospital. After he graduated he played with the Los Angeles Lakers for part of a season. He tried the same rough stuff, but it didn't work in the NBL. A couple of those animals on the Celtics smashed up one of his knees pretty bad and he never recovered quite well enough to make it in that league."

"That's our boy," I agreed. I recalled the story now. Adam Franklin had been a bay area star headed for the big time. Lots of speed and muscle and will to win, but no idea of sportsmanship at all. Even the pros draw a line somewhere. But not Adam Franklin. Knees in the balls and fingers in the eyes. That was his idea of sport.

"Okay," Pride said. "I'll take it from here. Since this is a twenty-four-hour locker, we can assume someone's going to pick up your printout between now and 3:00 P.M. tomorrow. Saxon, I'd like to see you in the morning and get the rest of your story. I know you're leaving a lot out and you'd better be ready to give me answers then."

"I will. Thanks, lieutenant." I was quite aware that he could have demanded my full cooperation at that moment, and I was grateful to him for giving me a little time. I think he knew I wanted to see George Hogan before talking to him. When you're working for a large, respected corporation you get a lot more leeway than you do when you're on some private citizen's payroll. Sometimes that ticks me off, but just now I was too happy about getting away from Pride's questions to worry about the social morality of the situation.

Yoder and Iwasaka weren't going to be that lucky. Pride told them, "I want you two to come down to the station as soon as my man gets here and fill out a formal complaint about the theft of this material."

CHAPTER 3

I LEFT THEM and got in my rented car and headed for InterComp. It took me fifteen minutes to cross Palo Alto in the late afternoon traffic. I wanted to cut through the Stanford campus, but when I tried to navigate the palm-treed circle in front of the law school I was stalled by a combination of cars and cyclists. Thousands of students at Stanford use bikes instead of cars. Toward the end of the day the campus begins to resemble some of the larger European cities as the streets swirl with students balancing heavy knapsacks of books on their backs or handlebars. But the traffic was so quiet and the delicate weaving motions of the bikes so harmonious that I welcomed their company on the streets, even though I did have to take a great deal of care to avoid running them down.

I finally found InterComp in the brown hills behind Stanford. The company was located on a secluded fifty or so acres in a small valley. A battery of dish-shaped radar antennas, some quite small and others as tall and wide as buildings, looked down from one of the nearby hills. They were probably part of the university's radio astronomy research. Except for their intrusion, InterComp would have appeared to be isolated in the California outback. It's a "profile" that many corporations prefer today; you can offer your employees a wholesome country environment and keep real estate costs down at the same time.

I drove down a long, curving driveway and around a stand of two-hundred-year-old oak trees into the parking lot. I avoided the section of the lot near the main entrance that was marked for visitors and found a less conspicuous area crowded with employee cars. There were four two-story wings connected to a three-story administration building by covered walkways. Much more attractive than the usual manufacturing plant. Lots of glass for good light. Horseshoe pits and Ping-Pong tables located here and there on the grounds. The low lines of the buildings kept them from dominating the rustic atmosphere.

When I parked I started strolling through the lot and in a few minutes I spotted a worn old pickup truck that had once been primed down to grey metal but never painted. Paul Avilla stood up on the tailgate and waved to me, then climbed down again.

"Good to see you, boss." We shook hands eagerly, glad to see each other. Paul and I work well together.

"You look great, Paul. The agricultural life agrees with you." His khaki work clothes and curly black hair and olive skin were covered with a fine layer of rich Santa Clara Valley soil.

"Come on. Let's sit in my cousin's truck and talk." Paul went around to the driver's side and got in, shoving a crate of apricots off the seat to make room for me. I climbed in next to him.

"Listen. You must eat one of these, Mike. They

are sweet. But . . ." one palm raised upward ". . . not too sweet." I accepted one and bit into it, enjoying its fibrous juices and meat.

"An army captain from the Criminal Investigation Division called on Lou a few days ago. He was looking for a Private Paul Avilla."

"A captain?" Paul rolled his eyes. "They used to send colonels and majors after me. How quickly they forget."

"They'd forget a lot faster if you'd knock off your annual valentine. It's foolish to goad them, Paul."

His wide shoulders shrugged lightly under the cotton work shirt. "They'll put their hands on me some day. I might as well enjoy myself while it lasts. What do you have here for me, Mike?"

"As I told you on the phone, someone's using a computer to steal the plans to a new product right out of InterComp's computer system. The name of the thief on the outside is Adam Franklin. But someone inside the company must have supplied him with the security codes he had to have to get into InterComp's system. I want to put you in here on an undercover basis to find out who the sellout is."

"I've got it. Sounds easy."

"Don't get overconfident. These people are tough and mean. I'd like you wait here in your truck for a while, Paul. I haven't met our client yet myself."

"I'll be here." Paul slid down behind the wheel and bit into an apricot.

The InterComp lobby was a bare blue place where all visitors were required to sign a book and pick up a numbered badge before they could be admitted. The entrance to the interior of the plant was guarded by a small smiling girl behind a large metal desk who inquired sweetly about my business. I told her I was here to see George Hogan. She gave me a swift extra glance to make sure I looked properly honored before calling his office. I was issued badge number eighty-five and instructed politely but firmly to return it to her desk before leaving the building. There was a locked box on one corner of her desk. I could drop my badge through the slot on top of the box if I left the plant after ordinary working hours.

"I'm afraid you'll have to wait for an escort," the receptionist informed me. "Visitors aren't allowed to walk through the plant by themselves. Miss Simpson, she's Mr. Hogan's secretary, will be here in a moment."

It didn't surprise me that a company paying so much attention to the trappings of security should be in danger of losing its most valuable secrets. That's often the case. Industrial security is a thankless, time-consuming business. It consists mainly of convincing employees to clear and lock their desks at night, to avoid talking business in public places like restaurants and planes, and to change their working procedures regularly. Identification badges and escorts for visitors don't help much when employees are careless with confidential information. Or when you have a disloyal employee.

A short while later Hogan's secretary arrived to escort me back to his office. Miss Simpson was a neat little brunette. She read me up and down and asked me to follow her, please. It was a pleasure. She wore a pants suit made out of a material built to stretch and the fabric was getting a good workout on her. On the way to Hogan's office we passed through a section of the manufacturing plant and I caught a glimpse of how computers are made. It looked very complicated. Men and women dressed in white smocks and mouth masks were putting tiny components together in sealed dust-free rooms. Other men sat on little stools in front of partially assembled computers frowning at oscilliscope screens. There were empty black metal frames on wheels and mini-computers everywhere that seemed to be used for testing the larger computers being assembled on the floor. All very "leading edge," as the front runner technologists are called. I was impressed and even more concerned about how serious a big information loss could be to a company like this. These people had families and homes with mortgages and doctor bills to pay. If I couldn't stop Franklin they might lose their jobs.

When we got to Hogan's office his door was closed. The neat brunette slipped behind her desk. She picked up her phone and dialed four numbers, her eyes on some papers on her desk. "Mr. Saxon is here," she said. "All right." She looked directly at me for the first time and I was surprised to see a pale tinge of fear in her expression. Swift contractions of tension pulled corners of her mouth. "He'll be right out," she said. She sat down and pretended to study the papers again. Something about me bothered her very much.

The door burst open and a sharply dressed man of about fifty bustled into the outer office. "Saxon? About time. Come in." He wheeled and disappeared back into his office before I could speak. I followed him, feeling like a feather being sucked into the eye of a hurricane. By the time I entered the office he

was already behind his desk again, blunt fingers flying through a stack of correspondence.

"Shut the door. Sit down there."

I shut the door. I sat down there.

"Yoder called. He's at police headquarters now
with Lieutenant Pride. Good man. Met him once at
Kiwanis. Glad you got that information back. Now
where do we go from here?"

I'd expected a vigorous hard-nosed businessman,
but Hogan was something more than that. He was
only slightly taller than average but gave an impression of towering over people. He was built along the
lines of a good Ivy-league football coach, pink-faced
with muscular jowls. His left hand clenched and un-
clenched on his desk as he waited for me to speak. I
felt uncomfortably like a schoolboy who'd come to
class unprepared for a verbal quiz.

"The most important job now is to find out who
leaked your security codes."

Hogan nodded. "You're right. I've been thinking
about those codes since we talked this morning." He
frowned. "Jesus Christ! Where did you get that
scar?" He cut me off before I could answer. "Never
mind. It's not important." He took a cigar out of a
shallow teak box on a table behind his desk and put
it in his mouth. He didn't light it. And he didn't
offer me one. "There are twenty-five codes. They
each consist of a series of eight letters making up a
codeword or phrase. Like MAILCARD or TINYTIDE or
PRATFALL. Any unusual phrase will make a code.
Each code must be given to the computer before you
can get into the area of information guarded by that
code. Do you follow me?

I told him I did and asked what kinds of information are guarded by each code.

"Engineering drawings. Cost estimating. Pricing. Programming documentation. Names of vendors who supply parts to us and detailed descriptions of those parts." He stopped to light the cigar. "In short, just about everything you need to know to build System/Sell."

"How can blueprints and drawings be handled by a computer?"

Hogan swung around and dropped a hand on a computer terminal mounted on a low table behind him. It was different from the one I'd seen that morning on Century Boulevard in Los Angeles. Both had typewriter keyboards. But the terminal in Los Angeles was built to print out information on the customary accordian-fold computer paper, while Hogan's terminal had a small televisionlike screen above the keyboard. Hogan said they call it a cathode ray tube. He punched a few of the keys and an engineering drawing flashed on the screen, appearing as white lines and lettering against the grey background of the screen.

"It would be fairly simple to photograph a terminal screen with any kind of camera—even a good Polaroid—to get the essential information in this drawing." He caressed the machine affectionately.

"And how many people have access to all the codes necessary to acquire the information to build System/Sell?"

"I knew you'd want that," Hogan said a bit smugly. Nice chance to show off his executive ability for anticipating questions. The blunt fingers slid a piece of yellow paper out of a folder and skimmed it across the desk to me. I caught it and looked quickly at a

51

list of names. I was hoping to see either Ann Lane's or Constance Morgan's names on the list. It would have simplified matters. But my jobs seldom simplify themselves. Just the opposite.

"There are nineteen names on that list," Hogan told me. He had anticipated me again. I was counting them. "These people are all top functional managers here at corporate headquarters. And I can't believe any one of them would sell this company out!" His fist slammed down on the desk to emphasize the point. Telephones and manila folders leaped to the air and fell back with a clatter. The blow had registered about a two on the Richter scale.

"You may be right, Hogan. An employee who works with one of these nineteen people could have stolen the codes. But it would be wiser to assume that one of the people on this list has sold you out."

His arms moved wearily. "I know. That's the logical answer. It just sickens me to think about it." He pointed at the list. "I trust those people. I've been to their homes. They've been to mine. They've given me help and friendship."

"I understand your feelings."

Hogan squared his shoulders. Threw off his melancholy. Rubbed his palms brusquely. "Tell me what you discovered today. And what you think we should do now."

"Do you know a man named Adam Franklin?"

"No," Hogan answered immediately. "What about him?"

"He appears to be the man in charge of robbing your computer. I tangled with him today."

"Is that why you're sitting so stiffly?"

"You're observant. I thought I was moving pretty

naturally again. Yes. He's big and very tough. Whoever is behind this scheme is willing to use violence. I suspect that's why Franklin is in charge. He isn't a computer expert. He's working with one or perhaps two women who know computers and know what they're looking for. The telephone company tells me that their front—a company called Computer Specialties—has installed computer terminals in five other cities during the past month. Each time for a period of just a few days. I'd say the chances are very good these people have gotten most of what they want by now."

The pink in Hogan's face washed out slightly as I spoke. "Who are the women Franklin's working with?"

"I'm only sure that one has been helping Franklin. Her name is Ann Lane. But the other knows something about this business. I don't know how much. Her name is Constance Morgan. They both live here in Palo Alto."

The cigar fell from Hogan's mouth, spreading ashes and sparks down his shirt front and across his desk. He seemed not to notice. He was staring at me with an immobilized expression. I jumped up and swept the cigar off the desk. Jabbed it out in an ash tray. It left a deep brackish burn in the polished walnut.

While I was dealing with the cigar Hogan had spun his expensive executive chair around and sat silently with his face lowered and covered by the back of one hand. He sat like that for quite a while. I waited, feeling much better than he did. Obviously these two women were connected with Hogan and InterComp in some way. Finally Hogan stood and walked over to open a door at the far end of the office. It led to an efficiency kitchen where I could hear him rattling bottles. I wasn't going to be left out this time. "Scotch or bourbon will be fine for me."

He didn't answer but when he emerged a little later he was carrying two glasses. I accepted one and followed him to a corner of the office where a trio of comfortable leather easy chairs were arranged for more casual conversation. This was probably where Hogan conducted most of his important business. As the Japanese become more like Americans, Americans become more like the Japanese. There is hardly a top level executive left in America who will close a big deal over his desk. Too cold. Too straightforward. Making deals isn't enough anymore. You have to have a *relationship* with your customer.

When we were seated Hogan started talking. "My wife died a little over a year ago, Saxon. She'd been an invalid for three years before that. I was faithful to her during that time. Always had been."

He looked into his drink as he spoke, instead of at me. It seemed uncharacteristic of him. "Shortly after her death I found myself waiting for a table for dinner in the bar of the Ox Tail restaurant. That's here in Palo Alto. A quiet place. Anyhow, a girl came in and took a booth near me. She was waiting for a table, too. Having a drink in the bar. I recognized her. Ann Lane. She worked here then as a systems analyst. We acknowledged each other. Chatted. I asked her if she'd mind sharing a table with me for dinner and she said she'd like to. We had dinner together and she insisted on paying her own check. That was on a Wednesday night, I believe."
54

He lifted his eyes at last and searched for disapproval in my face. He appeared relieved not to find any. "The following Wednesday night I went back there for dinner. I didn't kid myself. I knew why I was going. She was there again. We had dinner and this time I paid the full check. We went out together the next night. Within a week I was having an affair with her."

He stopped talking and stared at me over his drink. Presently I got the point of his silence. He'd given me as much spontaneous honesty on this subject as his position and character would permit. I'd have to wheedle the rest out of him. Fine. One of the first things a policeman learns is that people prefer to make their confessions by responding to questions.

"How long did the affair last?"

Hogan sighed. I sensed his gratitude for picking up the conversation from him.

"About four months. I broke off with her last January."

"Broke off? Sounds like it wasn't her idea."

"You're right. It wasn't." He put his drink down and patted his breast pocket absently. When he realized there were no cigars in it he picked up the drink again. "She was very bitter." He swallowed elaborately. "I couldn't blame her. But let me try to explain my emotions. After four years of sexual abstinence I was feeling young again. Jesus, there were some days I felt like a goddam bull! The more I got the more I wanted."

"And you started branching out."

He actually winced. It was quite a concession.

"One night we ran into a friend of mine who's

55

board chairman of one of the other companies in town. His name is Len Compton. He was with a beautiful girl, Connie Morgan. She worked for him as a secretary. I couldn't help noticing that Len was attracted to Ann, and I suppose he noticed me looking over Connie. The next day he called and asked me to have lunch with him. I did. He had a proposition. He could use a systems analyst in his company and he expected I could find a spot for a good secretary. He suggested that I hire Connie and he, in turn, would take on Ann."

"Just like the major leagues," I put in. "A straight player transaction."

"Yes," Hogan said grimly.

"And Ann Lane went along with the swap?"

"In a way she did. She cried when I broached the idea with her. Then said she was just as glad. Never wanted to see me again. That sort of thing. And she went to the other company and Connie Morgan came here as my secretary. I learned later, though, that Ann only stayed there a week. She quit and I hadn't heard a word about her until you brought up her name today."

"What about Connie Morgan? Did you have an affair with her then?"

Hogan cheered slightly at the memory. "Yes. She was quite willing. We had a marvelous time for six months. She's divorced from a chemistry professor at Stanford and is determined to simply have a good time and never remarry. She didn't mind changing jobs. Later I discovered why. At the end of six months she told me she was quitting and that she wanted five thousand dollars in severance pay."

"Blackmail?"

56

"Not really. There were no threats. She based the demand on the premise that I'd had at least that much pleasure out of her. She wanted the money in cash. From me personally, not from InterComp. I paid her and never saw her again. A few weeks later I was talking to Len Compton. He told me the reason he had wanted to make the swap was that Connie had made the same demand from him! After about the same amount of time. He paid her, too."

"You're two very generous fellows."

"Not really," Hogan said. "He's married and was afraid Connie would go to his wife."

"Do Ann Lane and Connie Morgan have the know-how to use the codes to milk your computers? And could they have gotten access to the codes while they worked here?"

"Ann's job was designing software systems. She would be able to use the codes. Connie wouldn't. Connie is a good secretary, but she has no hands-on knowledge of computers. Neither one of them could have gotten the codes while they worked here, though. At least, not the right ones. We change codes every month and we've had two new sets since Connie left."

I put down my glass and took out my notebook to make some notes on what Hogan had told me. When I looked up, Hogan was watching me warily.

"I'd say the girls have gotten together to ruin you, Hogan."

"That's a bit melodramatic."

"Is it?" I settled back and told Hogan in detail what had happened during the day. It took me about ten minutes and during that time his mouth opened and closed occasionally with the measured force of a Venus fly trap. But he didn't speak. Just as I was finishing my story there was a brief knock on the door and a young man entered without waiting for an invitation. He paused in the entrance when he saw Hogan and me huddled in the corner, but then he came on in anyway. He closed the door behind him.

"Dad? Sorry to interrupt. I didn't know you had a visitor."

Hogan jumped to his feet. "That's okay, Tom. Come on in."

As I stood up I glanced at the list Hogan had given me and confirmed the fact that Thomas Hogan was one of the nineteen people with access to all the computer codes.

"This is my son, Tom. Tom, Michael Saxon. I've called in Mr. Saxon to . . ."

"To audit your security procedures," I threw in. "I'm an industrial security consultant."

"Oh? I didn't think we had any problems on that score." Tom Hogan looked from me to his father with a bemused smile. "You must have noticed how tough it is just to get into this place." He laughed suddenly. "Why, we've got better security here than we had around the embassy in Bangkok."

"Tom came out of the Marines a few months ago." Hogan's voice rose an octave from pride. "He was deputy commander of the embassy guard there. Only a first lieutenant, mind you. But *deputy commander* of the embassy guard. You can guess what a hot seat that would be."

"You'll have to excuse my father's enthusiasm," Tom Hogan laughed. "He's never gotten over John Wayne." He grabbed his father's arm and gave it an

58

affectionate squeeze. The gesture was returned with a ritualistic flavor. They were obviously a very close pair. Certainly Tom Hogan resembled his father. He was a bluff, wide-shouldered young man in his middle twenties. Competent ex-officer demeanor. Tom's pallid, almost alabaster complexion was the only feature that kept him from being an exact but younger version of his father.

"I don't think I ever got over John Wayne either," I said. "That's probably one of the reasons I'm in the security business."

"Look, I'm sorry I broke in on you." Tom seemed abruptly aware that he'd interrupted a business meeting. As he backed away he shoved a heavy blue notebook into his father's hands. "Here's the market research report you wanted from the midwest division, dad. Mr. Saxon, see you again I hope."

When he had gone Hogan said crisply, "It wasn't necessary to hide your assignment from my son. I rather resent the implication that he can't be trusted."

"He's one of the nineteen people with access to the codes. And above that, I operate most effectively when as few people as possible know what I'm after."

Hogan grunted and went back behind his desk. It appeared that permission to question him about his private life had been withdrawn. Any more information I needed on that subject would have to come from other places. Like Ann Lane and Connie Morgan. I glanced at my watch. It was after five o'clock. Almost five-thirty. And I still wanted to talk with both of them yet this evening.

The phone on Hogan's desk rang with a muffled,

distant sound and he answered it. After listening a moment he said, "Send them right in." When he put the receiver down he told me, "Yoder and Iwasaka are back from police headquarters."

They were ushered in by Miss Simpson. Yoder looked harried and irritable and Iwasaka's head was hanging. "Someone really took us, George," Yoder said as soon as he sat down. "And I heard Saxon tell Lieutenant Pride that Ann Lane is involved. Ann Lane! I just can't believe that about her!"

"It's hard for me to understand, too," Hogan said cryptically.

"Have you discovered yet how much more of System/Sell we've lost?"

"No, I haven't," Hogan shot back. "But I will. Saxon and I have discussed the problem in depth and we have a plan for catching these people and retrieving our property. I can't tell you more than that right now, Karl. I'm sure you understand the need for secrecy."

At that point Iwasaka jumped to his feet and said somewhat hysterically, "I want to submit my resignation! Any unauthorized entry into our system should have been caught right away, and I accept the responsibility for not stopping those thefts when they began."

"Nonsense." Hogan's voice was so hard that Iwasaka folded back into his chair. "How could we have anticipated something so revolutionary?" Hogan's face lit up with the first genuine smile I'd seen since I met him. I was amazed. I couldn't see what he had to grin about. "I just had one of my inspirations," Hogan beamed. "If our computer can be robbed, so can the computers of other companies. This is a new technical problem faced by every firm using computers. We'll need new software . . . new hardware . . . changes in our on-line operations. And once we find our own solution we can turn around and market that package as a complete computer security system." His big fingers drummed on the desk. "I've got that old feeling in my bones, boys! I think there's big money in this."

Yoder laughed and even Iwasaka cheered up.

"Only you could find a way to make money out of a desperate situation like this," Yoder said admiringly.

Hogan chuckled. "When someone hands you a lemon, make lemonade! Mickey, I'm putting you in charge of a special project to devise a system for avoiding future teleprocessing thefts."

"Mr. Hogan. That's . . . good of you. I'll get going on it tonight." He jumped up and started out of the office.

"But keep it quiet," Hogan called after him. "Work independently until you need a staff. I'll have Neely sit in on your regular duties for a few weeks."

"Yes, *sir*."

I was impressed. I understood now why Hogan had been picked to fill Arthur Avery's job. Yoder left soon after Iwasaka, and Hogan slumped back in his chair. "I suppose I bucked them up a bit. Wish I had someone to do the same for me."

"Isn't that Miss Simpson's job?"

He straightened and glared at me. "What do you mean by that?" But the glare faded to an embarrassed squint.

"Didn't Miss Simpson take Connie Morgan's

place?"

"How did you guess?" He passed a hand through his glossy hair.

"She treated me like a syphilis carrier out there. I suppose she knows I'm a private investigator. Did you have her put your call through to me this morning?"

"Yes, I did. But why should that upset her?"

"I don't know. Where do you keep your codes? Could she have gotten at them?"

"You miserable snooper." He looked at me with a hearty contempt. "How do you know *I'm* not the one who's selling out?"

"I've considered that possibility. And I'll check into it. Believe me."

Hogan reared back in real exasperation. "Jesus, what a day! I need something for my goddam stomach." He opened a drawer and took out a box of old-fashioned Arm and Hammer baking soda. "I don't go for these new medicines," he grumbled, getting up and going into his private kitchen.

"I've got a man waiting for me in the parking lot," I said, speaking over the rush of tap water. "Do you think your personnel manager's still here?"

"He should be."

"Send for him. I'll be right back."

Miss Simpson's desk had been cleared and she was nowhere in sight when I came out of Hogan's office. I retraced my steps through the plant and out into the parking lot. Almost everyone had left, except for small pockets of people working overtime and a skeleton staff of second shift employees. The parking lot was spotted with just a few cars. Paul saw me and I waved to him. He ambled toward me, a brown paper sack under his arm.

"Sorry I took so long."

He shrugged elaborately. "I have more time than anything, Mike."

When we went up the steps to the lobby door I found that I couldn't get back into the plant. The door was locked. There was a compact metal box about four inches square attached to the door. It had a thin slit in the middle. I took from my lapel the badge I'd received when I signed into the building and worked it into the slot in the box. The door made a buzzing sound and I pushed it open.

"Magnetically coded badge?" Paul asked.

"Right. We use them in the plants that Saxon Security Systems provides guard services for. The badges are actually keys. When you put one into the slot on the door the magnetic code activates a lever that opens the lock."

We went back through the plant, and when we walked into Hogan's office he was talking with a greying, blinking man whose cheeks were beaded with sweat.

"This is Allen Sykes, our personnel manager," Hogan said. He pointed at me. "Michael Saxon. And I haven't met the other gentleman."

I introduced Paul and enjoyed their discomfort as they attempted to categorize him. They couldn't, of course. Paul was born to be a round peg in a world of square holes.

"I have a suit," Paul said helpfully.

Sykes cleared his throat. "I don't quite understand how you want me to make use of this gentleman." His question was addressed to Hogan but he never took his eyes off Paul. I answered for Hogan.

"I want Mr. Avilla put into a job here for a few days. Not a real job. A cover. He needs a badge with his name on it and an excuse to move around your executive offices."

Hogan swiveled toward Sykes. "Well, Allen. Any ideas?"

The beads of sweat grew and rolled down to Sykes' neck. He cast feverishly for a solution, and when he found one I could almost hear the little click in his head.

"Yes. He could be a service engineer." Sykes motioned us into chairs and tried to explain. "If you're interested in our executives at the functional level and above, each of them has a terminal in his office similar to the one here in Mr. Hogan's office. They need regular preventive maintenance, like any other machine. Mr. Avilla could, I suppose, pass himself off as a service engineer." He shrugged, as if he didn't think that much of his own idea. "We could provide him with the tools. Show him how to make a few simple tests of the terminals." Sykes turned to Paul. "If you don't talk to anyone in detail about what you're supposed to be doing, it might work."

"I can handle that," Paul agreed. He grinned so broadly that even Sykes started to look optimistic.

"That's it, then," Hogan said brusquely. "Put him on the payroll. Anything else?"

"I'd better use another name," Paul suggested.

"Give it to me now," Sykes said. "So I'll be ready for you in the morning."

Paul extracted a thick, hand-tooled leather wallet from his hip pocket and took a wad of social security cards out of one section. Each card had a different name and number. He thumbed through them and pulled one out of the pack. "How about Leon Marino? I haven't used that one for quite a while." He passed it over to Sykes, whose mouth was hanging open.

"This is quite illegal!" Sykes protested. "I can't knowingly accept a forged social security card."

Hogan squinted at his personnel manager. "You're making how much now, Allen? Twenty-two five? You're scheduled to move up to twenty-four any time now. Well you aren't worth that much money to me if you aren't prepared to take risks. If you have to break a couple of IRS laws, *break them*! I don't care. I don't even want to know about it. I *don't* know about it. But you'll have to handle this assignment just right if you expect to continue progressing here, Allen. I'm not exaggerating the importance of Mr. Avilla's project. You'll cooperate in any way he and Mr. Saxon suggest and you'll keep your mouth shut about it. Is that clear?"

Sykes could only nod dumbly.

"Why don't we move to your office and go over the details," Paul suggested to Sykes in a gentle voice.

"Yes. All right." Sykes was happy for an excuse to escape from Hogan's presence.

"These are the people we want combed," I said, handing Paul the list.

He took the piece of paper and folded it into a pocket without looking at it. "We'll have dinner tomorrow and I'll give you whatever I've come up with during the day. There's a little organic food restaurant on El Camino Real near San Antonio Road. My cousin sells them fruit. I'll meet you there at six-thirty."

As they left, the phone on Hogan's desk rang. I

65

reminded him that his secretary had left for the day and he answered the call with his customary charm.

"Hogan here." He looked quickly toward me. "Yes, Lieutenant Pride. I'm glad you called. I was going to phone you and tell you how much I appreciate the cooperation you gave my people today. Any additional news for me?" Hogan straightened and gripped the edge of his desk. "What? My God!" His eyes closed. "When? Oh, Jesus." He looked at me again and covered the mouthpiece with his hand. "Ann Lane has been murdered." The words came from him in broken chunks. "Saxon?" I shook my head violently and Hogan frowned but went along with me. "He's not here right now. I don't know where he is." A pause. "Yes. I know the girl. She used to work here. Surely. I'll . . . identify the body. I don't believe she had any relatives. Yes. What's the address?" He took a gold Cross pen from his shirt pocket and wrote an address on a scratch pad. The words came out shaky and uneven. "Certainly. I'll answer any questions." But his executive instinct did not abandon him completely. "I'll want my attorney to be present, of course. I'll be there as soon as I can locate him."

When he put the phone down I asked, "Where and when?"

"Her apartment. Before the police got to her about the printout. They found her door ajar . . . the lock sprung . . . went in and discovered her beaten to death. Who would do a thing like that?"

"Adam Franklin. He was after her. I knew that. I should have stayed with her instead of standing guard over your miserable pile of papers." I felt a

66

numbing shock of pain run from my wrist up through my arm. I discovered I had slammed my fist into the wall. "I have to get to Connie Morgan before Franklin does. When you talk to Pride try to keep her out of it, Hogan. And tell me one more thing: exactly how did Arthur Avery die?"

"You think it wasn't an accident?"

"Just tell me about it."

"It's very simple. Arthur always walked his dog before going to bed at night. The street he lived on isn't very well lighted and there are no street lights or sidewalks. A typical California development, you know. Everyone's expected to drive. He was hit by a car about 11:00 P.M. two weeks ago. The car was found the next morning, abandoned. It was a stolen car. An Oldsmobile. The police figured some kids had taken it joyriding and hit Arthur, then abandoned the car."

"What was his address?"

"He lived at 442 Meredith Lane."

"All right. Give Pride straight answers and tell him I called you after he did and that when you told me what happened to Ann Lane I promised I'd see him later tonight or in the morning. Don't leave out anything except the part about Connie Morgan's involvement. I have a feeling that if we want to salvage System/Sell we'll have to keep the police away from her. Unless, of course, it looks as if she's in danger, too."

"Do you think she is?"

"She is if Franklin got her name from Ann before he killed her. Connie Morgan is holding the key to the SP locker and Franklin doesn't know we've already recovered the printout from it."

Hogan rubbed his fingers across his brow in a desperate motion. "But are you *sure* Franklin's the one who did this?" He was clutching for straws. Looking for a way to avoid his part of the responsibility for the ugly fate of his former mistress. I didn't really blame him. I dearly wanted to find someone who would tell me that I hadn't been responsible in any way. But I was afraid neither of us could expect that much charity.

"I'm sure. I've seen Franklin." I said I'd talk to him in the morning and we shook hands with a grim formality. I'll give him this much. When I left there were pools of tears in the hollows under his eyes.

CHAPTER
4

I REACHED Connie Morgan's house on Emerald Drive in less than ten minutes by cutting through the Stanford campus again. I hit only three traffic lights on that route, one green and two red lights that I jumped. The little black MG was gone from the driveway. I went up to the door and rang the bell anyway. When no one answered I walked around the house looking in the windows. An elderly neighbor watched me with amusement as he watered his lawn.

"Riding," he called to me as I came back to the front yard.

"What?"

"She goes riding every day about this time." He shifted the stream of water about three feet into the base of a large fern.

"Where does she ride?"

"Connie? She owns a little chestnut mare. Boards her out in Portola Valley. You know the road that goes all the way around the valley?"

"Yes. I've driven through Portola Valley before."

"There's a farm just off the highway. Oh, five or six miles past the 280 overpass. Kelly Ranch. Big sign near the entrance. Be hard to miss. She rides the chestnut in one of the big fields. Jumps him sometimes, too. Dandy little horse."

"Thanks."

He continued talking as I walked to my car. "You don't see people watering by hand like this anymore. It's a way of relaxing without thinking, you know." His voice raised as I started the engine. *"These days people watch television instead."*

As I drove into Portola Valley ten minutes later the first fingers of evening fog were crawling over the coastal mountains between the valley and the ocean. I passed a number of small ranches, a sprawling religious retreat, hushed homes set far back from the main road, clusters of little stores that shared tiny parking lots. The long rows of elm and oak and walnut trees lining the road made it difficult to see the grassy fields beyond. I watched for the sign the old man had promised and hoped the fog wouldn't close in before I found it.

Portola Valley is one of those sleepy old places not yet broken into subdivisions. Very green and open, yet small enough to feel intimate. Even so, I've never greatly liked the valley. It's just a little too cutesy-pie for me. The kind of place where the local liquor store is known as Ye Olde Grogg Shoppe and the dry cleaner calls himself Tidy Town.

A stretch of the kind of white fencing you see in the Kentucky blue grass country suddenly appeared on my left and a hundred yards later I saw the Kelly Ranch sign and a dirt and gravel road going up over a hill. I turned and followed it. The little pebbles tinkled against the bottom of the car. The road ended at a low, luxurious ranch house built in the middle of a grove of olive trees. Behind that was a

70

stable. I parked next to a couple of horse trailers and got out and walked on past the ranch house and stables toward a fenced field farther back.

She was riding in the field and the old man had been right. The chestnut mare was a dandy. And Connie Morgan was a dandy herself. She had the horse cantering gently across the field in a sweeping circle. A jump had been set up at one end of the field and they were working in that direction. As they approached the jump Connie Morgan leaned forward and said something to the horse. Then she nudged the animal's flanks and raised herself slightly in the stirrups as they gained speed. Clumps of dirt flew up behind them as the horse's legs stretched and they went over the jump in a single beautiful movement. I could see Connie Morgan's face clearly in the pale light. She looked exultant. Fulfilled. Almost masculine in her command of the animal. There was a power and restless energy in her strong legs and arms that matched the strength of her horse. The mare's dark mane and her black hair moved in rhythm.

When she had slowed the horse to a trot and then a walk and was headed in my direction I raised an arm and waved to her. She waved back instinctively, then realized she didn't know me and continued toward me with an expression of friendly curiosity. She was too pleased with her horse and their jump to wonder about me.

"Mrs. Morgan? That was an exciting jump."

Her smile was wide and attractive. "Isn't she great? She'd do that all day if I let her. Do we know each other?"

"No. My name is Michael Saxon. I came here to

71

talk to you about your friend Ann Lane."

"Oh?" Her voice dropped into a suspicious register. "What about her?"

I didn't want to tell her Ann Lane was dead while she was up on that horse and I was down on the ground, so I said, "I'm working for George Hogan . . ."

"Go away! I don't want any little messages from George." She started to back the horse away and I reached up and took a firm grip on the harness.

"Don't do that!"

"We have something important to talk about, Mrs. Morgan."

Before I could continue, she put her right hand down to her waist and unfastened her belt and struck down at me. The buckle smashed across my face and I staggered backward and let go of the harness. Everyone was taking me today. On the way home I'd probably be mugged by a teeny bopper.

When I took my hands down from my face I couldn't see out of my right eye. Only blurred and muted colors. My left eye saw Connie Morgan dig her heels into the flanks of the mare and start her on a run across the field toward a wall of fog that was moving down the hill and through the trees in our direction. From somewhere to my right came a cracking sound, like a wet piece of wood popping in a fire, and Connie Morgan and her horse pitched forward. She went straight over the long neck of the animal and somersaulted onto her back. The horse crashed to the ground next to her. All four legs thrashed convulsively and then quivered into a heavy stillness.

I ran toward them and heard another crack. At

the same time I felt something tug at one ear.

"Stay down," I yelled, and lowered my own head as I ran. She had rolled to her side and was pushing on the ground with her hands. I dived toward her and knocked her back to the ground. Then took hold of an arm and began crawling and dragging her back into the protection of the hulk of the mare. We just made it there before another bullet plunked into the wide dead form. The shots were coming from behind the trees and bushes on the main road. A rifle. High-powered. But in the hands of a man who was not that good with it. Three easy shots and he'd only killed a horse.

"What . . . ?" Connie Morgan was still trying to rise. I held her down. Peeped over the horse. Saw nothing.

"Daisy . . . Daisy . . . What happened to her?"

"Somebody shot her trying to kill you. He's still out there."

"Why? What's happening?"

"Stay down!" I shoved her again. More roughly this time. She seemed unhurt by her fall.

"Daisy?" The situation was getting through to her now. She pressed herself against the body of the animal and hugged it. Petted it. Trying to bring it back to life with her love.

A swirl of fog had finally inched its way into the field, creating a vaporous barrier between the sniper and our position. I wanted to pick her up and get her out of there, but I was afraid the fog might dissolve at any moment and leave us exposed in the open. A second later the fog did just that and another shot kicked up the turf a few feet away. That bullet had come from a different angle. He'd moved farther

73

down the road to get away from the fog. We huddled there. Each of us breathing hard. Not speaking. I was grateful for her nerves. She looked alert and unafraid. Mad, as a matter of fact. Her body still against the sagging belly of her animal but her face toward me. The lean jaws were working silently.

"Can you move?" I asked her.

"Yes."

"Fast?"

"Faster than you if I have to. Why is this happening?"

"Ann Lane has been murdered. You probably know why better than I do. Is there anyone at that house?"

"Ann's dead? He did it. It's him out there. Oh, I told her that pig would hurt her."

"Adam Franklin?"

She was surprised. "Yes. That's the man."

"I asked you if there's anyone in the house."

"No. The Prestons were going out for dinner when I got here. They board . . . boarded . . . Daisy." Her chin trembled.

"Keep it together," I told her. "You're doing fine so far."

"I want to get that bastard," she said harshly. "That's the only thing keeping me together."

"The fog's shifting again."

A damp bank moved lazily on a breeze along the whole field and in a moment we were enveloped in it. I waited another minute, hoping the fog would extend itself clear to the house and beyond. Then I said, "Let's move!" and dragged her up. We fled together, my hand on her arm, through the whiteness. In and out of patches of fog and spaces that

74

were clear for ten yards around us. Our feet and breath sounded absurdly noisy as we ran.

As soon as we came to the stables I veered left and slowed us down to a walk. The two horse trailers emerged in front of us and I pulled Connie Morgan toward the back of the nearer of them.

"Get in here and stay down. Wait for me."

She listened attentively as I whispered to her. I pulled back one of the double doors of the trailer and eased her inside. She slid to the floor and I closed the door quietly.

The fog was still shifting. Still patchy. I went on in the direction of my rented car and found it in a crisply lighted hole in the fog. I swore to myself and ran to the trunk and opened it, expecting to hear another shot any moment and maybe feel the smash of metal against my spine. My overnight case was still inside. I yanked it out and moved away from the twilight and back to the safety of the fog. At the base of a tree I knelt and opened the bag and felt around for the tape recorder. I took out of it the Walther and loaded magazines. Then I pushed one of the magazines into the butt of the pistol and pulled the slide back. It jerked forward again with a nasty sound as a shell entered the chamber. Noise didn't bother me anymore. The man with the rifle didn't scare me anymore. I left my open bag on the ground and went to look for him. The sun had at last slid behind the mountains to the west and the normal ration of early evening light was canceled by the fog. Darkness had come with hardly a warning. A darkness in which a high-powered rifle would be no more effective than a .765 pistol.

As I passed my car and walked up the long drive

toward the road I raised the Walther and pulled the trigger twice. The resonance of the valley made the shots sound as if they came from a larger caliber gun than my little German automatic. The spurts of flame looked even bigger in the smoky darkness. I jogged to one side of the driveway and bent forward to avoid giving away my position through the gun flashes.

As I came near the top of the driveway a car engine started up. I ran the rest of the way, but before I reached the highway the car was gone. A vague pattern of taillights was disappearing toward Palo Alto.

Connie Morgan was still crouched at the bottom of the horse trailer when I swung its doors open.

"I heard more shots," she said. "I thought he killed you."

"No. He drove away as soon as I fired. If I hadn't had you to think about I would have moved up on him quietly."

"Don't worry about me, mister." She pulled her arm away as I tried to help her out of the trailer. We were back to our original relationship.

"Come on, Connie. Let's get out of here."

"What about Daisy?"

"We can't do her any good."

"You don't understand. There are other animals around. Wild ones. They'll make a meal out of her if we just leave her there." She turned abruptly and said, "Help me cover her."

I followed her into the stable and the other horses watched stoically as we heaved a large tarpaulin out of some shelving. Connie led the way and I staggered along behind with the tarp on my shoulders. We

76

found Daisy. While I spread the tarp over the horse Connie found some big stones and weighted down the corners and sides to stop animals from getting under to chew on the dead flesh.

When we got back to the house Connie used my notebook and pen to leave a message on the Prestons' door. I found my suitcase while she was writing and by the time we left the night was black and solid with fog.

"Where do we go now? The police? I'm sorry, I've forgotten your name."

"Michael Saxon. I'll take you to the police if you like. They'd want me to."

"Do I have a choice? And is it a real one or a Hobson's choice?"

"That depends on what you have to hide." The fog was worse. I couldn't take my eyes from the road to look at her. So I kept close to that elusive white line and told her everything I knew. About her. About Ann Lane. And about George Hogan and his troubles.

She interrupted me only once, when I described my fight with Franklin in Los Angeles. She said, "So that was you." By the time I'd finished talking we were out of the fog and approaching the Bayshore Freeway. I pulled into a gas station and parked next to a phone booth.

"I'll be right back," I told her. And just to make sure we didn't misplace each other I took the car keys with me.

I looked through the phone book and found Sandy Rawling's number and dialed it. When she answered I said, "This is Mike Saxon again, Sandy. I've got a favor to ask."

"What kind of favor?"

"I need a place to keep a girl for a couple of days. Can you help me out?"

"Wow! Some favor. Look, I was just headed for the airport. I'm going up to Reno with one of the girls for a couple of days. I don't have a flight till Wednesday."

"Can I use your apartment while you're gone?" When she hesitated I added, "Do you remember that girl on the plane today? Someone murdered her. They just tried to do the same thing to a friend of hers. I'm with the friend now and I need a safe place to hide her."

"Murdered?"

"Yes."

"The girl on the plane? Where were *you*, Mike?" She groaned. "Oh, never mind that. All right. You've got my address from the phone book. I'll leave a key under a geranium pot just outside the door to the apartment." She waited for me to say something and when I didn't she asked, "Are you still there, Mike?"

I was still there, but Sandy's question had hurt. I should have stayed with Ann Lane. I should have realized Franklin would find her damned fast. "I'm here. Thanks, Sandy. I appreciate this. You're better than I deserve."

"As a matter of fact, I am," she said simply. "Gotta run."

Fifteen minutes later I coaxed the door key out from under the geranium pot and we let ourselves into Sandy's apartment. I recognized most of the furniture from Sandy's San Diego place. A few deep,

78

low chairs and a couch in Mediterranean style. An old dining room set Sandy had painted green and antiqued herself. Posters of all the cities Sandy wants to visit hung on the walls.

"Why don't you get more comfortable," I told Connie. "Sandy—the girl who lives here—is about your size. There should be pajamas in the bottom drawer of the bedroom chest and a yellow robe in the closet. I have a couple more calls to make."

She went into the bedroom wordlessly and closed the door. I was getting edgy with her. She was too cool. Too tough.

I called the Palo Alto Police Department and asked for Lieutenant Pride.

"Pride."

"This is Mike Saxon, lieutenant. I called George Hogan and he told me about Ann Lane's death. What happened?"

"Where are you?"

"In the apartment of a friend."

"Where were you between 5:15 and 5:45 P.M.?"

"With George Hogan. Is that when she was killed?"

Pride grunted. "Must have been. A neighbor coming home from work at 5:15 saw the Lane woman pick up her evening paper on the doorstep. My officers arrived there at 5:45 and found the front door ajar. She'd been beaten to death. A real mess."

"Do you want me to come in?"

He sighed and ground his teeth. "Yes. But I don't have time to talk to you right now. Detective Canary, the officer I put at the SP station to watch the locker, was attacked half an hour ago. He just regained consciousness. I'm going to the hospital."

"Was it Adam Franklin?"

"Apparently he didn't see who clobbered him. But the locker was jimmied open afterward. Canary was sitting in his car watching the door to the station when someone leaned in and slugged him. Tore up one side of his face pretty bad."

"Franklin has a knuckle sap glove. He probably used it on both Ann Lane and your man at the station."

"*If* it was Franklin," Pride said pointedly. "No one has seen him or used his name in connection with this case except you. I need proof."

I thought about that and remembered Jockey Joe. "There's a tip sheeter who has a booth on Century Boulevard in Los Angeles near Hollywood Park. He saw Franklin chase the girl out of a building there this morning."

"Name?"

"I don't know his full name. He calls himself Jockey Joe. He should be pretty well known around there; he says he won forty-two races at that track."

"I'll check him out. If we don't have any solid evidence against Franklin I don't see how we can pick him up for anything but questioning. And I'm not yet absolutely sold on you as a reliable witness, either. I don't care who you're working for. Be in my office at 9:00 A.M. tomorrow. If you aren't, I'll put out a pickup on you at 9:05."

"I'll be there," I assured him.

Connie had still not emerged from the bedroom when I finished my call to Pride, so I looked in my address book and put in another call to Paul at his Santa Clara number.

The same booming voice answered me and when I

told him my name he yelled, *"I'm sorry for the swearing before. Come over now and we make a party."*

"I'll have to pass again," I told him. "I just need . . ."

"You don't want to make a party here? You're too goddam good to make a party at my house? I get my hands on your throat mister and . . . Let go . . . I'm telling this man . . ."

There was a scuffle at the other end of the wire and finally Paul's voice came on.

"Mike. Is that you?" He sounded winded.

"Yes. Tell your cousin I'm sorry. I really would like to come to his house, but I'm doing something important."

"You called about tomorrow?" Paul asked. "Everything is set up with that personnel manager. He's a real nervous man, but I think my cover will work anyway. I've got a tool box and a badge and I'm memorizing some very impressive words. I can even take the hood off a computer terminal and adjust some screws without ruining the thing."

"Sounds good, Paul." I hesitated. "I wanted to let you know this has become a very personal job for me. The girl who led me up here today was killed while we were at InterComp."

"Jesus! Who was she?"

"Ann Lane."

"Where is she now?"

"At the county medical center. In the morgue."

"Does she have a family?"

I remembered what Hogan had told Pride over the phone. "I don't think so."

Paul had a hasty discussion in Spanish with sever-

81

al other people. When he came back on he said, "My people are going to get her. We'll see that she is buried with dignity. Is there a particular religious belief to be observed?"

Connie had just come out of Sandy's bedroom, dressed in a pair of bell-bottomed pajamas and the yellow robe. She was combing out her hair. I repeated Paul's question to her.

"She was a Catholic," Connie said.

I told Paul and he said his people would take a priest to the morgue with them in case there were any problems in claiming the body. He said they would say she was a cousin.

"Thanks, Paul. When you're working at Inter-Comp tomorrow I think you'll find that one of the nineteen people on your list is very nervous."

"The killer?"

"No. The one who gave the killer his orders. Keep your eyes on anyone on that list who acts erratic or nervous or overly secretive. Comb their desks. Comb their cars. Listen to their phone calls. Get me *something* to work on."

"I will," Paul promised.

When I hung up Connie asked if I was hungry. I realized I was and she went into the kitchen while I took off my jacket and stretched out on one of the low chairs. I thumbed through the collection of records next to the chair and found a Beatles album I'd given to Sandy. I put the record on the stereo and closed my eyes.

"Too tired to eat?"

I opened my eyes and Connie was standing above me with a tray.

"No. Put it down here." I pulled the coffee table

82

over between us and turned the volume down on the stereo. Connie put the tray down and sank to her knees, sitting back on her heels. I started to reach for the glasses and noticed they were the heavy mugs Sandy and I had picked up on a shopping spree in Tijuana. The beer was Thor, a heavy and splendidly aromatic brew that Sandy used to keep stocked for me. I was surprised that she still did. Even the cold roast beef sandwiches on the platter were favorites of mine. It occurred to me now that Sandy had been expecting to see me tonight. When I called her she wasn't on her way to Reno; she was waiting for me. She'd stocked up on my favorite foods certain I'd phone her for a date. When I called instead to ask if I could bring another girl over, she invented a trip to Reno to get out of my way. That's me, Mister Charm.

"Anything wrong?" Connie was watching my frown.

"No, nothing." I poured us both some of the beer.

She picked up one of the triangle cuts of sandwich and said, "The girl who lives here is something special to you, isn't she?"

I shrugged. "She was. She might still be. I don't know."

"I'm sorry. Maybe we should have gone to the police instead."

"You don't seem too shaken by this whole affair, Connie."

Her eyes flicked up at me, then back down to her sandwich. She nibbled at a corner. "I've had a lot of experience at surviving, Mr. Saxon."

"My first name is Mike. Why don't you tell me how you got involved in all this while we eat." I added a thin layer of horseradish to the rye bread. "And while you're at it, tell me how you came to be such a professional survivor."

"All right. I'll tell you about me and Ann Lane first. You know how we met. Old shy George Hogan and my former boss, Len Compton, swapped us. I never expected to see Ann after that, but we ran into each other a few weeks later at a beauty salon. Just for jokes I suggested we have lunch together. I discovered over a chef's salad that Ann hadn't stayed with Len. She went through the motions of the swap, then quit her job. Ann really had a thing for George, and she was badly hurt when he tried to use her like a bubble gum card. When I got to know Ann better I learned that she usually had man problems. Her men were always surprising her somehow. And she invariably went for the very strong, very aggressive type."

"Like Adam Franklin." I added some of the beer to her glass. "When did she meet him?"

"About two months ago. We were still seeing each other for lunch on occasional Saturdays and this particular day Ann was full of news about her new boyfriend. He'd called her for a date out of nowhere, saying he'd seen her shopping at Town and Country and followed her home and had to meet her. She said he was so charming and honest about it that she agreed to go out with him. She described him to me and he did sound pretty good. About thirty. A former basketball star, six feet five. Good job with a growing company . . ."

"What company?" I asked quickly.

Connie put her sandwich down and closed her eyes. "Den . . . Dac . . . I'm sorry. She men-
84

tioned it but I can't remember the name."

"That's all right. Go on."

"Well, she'd changed her whole style of dress."

"I saw her today. The street look. Almost a disguise."

"That's what I thought! I became a little suspicious when she told me that her new boyfriend insisted she dress like that."

"I'll tell you why he wanted her dressing differently. He took her from city to city to help him steal material from Inter-Comp, and he was trying to mask her identity. I believe that he didn't want her recognized because he planned to kill her when she finished her job for him."

She nodded. "I sensed from her new look that she was being manipulated. But I didn't understand how until today. Ann showed up about three o'clock . . . you were outside, you said, so you know why . . . and she told me what she'd been doing for Franklin. Using computer terminals to steal industrial secrets from InterComp. She was almost hysterical about it; the guilt had been building up in her and when you and Franklin were fighting she ran away from him."

"Why did you put the printout in the locker at the SP station?"

"That was my idea, I'm afraid. Franklin sounded dangerous, but I was convinced he wouldn't hurt Ann if he couldn't get his hands on the printout. That's why I kept the locker key. Obviously . . . I was wrong."

We had both finished our sandwiches and beer. Connie took the tray into the kitchen. I followed her and stood leaning against the cabinets while she

85

found the coffee and spooned some into a percolater.

"Where are you working now, Connie?"

"The regional sales office of an insurance company. I'm secretary to the general manager." She regarded me coolly for a moment, then continued with the coffee. "I see what you're getting at. Do I have the same relationship there that I had with Georgie boy at InterComp? Yes. I do. In fact, I went to the insurance company the same way I went to InterComp. George and my present boss are both members of the Bay Tennis Club. They had a little talk and Miss Simpson went to InterComp and I started learning the difference between term and ordinary life insurance."

"Just like that?"

"Sure. You wanted to know how I came to be such a cool survivor. Okay. When I explain it maybe you'll understand how I can change . . . jobs . . . so regularly.

"My father is a sergeant major in the Army. I grew up moving from one army post to another. My mother died when I was ten, from alcoholism. Whiskey costs only twenty cents a shot in the noncommissioned officers clubs and she used to have breakfast there most mornings. When I lurched into puberty my father finally found a use for me. He started trading my young little body to his company commanders for stripes. I was fifteen when he made staff sergeant at Fort Leonard Wood, Missouri. Then he made sergeant first class at the Presidio in San Francisco and master sergeant at Fort Dix, New Jersey." I must have had a queer look on my face, because when she handed me my coffee she kept her head turned away from me. I followed her back to

86

the living room and we sat down in the same places. Me in the big chair and Connie lounging back on her heels across the low table from me. The oak table and the coffee cups between us seemed to bring us closer together instead of separating us.

"He made sergeant major in Germany," she continued. "I was here in the states when he wrote me about it. He sounded quite proud. It was the first promotion he'd gotten without help from me since he made corporal. By that time I was working here in California. When I met Bill he was a graduate student in chemistry. We were married and he got a job teaching here at Stanford. That was three years ago. We were divorced last year."

"What went wrong?"

"Nothing went wrong. We just never got started. I guess I married Bill because he was so different from my father. Quiet and civilized. Intelligent. But that wasn't enough. He seldom really thought about me. He was too busy trying to grow life in test tubes to look at the life around him. Even when we made love I could hear equations running through his head." She gave a sardonic laugh. "I'm not sure he's completely aware yet that I've divorced him."

"I still don't see the why of it," I told her. "Why you let your father sell you . . . why you're letting yourself be used now."

"My father has a punch that would stagger even a man as big as you, and he was always smart enough to leave my face alone. He didn't want to damage the merchandise. As for my life these days—I suppose George told you about the five thousand dollars I collected from him?"

"He did. And the five thousand you took off Len

Compton."

"Pfui." The mass of dark hair flew as Connie twisted her head in contempt. "Then I might as well tell you all of it." She sighed. "Russia and China have their five-year plans, and I have mine. After my divorce I decided my luck with men would always be bad. I wanted to just get away from them and stay away. But even dropping out costs money these days, especially when you aim to be a particular kind of dropout."

"What kind is that?"

"I want to own my own horse ranch. When I was about twelve we were stationed at Fort Riley, Kansas. The home of the cavalry. They still run a few horses there, to satisfy tradition. They had an old horse soldier in charge of the stables and he let me ride and help clean the stalls and brush down the horses. It was the best time of my life. I've been hooked on those big stupid beasts ever since. And so I set out to save fifty thousand dollars over five years. I decided I'd find ten wealthy men and give them each six months of the best sex life they've ever had. For that, I'd take five thousand dollars from each of them. A fair exchange, I think."

"That's called blackmail," I pointed out.

"Pfui. I didn't threaten George or Len Compton. I just told them I was leaving and that I wanted five thousand dollars. I wouldn't have made any trouble for George and I wouldn't have gone to Len's wife."

"But you knew Compton was afraid you'd go to his wife. The threat was implicit."

She grinned impishly. "Maybe I counted on that. Just a little."

"And one other question, Connie. You're working

pretty hard to convince yourself that what you're doing is legal, but did you declare the ten thousand dollars you've made so far as income on your tax form?"

"Oh! You men are impossible! All you think about is *money*. And *taxes*. And *capital gains*. Now do you see why I prefer animals?" She picked up our two empty cups and slammed them down on the tray. "Give me the company of a *real* horse's ass any time."

She flounced away and while she was in the kitchen I tried to sort out my feelings about her. In many ways Connie Morgan was the most outrageously disreputable woman I'd ever met. But in others she was incredibly appealing and genuine.

When she came back she asked me, "Now how can we get this Adam Franklin for what he did to Ann?"

"I don't know yet. I'm going to see the police in the morning. So far they don't have any evidence that Adam Franklin and Ann were connected in any way."

"I'll tell them what I know," she said promptly.

"That might help my credibility with Lieutenant Pride. But what he needs is the evidence that Franklin killed her. I've given Pride the name of the race track tout who saw Franklin go after her yesterday, but that's very circumstantial. The police will have to somehow place Franklin in Ann's apartment late this afternoon."

"How can we help do that?"

"My best bet is to find the man inside InterComp who's giving Franklin his orders. I know Ann spent only a few minutes with you this afternoon, but did she say anything that might indicate who Franklin is working with?"

She thought about that. "No. But she did say some puzzling things. I couldn't really tell you everything she said because she was crying and pouring things out and drinking hot chocolate I made for her all at once. But she said something like this: *I'm so sick of it . . . so damned tired of taking orders from a computer . . . even Adam's tired of that . . . wants to know who he's dealing with . . . I've got to break away from him.*"

"Franklin taking orders from a computer? I don't see how. Unless the inside man at InterComp gives Franklin his orders and the information he needs to carry them out over a computer terminal."

Connie shook her head. "I don't understand."

"I can't be sure of this either. But see if it sounds logical. Someone in InterComp wants to steal the complete plans for their new product, System/Sell. He can't do it himself from inside without being caught or at least suspected. As soon as he gets the plans he'll quit InterComp and set up his own company, or peddle the plans for a big price to some other company. A competitor. But he knows there could be trouble. Violence. So he finds a man who can do the dirty part of the job for him. Adam Franklin. Let's say he offers Franklin a sizable part of the loot. He gives Franklin the codes he needs to steal the information and tells him that Ann is so mad at George Hogan that she'd help steal the information if she's approached correctly. But let's add one more bizarre element. The inside man at InterComp doesn't want to be known to Franklin, so he uses a computer terminal located somewhere around

90

here—maybe even in InterComp—to give Franklin his orders."

"I suppose that's possible," Connie conceded. "Every executive at InterComp has a terminal next to his desk. The man you're looking for could contact Franklin by computer without even leaving his office. He could reach Franklin anywhere in California that way."

"Sure," I continued. "The person behind all this probably recruited Franklin through an intermediary."

"It sounds so complicated, though. Anyway, when the inside man at InterComp starts his own company Franklin will find out who he's been dealing with."

"Not necessarily. They could set up a corporation and sell the corporation's assets—the plans for System/Sell—to one of InterComp's competitors. That kind of deal is made very quietly every day. Franklin would be paid for his shares of stock. The inside man would collect for his block. The competitor would own the plans. It would be almost legal. Proving the origin of industrial secrets is almost impossible in court."

"This whole thing sounds incredible."

"It is incredible. But it fits what Ann told you." I looked at my watch. Ten o'clock already. "Franklin was after the locker key tonight, but he'll also be wondering just what Ann Lane told you about him. He may try again to shut your mouth. I want you to be very careful tomorrow."

"I suppose that before he killed Ann she told him where we had put the printout and that I had the locker key."

"Yes. He beat that out of her. When he couldn't get the key from you he went to the station and slugged the policeman watching the locker, then jimmied it open. He must have been shocked to find the locker empty. He had almost everything he needed."

I got up and went to the couch. "Come on. Help me open this thing. It folds out into a bed."

"I won't ask how you know that."

"Thanks."

We shifted some of the furniture around to make room for the bed. "I have to be at Palo Alto police headquarters at 9:00 A.M. What time do you start work?"

"Whenever I feel like it. One of the fringe benefits of my position."

"I see. Is that why you were home by three o'clock on a Monday afternoon?"

"Yes."

"Well tomorrow I want you to work a straight nine to five shift. Don't even go out for lunch. Don't let yourself be left alone in your office. And don't make any dates with your boss for tomorrow night. Or the night after that either. I'll pick you up at five."

"Are we going steady so soon?"

"I just don't want to leave you around where Franklin can get at you."

Connie straightened suddenly. She'd been bent over the couch pulling the sheets taut under the metal frame. "Why do you care what happens to me? I'm an embarrassment to your boss and to you. Two or three times tonight you've looked at me as if I had the proverbial scarlet letter branded on each of my boobs."

92

"It's not a question of caring. This is my professional responsibility. I try to look out for people involved in my cases the way my father looked out for the people on his beat."

"Your father is a policeman?"

"Was. He was a cop on the Chinatown squad in San Francisco. I was still in high school when he got worried one night about a Chinese grocery store that was late in closing. He walked into the store in the middle of a holdup and got shot twice through the chest."

"I see." She spread the blanket over the hide-a-bed. "You're all thumbs, by the way. Just stand back a little. You're a strange man, you know. A walking, talking case of hero worship. I haven't met one since the Army. Why you're an old-fashioned romantic! No wonder my little tale of woe shocked you. You can at least make a hospital corner, can't you? Good."

"I'm *not* a romantic," I said. "I'm a successful, hard-headed businessman. I have the debts to prove it."

"Maybe. But you're the most emotional hard-headed businessman I've ever met. And you know how well I understand that kind of man. You're different from them in many ways. You show everything you're thinking on your face, you know. I'd think that would be inconvenient for a detective."

I don't know why her words stung me so. But I snatched up a pillow from the closet and threw it on the freshly made bed. She sniggered and went into the bedroom. I took off my shirt, accidentally yanking one button loose. It flew across the room and I didn't bother looking for it. The blood pounded in my ears and I couldn't seem to get a deep breath. What the hell had she meant by hero worship? I'm not in business to carry on after my father. I'm in it for money—more money than he ever dreamed of.

The door to Connie's bedroom was partially open and she passed by as I put my shirt aside. Put it aside hell! I hurled it against the wall.

She gasped. "Look at your shoulder! And your stomach!" She came back into the living room. "Did Franklin do that to you?"

I looked down and saw enormous mottled purple spheres on my left shoulder and over my ribs. Those areas had been throbbing on and off since the fight that morning, but they looked worse than they felt.

"You need something to loosen those muscles or you won't be able to move in the morning," Connie insisted. She went into the bathroom. While she was gone I took off my pants and socks and slid under the blanket, sitting with my back against the cushions of the couch. Connie returned carrying a silver tube of lotion she'd found in the medicine cabinet. The label promised *fast, penetrating relief from minor aches and pains.*

"Let me work on those bruises." She sat down on the bed and loosened the cap on the tube. She filled one palm with lotion, rubbed her hands together, and began rhythmically kneading the lotion into my shoulder. She gave my bruises all her concentration, and I relaxed as I watched her work. The smooth tanned face began developing a light sheen of sweat. Her jaws worked too, as if I were a tough piece of meat to be chewed up.

"This is how I used to rub down Daisy. Except I'd start with her neck. She liked what I did at the base

94

of her ears. I'll show you."

Connie's hands moved up to my neck and began massaging the bones behind my ears with just her index and middle fingers. My eyes closed under the relaxing pressure.

"Daisy used to whinny when I did that."

I whinnied for her. She giggled and I reached up and took hold of her wrists. I slid down, dragging her with me.

"Please don't," she begged. "I wasn't trying to turn you on. Honestly."

"I know that. You started getting to me when I saw you take Daisy over her jumps. Now I'd like to take you over my jump."

Her color began turning. The rose circles on her cheeks darkened and new sworls of pink presented themselves along the flexing lines of her arms.

"It's too soon," she said angrily, twisting and trying to reach her feet.

"You're wrong, Connie. It's now or never for us."

She stopped twisting. She looked surprised and seemed to understand what I was saying. I pulled her back. Took the pillow from behind me and threw it at the lamp on the corner table, the only light left on in the living room. The lamp rolled on its base, tipped and fell. The bulb broke with a pop and we were in darkness.

"Now we'll find out what this is between us," I told her.

She surprised me by whimpering. I hadn't expected her to be the whimpering type. It drove me wild. Like an animal scenting blood I rose up and drove her down under me. My hands were inside her clothing and things came off with ripping sounds. My own shorts jerked downward and I lifted my knees to let them slide off.

"Too damned sweet," she said into my neck, giving it a swift and clumsy bite.

We met in the air. A hawk hitting a sparrow. Wham! Straight into her. My hands clamped around her waist. "Right now!"

"No," she begged. "This first." She rotated. Wrung me out. "Now!"

It happened. And it kept happening. A long, drawn out convulsion. A painful tide. "Don't stop!" one of us said. And we didn't. It went on until I wanted to yell. Until I thought it was still going on when it wasn't. We were apart and gasping.

"Now we know," she said a few minutes later. "Pfui. I wanted a horse ranch."

"I'll get you one," I managed to say. "I'll need a horse myself. I don't think I'll ever walk again."

"Go to sleep."

I went to sleep. Or passed out. And during the night I dreamed of horses. Massive circus horses jumping through hoops of fire. Little Mongolian ponies pushing their way through snow drifts. Wild free palominos copulating in mountain pastures. Hairy-hoofed work stallions pulling giant wagons filled with beer kegs. All kinds of horses all through the night.

Chapter 5

In the morning Connie dressed in one of Sandy's outfits and I dropped her off at her insurance office and cautioned her again not to go outside the office until I called for her about 5:00 P.M. She gave me another "Pfui" and I went on to police headquarters where I found Lieutenant Pride drinking coffee at his desk and staring at a plastic envelope in front of him. It was about the size of a tobacco pouch and sealed along the top with tape. It held perhaps an ounce of almost transparent fluid colored here and there with bits of darker matter.

"What's that, lieutenant?"

"This is what's left of Detective Canary's left eye." He looked at me moodily. "Your friend Adam Franklin can't have that hard a punch. Your story about his using a knuckle sap glove sounds more plausible."

"Have you found him yet?"

"No. But we did find two of his fingerprints on the locker at the SP station. That's good enough for me. We've issued a warrant against him for assaulting a police officer and for mayhem. When we've got him in custody for that we'll see what he can tell us about Ann Lane."

"There must have been prints of his at her apartment."

Pride picked up the plastic envelope and put it carefully into a desk drawer. "There were plenty of his prints there. All over the apartment. So what? He was going with the girl and his prints would be in the house quite naturally. We can't make anything out of that."

"All right. What about Jockey Joe? Has anyone found him yet?"

A secretary was going through the office distributing cups of coffee from a tray. Pride went out and snagged one for me before he answered. "Too early. The tip sheeters don't start setting up their stands on Century Boulevard until just about this time." He examined a sheet of paper lying on one corner of his desk without picking it up. "The L.A. police did give me a rundown on Jockey Joe. His name is Joe Gambino but he never rode any forty-two winners at Hollywood Park or any other track. He was an apprentice jockey about fifteen years ago. He didn't have the strength or nerve or whatever it takes to become a pro. His first time out he took a bad fall. The second ride he fouled everyone in sight and still finished last. I guess they don't give third chances in that business. He was washed up as a jockey before his career started. Since then he's been on the fringes of racing. Exercise boy. Tout. He even made book for a while." Pride scowled. "What the hell are you smiling about, Saxon?"

"Huh? I'm sorry, lieutenant. I was just thinking about horses. And I might have another piece of evidence against Franklin. Yesterday Ann Lane managed to lose him in the terminal at L.A. International. He was looking for her and I think the ticket clerk who was checking in passengers on Pacific Airline's noon flight to San Francisco would remember Franklin. He could corroborate Jockey Joe's word that Franklin was after her."

"*If* Jockey Joe has any evidence," Pride added sourly. "And *if* the L.A. police find him."

Pride was more pessimistic than he had a right to be. He knew that Jockey Joe would be found sooner or later at one race track or another. A man with Jockey Joe's pattern of life is the easiest kind of person to track down. What Pride was sour about was the crippling injury to his man.

"Now about Franklin," Pride went on. "He doesn't have much of a police record."

"I wouldn't expect him to," I said.

"But the record that exists is pretty interesting," Pride continued. "Franklin was charged with child beating four years ago by his wife, Irene. She brought their boy into San Francisco Presbyterian Hospital one night. His name is Mark and he was five years old then. Mrs. Franklin said her husband had hit the boy repeatedly for failing to clean his room to suit his father. She said Franklin was in the habit of doing that. A firm disciplinarian. One of the boy's kidneys was swollen and he had a number of bruises, some recent and some old. There was blood in his urine. Franklin was arrested and released later on bond. Then Mrs. Franklin dropped the charge about a week later. A month after that she filed for divorce. She got the divorce court judge to forbid Franklin to see his son, so there must have been a very consistent background of child beating."

"Does Mrs. Franklin still live in San Francisco?"

"Yes. Two men from the San Francisco Sheriff's Department called on her about an hour ago. She told them she hadn't seen or heard from him since the divorce. She said she refused to accept alimony or child support from Franklin so that she wouldn't have to see him again."

"What's her address?"

Pride hesitated, then gave me Irene Franklin's address. I recognized the street and neighborhood.

"Are you planning to talk to her today?"

"I am."

Between sips at his coffee Pride thought that over. "Okay. Ordinarily I'd stop a private investigator from messing around in a case of mine. Especially when one of my men has been injured on the case. But I talked to your old boss in Los Angeles last night, Captain Twomey, and he said you're a smart-ass but all right otherwise. He also told me your old man had been a good cop. That kind of thing goes a long way with me." He made a face. "Maybe it goes too far. Anyway, you can go ahead and look for Franklin as long as you keep me informed."

"I will, lieutenant." You can't go wrong calling police officers by their rank instead of their names. There's a desire in every cop—no matter how good he is—to see the private citizen humble himself a little in front of him. Maybe that's one reason I had to become my own kind of cop.

Before Pride could begin asking me questions, I launched on a detailed account of how I had gotten into this case and what it was all about. He turned on his tape recorder and listened quietly, stopping me only occasionally to ask a question. I told him everything except that I'd made love to Connie last

100

night and that she made a business out of milking rich executives. I did tell him, though, that she and Ann had both been mistresses of George Hogan. I'd considered holding that back, but I reasoned that a policeman as good as Pride might already know that. I was probably right. At least he didn't seem surprised when I went into their relationships. I didn't go into detail about Paul Avilla, either.

"I'll have the cruise cars check out that insurance office every hour or so until five," Pride said when I'd finished my story. "What you told me agrees pretty much with what Hogan told me last night. But I don't think Franklin will try to get at Mrs. Morgan today. He has plenty of other problems. Incidentally, you can tell Mrs. Morgan that the county humane department picked up her horse this morning."

"Thanks for the information. She'll want to know what happened to Daisy."

"They took care of her. And some wild group of gypsies or Mexicans tried to claim the Lane girl's body. I had to stop them. The coroner hasn't finished gathering all his medical evidence."

"There's one more possibility I want to suggest, lieutenant." Hogan might fire me for bringing this up with Pride, but I felt I had to. "I believe there's a possibility Adam Franklin also killed Arthur Avery, Hogan's predecessor at InterComp."

Pride had been leaning far back in his swivel chair as we talked. When I told him my suspicion about Arthur Avery's death he straightened quickly and reached over to turn off the recorder. Then he hit the rewind button and let it run about five seconds. He jabbed the record button and sat in silence while my remarks about Avery were wiped clean from the tape. Finally he pushed the stop button.

"Now the reason I did that, Saxon, is that I don't want to clutter this tape with hearsay about another case already judged as a hit-and-run accident." His eyebrows shot up somewhere around his hairline. "Do you have any proof that Franklin killed Avery?"

"None," I admitted. "But the presidency of Inter-Comp changed hands at the same time someone began clouting their computers for industrial secrets. That's just too coincidental for me."

Pride picked up his phone and dialed another headquarters extension. "Jean? Go down to Traffic and pull the file on the Arthur Avery hit-and-run, please. Do it right away."

We talked some more about Franklin and where he might be until the young lady who brought coffee around came into Pride's office again with a manila folder. She gave it to Pride, who initialed a buck slip and opened it hastily. He stared hard at the photos of the accident, then passed them to me while he began reading the investigating officer's report.

The photos showed the body of a man lying in a street gutter. The usual amount of blood was running from various parts of his head, making it impossible to see what Arthur Avery once looked like. The other photos gave a wide angle of the street itself. A typical California suburban neighborhood. No sidewalks and very few street lights. The kind of place where pedestrians are hit by cars all the time. Just past Avery's body were skid marks where the driver had stopped. He had probably gone back to see if the man was dead. If the driver was Franklin, he wanted to make sure Avery was dead.

102

When he finished reading the report Pride looked up. "Wanta go out there and look around?"

"Sure."

"Where are you parked?"

"Across the street by the bookstore."

"I'm in the garage. I'll pull out in front and you follow me." He put on his coat and stuck the file under his arm and we left.

I followed Pride's unmarked police car from the center of downtown Palo Alto to the spot where Avery had died. A nice neighborhood. Big houses set far back from the street with lots of hedges and bushes forming natural screening from the street.

We parked and walked over to the spot where Avery had been hit.

"It hasn't rained since the accident," Pride said. He was explaining why the chalked outline of the body could still be seen at the edge of the curb. Some kids had added embellishments to the scene, drawing in a car with horizontal lines coming out behind it to denote speed. They'd also drawn a grotesque face on the outline and given Avery a bushy head of hair and a necktie.

"Bloodstains," Pride said, pointing to fading brown spots on the curb. "Skid marks. The driver stopped and came back to look at the man he hit. Saw he was dead. Got scared and drove away. The car was stolen and the driver dumped it about an hour later in a supermarket lot. Probably a kid joyriding. Maybe a bunch of them, high on pot. Or pills. Or acid. I don't see anything that says murder, Saxon."

"What kind of car was it again?"

"An Olds station wagon."

"That doesn't sound like kids to me. They like to clout something with guts. A Porsche or maybe a Mustang."

I walked on down the street in the direction the car must have been coming from. About a hundred yards away I came across a spot where a handful of cigarette butts were scattered in a neat little pattern.

"Take a look at this," I called to Pride.

He trotted over and I showed him the cigarettes. "Someone sat here in a car smoking and throwing butts out the window on the driver's side. Then he started his car fast. Burned rubber to get quick acceleration. Look at the marks."

Pride went down on his hands and knees. "Yeah. A big heavy car made these. They could be the same tread as the skid marks back there." He stood up and surveyed the street with new interest. "That's Avery's home." He pointed to a long ranch style house a few driveways ahead. "Franklin could have parked here, waiting for Avery to walk his dog. When Avery got a little way down the road he gunned his motor and drove into him flat out. He timed it so Avery would have been walking next to that big hedge and wouldn't be able to get off the street. Then he stopped and went back to make sure Avery was dead. Drove off and ditched the car. Hit-and-run. Accident."

We were walking back toward Pride's car. He was setting a fast pace. When we got to the car he leaned in and pulled out his radio mike. "This is car five-four-five, Lieutenant Pride. Car five-four-five, Lieutenant Pride. Patch me into Sergeant Batra at accident investigation." A loud background of static

104

faded, and a tinny, partially obscured voice answered, "Sergeant Batra here."

"Batra. This is Pride. I'm at the scene of the Avery hit-and-run. I want you to get out here with a crew and go over the site again. It appears Avery's death may have been premeditated."

"The Avery case? I don't think so," the tinny voice answered. "Bad light and no sidewalks. Kids in a stolen car. A very clear-cut case of felony hit-and-run. Not murder."

Pride's face went red. "Clear-cut? Did you reach that decision before or after your investigation, Batra? You must have prejudged the case because there's physical evidence out here that might prove you wrong." Pride's voice was rising with every syllable and I was glad I was not Sergeant Batra. I felt sorry for Sergeant Batra. The automobile has become such a wholesale killer of man that every auto death is routinely assumed to be an accident by most police departments. That makes the family car the most subtle murder weapon available. "Now you and your crew get your asses out here right away!" Pride concluded, hitting the off switch on his mike and throwing it through the car window.

A grey-haired middle-aged lady with rollers in her hair materialized from behind some shrubs. She was holding a pair of pruning shears. "Are you a police officer?" she inquired loudly.

"Yes, ma'am," Pride answered, astonished by the way she had appeared like an actress walking on stage on cue.

"Well, your language is shocking!" Her mouth was set in an angry line. "You should set a better example, officer. There are children on this street."

"I'm sorry, ma'am." Pride backed away. "Excuse me, please." He turned to me. "Let's take another look at the spot where the car started from." We retired quickly to poke around the bushes near the place Franklin's car had waited for Avery. Pride found part of the outer cellophane wrapping to a pack of cigarettes caught in the branches of a flowering hydrangea plant. He took a pencil out of his coat, wet the tip of the eraser with his tongue, and touched the eraser to one tiny corner of the cellophane scrap. It stuck and he lifted the cellophane out of the bush and put it carefully into a plain white envelope he took from his inside breast pocket.

"Might be a print on there. It's smudged." He gazed around at the lawns and shrubs. "I'll have Batra's crew go over the whole area. There's enough shrubbery around here to trap a good many of these cellophane pieces."

"I'll be on my way then, lieutenant."

"Yes. I'll see you later. Check in with me. And don't push too close to Franklin. If you get a lead on him tell me about it. Right away."

He wanted to thank me for turning the Avery case around, but he couldn't bring himself to do it. I didn't blame him. When I was a cop I had a few occasions to watch an outsider break cases of mine. As happy as I'd been to clinch a conviction, I hated to have my work done for me. That was how Pride felt now.

I drove to San Francisco and located Irene Franklin's home at the bottom of Nob Hill on the slope facing Alcatraz Island. You could just see the old prison buildings from the sidewalk in front of the house. The house itself was the kind you see only in San Francisco; three stories high but only about twenty-five feet wide, with similar homes built flush against it on both sides. A wide bay window stuck out above the sidewalk and over the door to a single-car garage. Despite its age the house was well kept. It would, in fact, bring about seventy-five thousand dollars in today's real estate market. I know because the house my father bought thirty years ago for eleven thousand was almost identical to this one. My mother was forced to sell it when my father was killed. For thirteen thousand dollars. To a kindly uncle who helped put me through college. Probably on the profit he later made off the resale of my father's house. But that's another story.

I climbed the dozen steep steps and rang the bell. A clever little chime announced me deep into the house. No one came and in a moment I rang again. This time the door opened and a boy of about ten stared at me. He was just beginning to get his height and his father's looks.

"Good morning. I'm looking for Mrs. Franklin. Are you her son, Mark?"

He looked at me suspiciously. "Who are you?" he demanded. "What do you want?"

A good reaction. I shudder to think of how many kids throw their doors open to every stranger who rings a bell. Franklin's boy seemed to have a healthy skepticism about his fellow man, but I suspected he picked it up in an unhealthy way—from his father.

"My name is Michael Saxon and my business with your mother is rather personal. I'll be happy to wait while you tell her I'm here."

He stared at me for another moment, then said,

"All right," and closed the door. I waited. When he came back he opened the door wide and told me, "She says you can come in. She's in the patio with *him*."

My heart skipped when Mark Franklin coated the word *him* with a thin veneer of venom.

"Who's she with?"

But he answered, "Uncle Gene."

I was just as glad not to find her with Adam Franklin. What I would have done to him—had to do to him—wouldn't be something for Mark Franklin to see.

Mark took me through the living room and dining room toward the patio in the rear. The house was expensively furnished with heavy modern pieces set against a profuse background of rubber plants and split leaf philodendrons. We came out on a rear porch one story above the long narrow garden and patio. You actually overlooked a score of similar gardens running up Nob Hill, each separated by high wooden fences. As I walked down into the garden I saw the man with Mrs. Franklin. When he glanced up at me he saw Mark Franklin in the background and called out, "Hey, Mark! Bring me down another bottle of bitter lemon. That's a boy."

"He won't bring it, you know," Mrs. Franklin said to him. "For some reason he seems to hate you." She sounded very amused. I was to learn that Mrs. Franklin is the kind of person who is very amused at just about everything, in a remote and disinterested way.

She was a long lazy woman about the age of her husband. She had frosted hair, a mouth that ticked downward at the corners every few seconds, and a plain face with very luminous brown eyes. Someone had obviously told her that her eyes were her best feature, because she had set to work with eyebrow pencils and eye liner and pots of blue paste and turned them into a pair of gaudy circus posters. She focused them on me and said, "You're Mr. Saxon?"

"That's right. I've come to ask a few questions about your ex-husband, Mrs. Franklin. I'm sorry to intrude on you, but it's important."

"I don't understand. The police were here this morning looking for Adam. I told them I haven't seen him in three years." She was sitting on a chaise lounge in a pair of tight pants and a see-through blouse and she moved slightly to adjust the nothingness around her shoulders. "You aren't a policeman," she said suspiciously.

"No. I'm not."

"Then what right have you to bother my sister?"

That question came from the man with her. Obviously her brother. He was mixing drinks at a small outdoor bar set up several yards away under a green and white aluminum canopy. He didn't look toward me as he spoke. He was quite engrossed in his intricate task.

"No right," I admitted. "But I'm part of the same police case your ex-husband is involved in, Mrs. Franklin. I'd like to find him and talk to him. I'm a private investigator. If you can't help me find Adam Franklin would you mind answering just a few questions about him?"

"I don't think you should," her brother said.

"Oh, relax, Gene. I don't mind talking about Adam. You might as well know, Mr. Saxon, that I'm rooting for the police to catch him. I don't know

109

what he did, but I'm sure it was violent. I'd feel safer if he were put away in some cozy prison." She gave me one of those twitchy grins. "With all the reforms he wouldn't be too uncomfortable. Would he?"

"He's threatened you?"

Her brother joined us and handed Irene Franklin a greenish drink with a cherry floating on top and what looked like a slice of avocado shoved onto the rim of the glass. He gave me a drink, too. Same concoction. "You might as well have one if you're staying," he said.

"Thanks." I sniffed the drink. It smelled strongly of creme de menthe. I hate creme de menthe.

"This is my brother, Gene Chase. Gene, Michael Saxon."

"How d'ya do," Chase said. He was perhaps ten years younger than his sister and had none of her features except the round brown eyes. He was angular. Lean. Tall. A young greyhound. Even to the ears lying back flat against his head. Handsome verging on prettiness.

"Threaten me?" Irene continued. "Not lately, no. But when I divorced him he said he'd kill me one day. Did you know that?"

I said I didn't.

"My father was alive then," she went on. "He hired private detectives to watch me around the clock. And Mark, of course. I went to Nevada for the divorce and the private detectives stayed with us for the whole six weeks. Father took them off when the divorce was final. He knew Adam wouldn't do anything to me once there was no way for him to profit from my death. Nothing to inherit. He only married me because dad was well off, you know."

"I don't think that's quite the whole story," Gene said in a severe tone. "You two were very much in love at first. Even I could see that and I was only . . . what . . . fourteen when you were married?"

"Don't pay any attention to Gene," Irene said brightly. "He had a crush on Adam. Still does, I think."

Gene Chase flushed and jerked the glass down from his mouth. "Shut up, Irene!" he said in a very controlled voice. Some of the sticky green liquid had splashed on the sleeve of his shirt and he picked up a napkin and wiped it away. It didn't leave a stain because his shirt, as well as his slacks and shoes, were also green.

"Don't be silly, Gene." She turned the huge eyes on me. "Everyone gets a crush on Adam at first, Mr. Saxon. He's so big and capable. All man. And so polite. Then . . . he becomes less polite."

"Where did you meet him?"

"At Cal. I was a pom pom girl. I led the cheers for the basketball team." She lifted her legs a few inches off the chaise lounge. "These were pretty good then. At least Adam thought so. And when he met dad and found out he was a wealthy investment broker, we were married."

"That was after his legs were hurt playing basketball?"

"About the same time. I didn't understand what all the fuss was about then. Everyone said Adam was the dirtiest player the league had ever seen, but I was practically on the court during his college games and I couldn't see him doing anything wrong.

111

I found out later, of course, that Adam is an expert at hiding that kind of behavior from the public." Her voice suddenly went colder and she dropped the stance of the amused sophisticate. "One evening we had some guests in and he romped all over the floor with Mark, showing them how strong his son was getting to be. Mark was about three. An hour before the guests arrived he'd whipped Mark with his belt for wetting his pants."

"What did he do after college."

"My father took him into the firm as a stock and bond salesman. Adam was quite good at it. But then came that year when the Dow dropped three hundred points and so many stock houses went out of business. Dad was forced to merge with another company and lost management control as a result. When the merger went through a lot of salesmen were let go and Adam was one of them."

Just then Mark Franklin appeared above us on the porch and called down, "Uncle Gene. You just had a phone call. Gumper Brothers Hardware says your order came in."

Gene went livid. "Why didn't you call me? I've told you before that I want to take my own calls when I'm visiting your mother!"

The boy flinched. "I'm sorry. He said he didn't need to talk to you. He just wanted to leave the message."

"Well next time call me anyway. Understand? Can you get that through your dim little brain?"

"Gene! Stop yelling at Mark or get out of my home. He did exactly the right thing and I want you to apologize to him this minute. Do you hear me? This minute!"

Gene scowled at his sister, but seemed to be pulling himself together. He drew a couple of deep breaths and looked up to Mark. "I'm sorry, fella. It's just a quirk I have about getting phone calls straight." He glanced from Mark to his sister to me, as if to make apologies all around. "I'm an interior decorator," he said directly to me, "and I've had a lot of problems with messages becoming garbled when they go through other people. If a woman wants blue wallpaper with a red pattern and you show up with red wallpaper with a blue pattern, you're really in trouble." He looked to Mark again. "Really, I'm very sorry, Mark."

The boy took the apology impassively and went back in the house.

All three of us lapsed into an embarrassed silence when Mark went inside. Finally, to break the mood, Mrs. Franklin said, "Gene remodeled my place recently."

"I like all the house plants," I said politely. "Sort of brings the outside world into the home."

Gene beamed. "That's exactly the effect I wanted! Green is the perfect color, you know. Goes with anything. The human eye accepts green in any situation, and do you know why? Because we see it constantly matched with every conceivable color in nature. Look around you!" He gestured forcefully, somehow giving the impression he had personally created the world as we saw it. "No matter what color a flower is it's always accompanied by a green stem. We'd be shocked to see anything but green stems. Green grass. Green leaves. Even the ocean is more green than blue. Did you know that? Instant compatibility and acceptance. That's what green gives you."

I laughed. "I get it now." I raised my glass. "The green drink. The green clothes. The slice of avocado."

"That's right. Green's my bag. Look." He stepped right up to me and thrust his face against mine. For one horrible moment I was afraid he intended to kiss me on the lips. Instead he said, "Take a good look at my eyes."

"I'll be damned. Green!"

He and his sister laughed at my surprise.

"Gene's contact lenses are tinted green," Irene explained. "When he's into a motif he goes all the way. You should have seen him when he was into stripes."

"I like green, too," I said. "But I prefer something a little more amber in a glass. Do you mind if I help myself to another drink?"

"Go ahead," Irene said. "And bring me something amber while you're at it." I took her empty glass and went over to the bar. A party mood was developing and I wanted to encourage it. Maybe I could even start Gene talking about Adam Franklin.

"What'll it be, Mrs. Franklin?"

"Make it Irene and make it Scotch. With a little soda please." The big eyes flared with a hint of invitation. Her adrenalin must have started flowing because she finally got up off the chaise lounge and came over to stand by me. "I think there's some J&B in here somewhere." She leaned over the bar and her shoulder touched mine. She stayed pressed against me just long enough to assure me the movement was no accident, then said, "Here it is," and pulled the J&B out of the jumble of bottles.

114

Gene was standing to one side looking morose. I had the feeling he was sorry he'd let himself get animated enough to make his sister relaxed around me. I fixed Irene's drink and found an honest old bottle of Jack Daniel's for myself. When I carried the glasses back I asked Irene, "What did your ex-husband do when the stock and bond business folded?"

She sipped and answered, "Dad helped him find a job at the Marlborough Bank. He became an assistant trust officer and later went into commercial loans. He was pretty successful at that, too. But not successful enough, I suppose. That's when he started becoming irrational as well as cruel."

"What do you mean by irrational?"

"Oh, I don't know." She clucked her tongue. "He started telling people he was being groomed for the presidency of the bank, for one thing. He wasn't, of course. And he embarrassed people. Then he'd take off by himself for long weekends in Mexico. He wouldn't even stay in a hotel down there. He'd camp out. Come home looking like a bum. And, of course, he started hitting me and Mark whenever we displeased him. He got into fights with people. One time he slugged a grip man on the Powell Street cable car when he stopped the car suddenly and Adam was thrown against one of the metal hand rails. Shortly before the divorce he began having terrible headaches that made him impossible to live with. If I tried to comfort him in any way he'd just swear at me and claim the headache was all my fault. He said he had a 'mission' in life and that I was holding him back. It was terrible."

"Sounds like he was developing some real mental hangups."

"He was. I finally talked him into going to a shrink. Dr. Lewis over in Marin County. After a couple of months of visits Dr. Lewis told Adam he was developing paranoid delusions. Adam got mad about that and stopped going to him."

Paranoid delusions. Now I understood how Franklin had worked himself up into a genuine frenzy against me at that little office on Century Boulevard. Paranoids often have the delusion they are marked for some kind of greatness, that they have a special destiny. And the violent ones smash down anyone they believe is trying to stop them from achieving that destiny. To Franklin I wasn't simply a detective trying to stop his swindle; I was the man who threatened to destroy his chance to become a millionaire and an industrial giant. He was prepared to kill me for that. Just as he killed Ann Lane and Arthur Avery. Just as he tore one eye out of Detective Canary's head.

"I assume your ex-husband doesn't work at the Marlborough Bank anymore." I knew the bank. A very rich independent operation.

"No. He was working there when I left him, and a few months later I heard he'd left the bank. I don't know what Adam's been doing since then."

"I'd like to talk to the man he worked for. Who would that be?"

"Cecil Mock," Irene answered. "But I think he retired from the bank. He bought a vineyard somewhere and moved out of San Francisco. We had a card in the mail from him a couple of months ago. An advertisement, sort of. Asking his friends to come out and visit his winery. Gene, I showed it to you. Where did Cecil move to?"

"I don't remember," Gene said. He had been sitting in a lawn chair crossing and uncrossing his legs, obviously fretting over the amount of personal information his sister was giving me.

"Of course you do," Irene said crossly. She put her hand next to her mouth and called, "Mark! Oh, Mark!" Her son came onto the porch again and she said loudly, "There's an advertisement somewhere on the desk by the phone. From Cecil Mock, your dad's old boss. Find it for me like a good boy."

"Okay, mom."

Mark went off and returned a minute later. "Here it is. Catch." He dropped a yellow oversized postcard over the porch rail. It fluttered downward, making odd loops that took it deeper into the yard. I walked toward the general area where I thought it would land. Just as I stretched to reach for it Chase came springing out of his chair and jumped in front of me. He missed the leaflet. It twirled down toward his ankles and he scooped it up.

"Gene!" his sister called. "What are you doing? Bring me that card."

"No." He danced away from me. "You shouldn't send a private detective out to see your friends, Irene. Prying and asking a lot of questions about things he has no business knowing."

"You don't even know Cecil Mock," Irene snapped. "You're being childish. That card is addressed to me and I insist you hand it over." She unlimbered herself from the chaise lounge again and advanced toward her brother.

"I won't!" he said, in a childish voice.

"You will!" his sister commanded. For a moment I could see them as they must have been fifteen

117

years ago, the older sister sternly commanding the little brother to return her toy to her. They weren't even concerned with me at the moment. They were acting out an old set of antagonisms that would always exist between them.

I settled the question by stepping forward and grasping Gene's wrist. He struggled and leaped and pulled and jerked and quivered in my grip. He was surprisingly strong and agile, with the staying power of the greyhounds he reminded me of when I first saw him and the fierceness of some of the twenty-pound Mackinaws I've pulled from the depths of Lake Tahoe.

"I'm sorry," I grunted, leaning into him and pulling the yellow card away from him. "But this is important to me." He stopped struggling the moment I took the card. I let his wrist go and he flounced away. Flounced. That's the only word for it.

"Don't ever treat a guest of mine like that again," Irene scolded. She came over to me. "I'm sorry, Mr. Saxon. Michael. I apologize for my brother."

Gene made a huffing sound.

"That's all right. I understand your reservations about me."

"Now let's see where Cecil has got himself to," Irene said. She moved next to me and slipped an arm under mine. "Livermore Valley. Of course. How stupid of me to forget. I've said a dozen times to Mark that we must drive out and say hello to Cecil and pick up a case of his wines. I'm sure they're very good. Cecil has wonderful taste."

I wrote the address in my notebook. Livermore Winery. Castillo Way. Livermore Valley. The card was a printed announcement stating in rather re-

118

served language that the winery was now under the new proprietorship of Cecil J. Mock. I hadn't heard the word "proprietorship" in years and I formed an immediate impression of Cecil Mock from it. The fact that he'd been president of an ultra-conservative bank helped. A handwritten note on the card said simply,

Dear Irene: Hope to see you one day. I've heard you and your son are getting along well. Glad to know that. Cecil.

I turned the card over. It was postmarked about four months ago.

"Thanks very much for your help," I said to Irene, handing the card back to her.

A very small pout presented itself on her lips. "I was hoping you'd stay for another drink. Gene has to go in a moment anyway."

Her invitations were becoming more explicit and I wondered how she handled male visitors with Mark in the house.

"I'm sorry. I have a lot of ground to cover today. Can I take a raincheck on that?"

"Surely. Mark will show you out. Do come back."

I moved slowly but steadily toward the stairs, trying not to appear as if I were making an escape. Which is how I felt.

"Thanks again," I said from the safety of the steps. And to her brother I added, "Nice to meet you, Gene. I'm sorry we had a disagreement."

He didn't answer. Didn't look at me. Old green Gene. Gene and Irene. What a pair and what a house. No wonder Adam Franklin went paranoid. I wondered what her old man had been like.

Mark was putting together a model of a World

119

War II P-38 at a table in the corner of the dining room. "I'll let you out," he said.

"Thanks. You don't like your Uncle Gene very much."

He grimaced and shook his head. "No."

"Why not?"

"He puts his hands on me too often."

"Why don't you tell your mother about that?"

Boys have a way of shrugging as if huge weights were welded to their shoulders. Mark did that and said, "She thinks he's funny. She doesn't know how weird he is."

"All the more reason to tell her."

"Maybe."

"Think it over, Mark. Goodbye."

"Mr. Saxon, are you looking for my father?" Mark said the words in a rush, staring at me with his head cocked to one side. I realized then that he'd been crouching behind the porch rail listening to us. That's how he was able to appear so fast when his mother called him.

I had to give him a straight answer.

"Yes, Mark. I am."

"Are you going to send him to jail? Has he done something that bad?"

"I'm not a policeman, Mark. I can't send him to jail. But yes, he may have done something pretty bad."

"Will you be seeing him?"

"I might."

"If you do, I'd like you to tell him something for me."

"Sure. What shall I tell him?" I couldn't see his eyes. He was looking straight ahead, into my necktie.

120

"Say I still love him no matter what he's done."

"I'll be glad to tell him that."

I stepped out and Mark closed the door behind me. I found as I went down the steps that my legs were shaky.

On my way out of San Francisco I cut over Broadway along the fringes of Chinatown. As I waited at a red light I glanced across the street and realized with a shock of recognition that the old-fashioned narrow building directly across from me was the Chinese grocery where my father had been killed. I hadn't seen it in fifteen years. Seeing the place now, right after talking to Mark Franklin, made me realize how much I still miss my own father and try to pattern myself after him. Connie had been right. Consciously or subconsciously, I am your standard brand father/hero worshipper. But Mark had been right, too. Your father doesn't have to be a hero to be loved. You can love a mean, murderous son of a bitch if he's the one who taught you how to throw a football or took you trick-or-treating or put that shiny new Schwinn together for you on Christmas morning.

The light turned green. I put my foot down and gunned away from the intersection at an illegal speed.

CHAPTER

6

LIVERMORE VALLEY is on the east side of San Francisco Bay. The mountains to the west of the bay—the peninsula—are green and heavily wooded. But on the eastern side the hills are a soft rolling brown and practically bare of trees. You cah grow premium wine grapes on those slopes and in the wide valley below.

I found Cecil Mock's winery nestled in one of the smaller enclaves of the valley and drove up a long winding gravel road to a pair of low stone buildings. One of the buildings was Mock's home. The other had a small "Tasting Room" sign on the door. I went into that one.

The tasting room was twenty degrees cooler than the air outside and very dark. Rows of aging casks stood patiently in the back, waiting their time to be opened. Nearer the door stood a sort of bar that had been made by turning four fifty-gallon casks on their ends and resting a long slab of black polished wood across them. The roof of the building was arched and the whole effect of the place was to take you about three hundred years into the past when things happened at a slower, more natural pace.

"Hello there."

The greeting came from a tall white-haired man in a grey turtleneck sweater and slacks who emerged from the maze of aging casks at a leisurely stroll. As he stepped behind the bar he dragged one leg slightly. I couldn't see that in the dim light, but the acoustics were so good I could hear the faint shuffling sound.

"Mr. Mock?"

"Yes."

"My name is Michael Saxon."

He extended his hand and I shook it.

"Would you care to sample our wines?"

"I'm here on business but I would like to taste your wines. Very much."

"Good."

In some of the wine-tasting rooms in California they give you a little paper cup and half an ounce of vinegarish fluid and then pressure you to buy a couple of bottles. Cecil Mock produced a sparkling wine glass and a half-full bottle of a rich red wine. He filled the glass almost to the brim and stood back.

"That's a Chardonnay. One of our nicest dry red wines."

After sniffing briefly at the Chardonnay's aroma, I took a long sip. "That's an excellent wine," I announced.

Cecil Mock beamed and brought out a jar of bread sticks. I hadn't eaten any lunch so I took one and nibbled at it. The blend of the crusty bread and the wine was very good.

"What kind of business are you here on, Mr. Saxon?"

I had been studying Cecil Mock and I decided he was not the kind of man to con. His mouth was set too firmly and his eyes looked too directly into mine. I brought out one of my cards and gave it to him. I hoped he would be deceived by the impressive sound of *Saxon Security Systems*.

"So you're a private detective," Mock said, destroying the careful ambiguity of my business card. "What kind of information can you possibly want from me?"

"I know that you were president of the Marlborough Bank in San Francisco until you retired. I'd like some information about a man who worked for you. His name is Adam Franklin."

"So that's it," Mock said flatly. "I'm sorry. But I don't gossip about friends, relatives, or former colleagues. Enjoy your wine, Mr. Saxon. But no personal questions, please."

I shrugged as if to say the matter was closed. As if I'd drive all the way out here to be put off so easily. Both of us knew better. I caught a little flush of interest when I asked him about Franklin. As a banker Mock had lived in a forest of secrets that people wanted to get at. He was probably enjoying my pitch the way an old baseball player enjoys the sounds of spring training. If I could be clever enough to arouse his interest he might reward me with some solid information about Franklin.

"How long have you been retired, Mr. Mock?"

"About a year. I bought this small vineyard and I must say I'm enjoying the life of the country gentleman. I've been up to the University of California agriculture school at Davis for some courses in viticulture."

"Was it the stroke that caused you to retire?"

He bristled. "You noticed my leg. Very observant.

125

It was a mild stroke, thank God. But severe enough to get me out of that pressure cooker back in the city."

I'd finished the Chardonnay. Mock brought out another bottle. A white wine. Somewhat less dry. A Chenin Blanc that had a pleasant little snap to it. I took another bread stick. Like Pavlov's dog, I wondered just what I should do to receive my next reward.

Mock moved away and picked out a bottle and poured himself a few ounces of wine. From a desk behind him he took out a pale grey folder and spread it open on the counter between us. There were a half dozen large advertising layouts done in rough format in the folder. I assumed an agency had given them to Mock to select one to use in selling his wines.

"Look at this. I asked for a simple, understated ad that would bring some discriminating people out here to buy a few cases of wine, and the fools send me this trash." The ads featured young men and women drinking wine with huge smiles on their faces against various backgrounds of leisure—at the beach, on a yacht, at parties.

"What I really wanted," Mock continued intensely, "is just a photograph or drawing done in generous colors of a glass of wine sitting next to a platter of cheeses and breads and worthy cuts of meat. It should have a caption that sums up the improvement wine makes to the simplest meal." Mock appeared so frustrated at his inability to hit the right note for his ad that I decided to put my expensive education to work for a change.

"What about something from Walt Whitman," I suggested. "I recall a very succinct phrase from *Song*
126

of Myself that might make a caption for your picture. I think it went, '*This is the meal equally set.*' If that one doesn't do it I'm sure you'll find plenty of other good one-liners in Whitman; he was the supreme sensualist."

Mock tilted back on his heels. "My God! A private detective with a classical education." He glanced at my right hand to see if I was wearing a school ring. "And a USC man at that. You fellows push your way into all the businesses on the coast, don't you."

"We are ubiquitous," I admitted. Bankers love big words.

Mock chuckled and found a pencil and a pad of paper. "What was that quote again?"

I repeated the quote and the name of the poem. Mock wrote them down carefully. He folded the paper and put it into his wallet. "I have something that might interest you," he said, sweeping the folder of objectionable ads out of sight. He went into the maze of aging casks and returned carrying a very dusty bottle. "Port," he announced. "Twenty years old." This time he had a silver corkscrew hanging around his neck from a silver chain.

I put the last piece of my fifth bread stick in my mouth and said, "I'm ready for it. I'm practically making a meal of your bread sticks. They're very good."

"I bought this place from the widow of the man who founded it twenty years ago. His first year he put down a hundred bottles of this wine as a sort of commemorative act. There are twenty bottles left." The cork came out with a very soft pop. "Nineteen." Mock poured two glasses very carefully and we

127

drank in silence for several minutes.

At last Mock said, "What kind of information do you want about Adam Franklin?"

"The police in Palo Alto want him in connection with a crime committed in that city. I'm looking for him, too."

"What kind of crime do the police think Adam committed?"

I hesitated, then decided to tell him. "Murder. They think he killed a girl who was helping him steal industrial secrets from my client."

Mock set down his glass with a clatter. "Murder? Adam Franklin?" He closed his eyes and seemed to be casting his mind back in time. When he opened them he said, "Yes. I'm afraid Adam is capable of murder."

"Why do you say that?"

"Let me tell you what I know about Adam Franklin. Then you'll understand. I hired him about four years ago as a trust officer for the Marlborough Bank. He'd been let go by the brokerage firm he'd been working for. Not his fault. There was a merger in his father-in-law's firm and when they consolidated they let people go. Good people and bad. Adam made forty thousand dollars in commissions the year before, but the new management thought he wasn't worth the business he brought in. Adam liked to think of himself as a big operator. He spent a fortune on long distance calls. Sent out tons of material in the mail. But more important, his specialty was churning and that sort of business didn't appeal to the new management. I imagine you're familiar with the technique."

"Yes. I know what churning is." In the brokerage

business churning means getting customers to buy and sell stocks instead of holding them for long-term gains. The customer's capital usually erodes over the long haul but in the meantime a lot of commissions are generated for the salesman. Churning fitted into Franklin's pattern.

"His father-in-law asked me to find a spot for Adam after the merger. He didn't like Adam, but he'd do anything for his daughter and he felt somewhat responsible for Adam losing his job. I talked to Adam and was impressed by him. He knew the securities market. I wasn't especially put off by his experience in churning; that's the stock and bond business. I explained that if he joined the bank he'd have to adopt a new investment philosophy. We don't gamble with our trust accounts. We put people into good investments and keep them there." An edge of pride appeared in Mock's voice. "At any rate, Adam understood that and when he joined the bank he did a fine job. So good, in fact, that I soon put him into commercial loans. He was very aggressive. Some people said he was too aggressive. He had not just a *desire* to succeed, but a *compulsion*."

"A compulsion," I repeated. "I saw his ex-wife this morning and she intimated that Franklin has psychiatric problems."

"I'm not surprised," Mock said promptly. He looked at our glasses. "Shall we finish this fine bottle?" He poured each of us a final glass and paused to read the label before putting the bottle aside, the way an English professor might glance at a first edition as he put it back on the shelf. The label told not only the year the wine had been bottled, but the number of the cask and the bin the bottle had been

129

drawn from.

"Adam Franklin is an unfortunate by-product of our success-oriented society," Mock went on. "He had to constantly be given new signs of his worthiness to be even a moderately happy man. Promotions. Raises. Better-sounding titles. I started him at twenty thousand a year and he was soon making thirty. It wasn't enough. He was unhappy and restless. He and Irene were divorced soon after he was promoted to commercial loans officer. But he and I still got along fine until the vice presidency opening came up."

"That was how long ago?"

Mock frowned. "About two years ago. One of our vice presidents retired and Adam expected the opening would go to him. Instead I promoted another man, Arnold Thompson."

"Had you considered Franklin for the job, and did he know he was being considered?"

"Yes."

"And why did you promote the other man—Thompson—instead of Franklin?"

"That's a very good question. The answer lies at the very heart of today's philosophy of banking." Mock was warmed up to his subject now. I don't suppose I could have stopped him from talking about Adam Franklin if I'd wanted to. "Adam was aggressive and a top producer. He knew where to find the opportunities to make good loans. So did Arnold Thompson. But Adam was a little too conservative about who he made loans to." Mock looked at me with amusement. "That may sound strange coming from the former president of San Francisco's most conservative bank, but it's true. Adam would never waste his time talking to the screwballs who come into banks looking for loans. The odd professors and the mechanics with inventions and the engineers who want a thousand dollars to start a little business in a garage. Adam was after the big loans. But every now and then a screwball walks in off the street with an idea that's really good and the ability to make something out of that idea. But you never meet that one man unless you're willing to listen to the two hundred genuine losers who came in ahead of him. Do you understand me?"

"I think so."

Mock sipped his wine and slipped into a reminiscent mood. "I remember a man who came to see me one day with a scheme to standardize a particular kind of aerospace part in order to sell it to every big airplane maker without the constant costs of retooling. He stammered and couldn't look me in the eye and he had food stains on his tie. Adam would have ushered him out. I listened and loaned him some money. Not much. A few thousand. Do you know who that man was?"

I told him I didn't and Mock gave me the name of one of the biggest industrialists in California. I looked appropriately respectful.

"He banked with me from that day on. Wouldn't go anywhere else no matter how big his company became. Every other bank had turned him down when he was trying to get started, you see. There's a lot more sentiment in a really big businessman than most people realize. Oh sure, you write a few bad loans when you get caught up in people's dreams. But that one big success more than repaid all the little losses over a lifetime of banking. Adam never

131

understood that, but Arnold Thompson did. It's
something the conglomerate boys don't understand
either," Mock added with a touch of bitterness. He
stopped to sip his wine and, I suspect, think hateful
thoughts about conglomerates.

"How did Adam react to losing the promotion?"

"What? Oh. He was surprisingly civil about it.
Congratulated Arnold heartily and even took him
out to lunch to celebrate. It was later, after Arnold
had the accident and I decided to let the vice presidency remain vacant for a while, that Adam got
furious with me and quit."

A quite small chill had wormed into my back.
"What kind of accident did Thompson have?"

"Hit-and-run. He was struck by a stolen car late
one evening near his home. Just a few days after his
promotion, in fact. The police found the car the next
morning. They theorized that some kids took it to go
joy riding and when they hit Arnold they just kept
going and later abandoned the car."

"A large heavy car?"

Mock squinted. "I believe so. Yes. A Buick Ri-
viera." He noticed the expression on my face.
"What's wrong?"

"One of the people involved in the case I'm working on was struck and killed by a hit-and-run driver
in a large heavy car. A stolen Oldsmobile, found the
next day. The police thought kids had caused that
accident, too, until some new evidence came up just
this morning. Now there's a possibility Adam Franklin may have been behind the wheel of that car and
run down the man deliberately. His name was Arthur Avery."

"Dear Jesus. I remember reading about that in

132

the paper. I'd met Avery a few times. Is it possible Adam ran down Arnold Thompson, too?" Mock's voice was shaken and hoarse.

"I'm afraid so. Did Franklin quit the bank when you failed to promote him to Thompson's spot?"

"He was respectfully reserved about Arnold's death for two weeks. Then he came to me and asked point-blank when he was going to be promoted to vice president. Not *if*. *When*. I was appalled by his crude display of ambition and told him I'd made no decision about who would succeed Arnold. Adam flew into a rage and quit on the spot." Mock removed the silver chain from around his neck and put the corkscrew on the counter between us.

"I saw Adam recently. I'm glad I didn't know this when we met. I'd have tried to kill that merciless brute myself." He smiled grimly, holding up his thin banker's hands. "And failed."

"When and where did you see him?"

"About two months ago. I think I mentioned to you that I've been taking some viticulture courses at the university's Davis campus. Well, I was up there for a lecture and bumped into Adam on the library steps. He looked very tan and fit and said he'd been in Mexico. I asked him what he was doing with himself and he told me he'd gotten in on the ground floor with a new company."

"Did he give you the name of the company?"

Mock ran a finger across his temple. "Yes. The . . . Darby Corporation. Darby? I'm sure of it. The Darby Corporation."

I wrote it down. I wouldn't forget the name, but I wrote it down anyway. Police training. Habit. Quirk. I never feel I've quite captured an important piece of

133

information until I write it down.

"That's very helpful, Mr. Mock. I appreciate your time and candor."

"But what about Arnold Thompson?" Mock gestured vaguely. "We can't just ignore the possibility you've brought up. If Adam did kill him the police should know about it."

I'd been thinking about that myself. "Was Arnold Thompson married?"

"He had a fine wife. He and Ellie had two children."

"Was he insured?"

"I see what you're getting at. Arnold's insurance carried a double indemnity clause. The policy had a face value of twenty-five thousand but she collected fifty thousand because Arnold's death was accidental. So if murder were proved she might have to return half her insurance money." He looked troubled and pained. "We wouldn't be doing her much of a favor by bringing this to the police, would we."

"No, we wouldn't," I agreed. "Besides the money, she might feel even worse about losing her husband by murder than by accident."

"You're right. I just hate to think of Adam getting away with it."

"He won't get away with anything," I promised. "The police in Palo Alto are working very hard to nail him for killing his girl friend and Arthur Avery."

"They may prove he killed those people, but I have a feeling they won't catch him."

"Why not?"

"I think Adam is back in Mexico by this time. He knows the interior of Baja California like a native.

134

Better than a native, perhaps. He used to spend weekends and vacations tramping through the mountains there, meeting the people and camping out. I'll tell you one more thing that may help you. I didn't take Adam seriously about this at the time, but he often talked of buying land in Baja California and starting an empire there. That's what he said. An *empire*." Mock laughed shortly to indicate how foolish the idea was. "He always had books in his desk on international law. I asked him once what he was studying and he said he was looking into legal ways for territories to secede from nations. I can see now he was quite serious about his empire. When I saw him at the university he had more books under his arm and I'd be willing to bet he's still planning on forming his magical empire."

I finished my wine. It left a slight skim of sweetness in my mouth but I couldn't think of a decent way to ask for a glass of water. "I met Franklin briefly yesterday morning," I told Mock. "He beat me right down into the ground because he thought I was trying to deprive him of that empire. He used the word with me, too. I'm afraid he's mentally ill in a very vicious way."

"I'm so sorry," Mock said, as if he had personally pushed Franklin over the edge of sanity. In some ways Mock probably had contributed to his sickness. To Franklin the Marlborough Bank was an altar in the religion of materialism and Cecil Mock was a high priest. Franklin worshiped at that altar along with a hundred million other Americans. Like too many others, he went literally mad in his quest for wealth and power.

I left Mock alone with his silver corkscrew and

135

aging casks and drove back toward Palo Alto, taking the Dumbarton Bridge over the bay for the pleasure of skimming along a few feet above the water. When I reached the west side of the bay I stopped at a phone booth to call Roger Max in Los Angeles. He told me he'd talked to George Hogan in the morning and had given him the dates and times that long distance phone calls were made to InterComp from the phony computer company offices Franklin had set up around the state. Hogan was using that information to piece together the amount of data Franklin had stolen. I asked Roger to find out where in the state the Darby Corporation operated and whether they leased any teleprocessing lines. By the time I reached InterComp it was past three in the afternoon and I was beginning to wonder just how much I'd accomplished during the day.

The receptionist greeted me with an arched eyebrow. "You didn't turn in your badge last night," she said in a disappointed voice.

"I'm sorry, I forgot." I fumbled around in my pockets until I found the badge and started to give it back to her.

"Never mind," she sniffed. "Mr. Hogan has instructed us to give you the run of the building and whatever cooperation you need." She appeared to consider Hogan's judgment questionable in this case.

I had a sinking feeling. "How did Hogan communicate that order to you?"

"He sent around a red memo," the receptionist replied in hushed tones.

"A red memo?"

"Mr. Hogan uses white memos for routine corre-

136

spondence, blue memos for important subjects, and red memos for the highest priority messages. This is only the fourth red memo he's sent around since I've worked here!"

I gathered that God would certainly not have used those crummy tablets to give Moses the ten commandments if he could have gotten his hands on a red memo.

"May I see the memo about me?"

"I suppose so."

The memo said:

> Michael Saxon, a consultant on industrial security, is making an audit of our security procedures this week. I expect management to give him its full cooperation. He has complete run of the plant and access to all confidential information.
>
> *G. F. Hogan*

"Jesus Christ! Who got this memo?"

"Why, all functional managers. And he sent it out here so you could get into the plant without an escort. Is something wrong?"

"Oh, no. Everything's just fine." Except that all the high level people in the plant must have realized as soon as they saw the red memo that InterComp was having some kind of security problem. "Thanks very much," I told the troubled receptionist. "I'll find my own way."

I took the familiar route to Hogan's office and as I reached the executive corridor I spotted Paul Avilla talking to a secretary in a corner. She was a well-dressed girl with upswept hair and she was moving in on Paul like Patton moved in on Hitler's panzers. I almost didn't recognize Paul; he was dressed in a

137

dark suit, white shirt, and solid color tie and he held an attaché case in one hand. He looked every inch the corporate climber. He saw me as I went past but took no notice of me. I thanked God I'd gotten him into the plant. Hogan's red memo made it impossible for me to talk to people casually.

Joy Simpson greeted me as coolly as she had the day before and ushered me into Hogan's office.

As soon as the door was closed behind us I said to him, "Your red memo was a dumb stunt, Hogan."

"Why?" he asked, sitting back startled behind his desk. "You said you wanted to talk to my top people. They wouldn't give you any information about the company without my approval."

"But you didn't have to admit I'm here on a security matter."

"That's what you told my son," Hogan shot back. "I couldn't very well tell Tom not to talk to anyone about you without arousing his suspicions; he's one of the people on the list. Besides, the memo will draw all their attention to you and away from your man Avilla."

I calmed down a little. Hogan made a couple of good points. His memo wouldn't do that much harm in normal circumstances, but with a murderer floating around I wasn't looking for too much publicity.

"How's Paul doing? Have you had any word on him from your personnel manager?"

"He's certainly been all over the executive offices," Hogan grumbled. "I can't go out there without tripping over him."

"Glad to hear it."

"Do you think Avilla might be interested in a permanent job here?" Hogan asked suddenly.

"Paul? Doing what?"

"Just what he's doing today. Our service manager passed the word to me that his new man is a genius with teleprocessing equipment. Avilla found a bug in one terminal that had been eluding his other engineers for a week; according to my service manager Avilla is pretty close to a genius. He picked up all the basic operations of the cathode ray tube terminal in an hour's time."

"I'm not surprised, but I don't think Paul wants a permanent job."

"Do you mind if we ask him?"

"God, no." I wondered what Hogan's reaction would be if I told him Paul lives his life two jumps ahead of the Army's Criminal Investigation Division. "I talked to Roger Max at the phone company today. He told me you're trying to determine what information has been stolen by matching phone company records of long distance calls from Computer Specialties with your own computer records."

"That's right." Hogan's jutting chin dropped a little. "It's been a very depressing day. Mickey Iwasaka has estimated the amount of computer time used in getting into our system. They apparently had enough time to take just about all the pertinent data on System/Sell out of our computer." He stood suddenly, like a pop-up toy. "I hope to hell you can get it back, Saxon."

"There's a good chance we can. Have you heard of the Darby Corporation?"

"No."

"Well, keep the name to yourself. The Darby Corporation may be your future competition."

Hogan trembled as if he'd been electrified. "You

139

mean you've found the people who have our plans!"

"No. I just have a name. Roger Max is trying to pin down their location. It's probably another rented office with a terminal installed. They won't be able to put together a manufacturing team until they've culled through all the material taken from your computer. How important were the engineering changes we recovered yesterday?"

"You could build System/Sell without them," Hogan admitted in a grudging voice. "It wouldn't be as efficient as it could be."

"But would it be profitable?"

"Yes."

"Then we have to assume they'll go ahead without the engineering changes. That means we have very little time to recover your plans."

From the parking lot outside Hogan's window came the sounds of hundreds of cars starting up and creeping into lines leading toward the highway. I glanced at my watch. Four o'clock.

"The first shift is leaving," Hogan explained. "They start at seven in the morning."

"Let me use your phone."

I called police headquarters and asked for Lieutenant Pride and was told he was in superior court. They gave me the address and told me to look for him in courtroom number three.

"I want to talk to Pride and then I have a meeting with Paul Avilla. We'll see what he picked up today. Will you be home tonight?"

Hogan hesitated, then said he would.

"There are two questions I've been meaning to ask, Hogan. What would all the information taken from your computer look like? And have you figured

140

a precise value on it yet?"

Hogan raised his hand and made a leveling mark with it at just about my eye level. "The System/Sell plans could be contained in a stack of printout paper about that high, and the value is three million dollars."

"At least I know now what the stuff I'm searching for looks like. I'll call you tonight if I turn up anything."

As I started to leave Hogan cleared his throat ponderously. "Did you have something else for me?" I asked.

He went to his desk and slid a plain white number ten envelope out from under the blotter. "A messenger arrived with this envelope just after lunch. Did you have anything to do with recovering what's inside?"

I took the envelope and opened it. It contained a cashier's check for five thousand dollars and a handwritten note. The check was drawn on a Palo Alto bank. The note said: *I don't seem to need this much money after all, Georgie boy. It's all yours. Good Luck. Connie.*

I grinned at him. "Yes. I definitely had something to do with recovering that money for you."

"I suppose you'll want an additional fee," Hogan said stiffly.

"Not a penny. Not a sou. Not a peso. Not a franc. But I'll tell you what I would appreciate. Since my fee is a minimum of twenty-five thousand, why don't you just endorse this check over to me as a down payment."

"That doesn't sound very businesslike," he said with a dubious frown. "But I suppose it would be

141

legal."

As he endorsed the check he said, "Len Compton called me this afternoon. He got his five K back, too. The same way. He's afraid Connie has decided five K wasn't enough and that she's getting ready to hit him for a bigger sum. The idea's really making him sweat. Most of his money is in his wife's name, from an inheritance."

"Tell him to relax. He'll never hear from Connie again. I guarantee it." I felt light-headed. Buoyant as a cork. Either my day's consumption of creme de menthe, bourbon, port and so forth had finally gotten to me, or I was beginning to feel something very special for Connie. Something akin to what the poets call love. Something that was revving up my metabolism and making my ears hot.

When I left InterComp I noticed a red Mustang with white racing stripes behind me. The car followed me as I skirted the Stanford campus and found a maze of side streets to take me back to Camino Real. No one would take that same route by coincidence. I made a few unnecessary rights and lefts and the car stayed behind me. Far enough back so that I couldn't see who was behind the wheel. When I turned onto Camino Real a second time I spotted that rare animal, a gas station in the middle of the block. I pulled into it. The red Mustang slowed down almost to a stop, but the cars behind it started honking. The driver made a futile attempt to U turn and was blocked by a steady stream of cars coming in the other direction. In the end the driver of the red Mustang had no choice but to continue straight ahead. She turned her face away as she gunned the car past the gas station, but I recognized
142

her anyway. It was Joy Simpson, George Hogan's secretary and part-time mistress. Or mistress and part-time secretary. I didn't know which, but now I was interested in finding out. There was no logical reason for her to follow me, unless she were somehow involved in the theft of the System/Sell plans.

CHAPTER
7

FROM THE GAS station I drove downtown to the courthouse to look for Lieutenant Pride. I found him being sworn in as a witness against a young man in his mid-twenties who was accused of possession and sale of narcotics. Pride had been the arresting officer. He saw me in the back of the courtroom and tipped his head toward the benches, indicating that I should sit down and wait for him.

I was reluctant to do that with only an hour to spare before picking up Connie and meeting Paul for dinner. But I sat down and hoped the cross-examination wouldn't take too long.

Fortunately the prosecutor asked Pride very few questions. In answer to the questions Pride swiftly explained that he had entered this case when he captured a Palo Alto high school student following a liquor store holdup and auto chase. After his arrest the student told Pride he pulled the robbery to get money for narcotics. He said he purchased his supply from Ronald Cummings, as did several other students at the school. Pride had staked out the home where Ronald Cummings lived with his parents and had seen several high schoolers meet with Cummings in his parents' garage. One evening

145

he and two other officers, armed with search warrants, burst into the garage soon after Ronald Cummings went in there with two other boys. He caught Cummings with four "baggies" of marijuana in his hand and found a stash of pot, amphetamines, and even some heroin hidden behind the hot water tank in the garage. The two boys were also high school students.

Pride's evidence was simple and damning, but to my surprise Ronald Cummings smirked throughout the testimony and the defense lawyer doddled on a scratch pad. When the lawyer rose for the cross-examination he was smiling, too. He started quietly enough, asking Pride to repeat various portions of his testimony and bringing up side issues that might have confused the case. Pride refused to be drawn into those side issues and stuck to his simple facts. Obviously the lawyer thought he could get Pride to prejudice parts of his own testimony. As he began to realize Pride would not damage his testimony, the lawyer's questions became sharper and more demanding and Ronald Cummings sat up straight, dropping his amused manner. At one point he turned and held an intense whispered conversation with a tall well-dressed man sitting on the bench directly behind him. From the facial resemblance I assumed the older man was Cummings' father. The father's face was twisted and ugly by the time the defense lawyer gave up on Pride and excused him from the stand.

Pride walked past them and motioned to me. I joined him in the hallway outside the courtroom.

"What was all that about?" I asked.

"Albert Cummings is a big banker here in town.

President of the Chamber of Commerce and a member of the city planning commission. You know the type. He 'accidentally' bumped into me the other day and told me how much he admired me and what a big future I have if I keep up my fine work. Hinted I could make chief some day. Then he said he hoped his son's trial wouldn't last too long, but he was afraid it would if everyone got their testimony as tangled up as they usually do. He cleared his throat a couple of times and gave me a big wink as he said that. Subtle as hell." Pride took a stick of gum out of a shirt pocket and unwrapped it. "Guess I won't make chief this year."

"Albert Cummings didn't look too happy in there. I hope you don't have any loans at his bank."

Pride chuckled. "I don't. And now I never will." He put the gum in his mouth and changed the subject. "I've got some news about Franklin. There were no prints on those little pieces of cellophane we found in the bushes, so I went back to the man whose Olds Franklin stole for the job. I borrowed back the car again and found another cellophane scrap way down under the front seat. This one did have a print on it."

"Franklin's?"

"His right thumb. Good thing the car hadn't been cleaned since we returned it to the owner."

"So you can prove Franklin killed Avery."

His teeth smacking at the gum, Pride considered that with a sour expression. "I don't think so. The car had been out of our hands for a week and a half, long enough for a smart lawyer to show that Franklin's thumb print could have been planted. No. That print is just a piece of the pattern. You see, the Los

147

Angeles police picked up Jockey Joe this morning and he confirmed your report that Franklin chased Ann Lane out of a building in L.A. yesterday. The ticket agent at L.A. International also confirms that Franklin was looking for her. The department there took his photo out of the sports files at the *Times* and wired us a copy. We showed it around Ann Lane's neighborhood and came up with the best piece of evidence yet. A woman who lives in Ann Lane's apartment house saw Franklin in the entranceway when she checked her mail. The time was slightly after 5:00 P.M."

I was about to ask Pride if he'd gotten a line on Franklin's whereabouts when the courtroom emptied out a jostling crowd of people around us. We stepped out of the way, but not soon enough. Ronald Cummings pushed past, slowing to give Pride a sullen scowl. The lawyer's attitude was frigidly correct, but when Cummings drew up next to us he stopped and tried to make Pride shrivel under his angry glare. Pride does not shrivel worth a damn. When Albert Cummings finally realized this he said to Pride in a shaky voice, "I thought we had an understanding."

"We didn't," Pride answered, keeping his voice low.

"You're going to regret that. I have many friends in this city, Pride. They're as shocked as I am at the way you're hounding my son."

"Your son is a drug dealer, Mr. Cummings. Not entirely out of choice, I know. He's paying for his own habit. I think if you assure the judge you'll get competent help for your son, he'll suspend his sentence." A smile of concern momentarily softened Pride's blocky profile. "Why don't you take him to

148

Synanon or one of the other places where he can get help from people who have been through the same grinder. Give your son a break, Cummings."

The banker went white. "I don't need *your* advice. What I needed was your help. Since you refused that I just want to let you know you're finished in this city. You'll never get a promotion or a bank loan or a building permit to add a den to your house or even a simple charge account at any store in this town."

"We'll see," Pride answered, his features quickly hardening again.

With a rude noise Cummings turned and stalked away. Pride touched my arm to guide me away from the knot of spectators who had stopped to catch pieces of the argument.

"I might have given young Cummings a break if he'd told me who his supplier is," Pride said. "There's a new operator in town who's hooking a lot of dummies like Ron Cummings and turning them into pushers. I thought Cummings was the big operator until I saw what a small cache he had; I should have tailed him a few more days, but I couldn't sit in my car and watch him turn on all those babies at the high school." Pride sounded disappointed in himself, but I liked him as much for his occasional weaknesses as a human being as I did for his excellence as a cop.

On the way to the parking lot I told him what I'd learned about Franklin and gave him the phone number at Sandy's apartment. He was interested in the Darby Corporation and thought he'd seen the name. He couldn't remember where, but I bet myself that he wouldn't stop leafing through his mental files until he came up with that answer.

The last thing I said to him was, "Do you think he might have skipped to Mexico already?"

"No. He's too motivated to quit this soon. He's sitting on three million dollars' worth of computer loot and his name hasn't been mentioned in any of the papers in connection with Ann Lane's death. No, he's still here. He wants the money to build that empire you told me about."

From the courthouse I drove to the insurance office where Connie worked. She was sitting in a chair by the front door with a brown grocery box in her lap. When she saw me pull up she struggled up and came outside before I could park and help her with her load.

"What's all this?" I pushed the front seat forward so she could dump the box in the back.

"Stuff," she panted, moving the seat back again and sliding in next to me. "I quit my job today and I had to clean out my desk."

"You quit? Just like that?"

"That's the way I always quit jobs. I bought you a present, too." She reached back as I moved out into the traffic and pulled a long thin box from the clutter. "A new tie. Do you like it?"

I glanced to the right quickly and turned my eyes to the traffic again. "Very nice. But you shouldn't spend your money on me."

"I just couldn't bear the thought of looking at that tie you're wearing today all through our dinner." Before I could stop her, she reached over and loosened the knot on my tie and slipped it over my head.

"Hey look out! I'm driving."

"Haven't you heard it's unsafe to drive under the influence of an ugly tie?" Her fingers moved deftly

150

around my neck. I was powerless to stop her from flapping the new tie in my face as she manipulated a bulky knot under my chin. "There! Much better." She took a matching handkerchief out of her purse and arranged it in my breast pocket. "Now you look handsome enough to have dinner with. Where are we eating?"

I told Connie we were meeting Paul at a health food restaurant near the Stanford campus. She was familiar with the place and gave me directions. I already knew how to get there, but I listened patiently and took the streets she suggested. There was an undercurrent of nervous exhilaration to her chatter and I thought I knew what was causing it. Connie had not enjoyed a normal relationship with a man in a long time. Maybe never. Certainly not with her father's commanding officers or her remote ex-husband or the men she collected those five-thousand-dollar fees from. And now that something curiously honest had developed between us she was trying desperately to establish some form of domestic relationship with me. Hence the little gifts and the mild henpecking of telling me what route to take to the restaurant. She was trying to show me she could handle a normal love affair.

"How did you buy a present for me anyway? I told you not to leave your office today."

"Pfui. There's a men's store next door to the insurance office. If you're such a great detective you should have noticed that."

"And how far was the bank?"

"How did you find out about that? I wanted to surprise you."

"I saw Hogan today. He'd just received your cash-

151

ier's check and wanted to know if I had anything to do with recovering his money."

"And what did you say?"

"I told him I did."

"Male chauvinist ultra-pig. I suppose you think you were so *marvelous* in bed that I rushed out to renounce my illicit money for you." She laughed nervously.

We found the organic foods restaurant a moment later. Paul was in a spotlessly white booth sipping a glass of carrot juice. When I introduced him to Connie his eyes narrowed slightly. Not enough for Connie to notice, but enough to tell me he'd learned of her affair with Hogan during his long day of snooping.

Paul lifted his glass. "I highly recommend the carrot juice."

I looked at the menu. "I see about three things I can eat without needing a transfusion of beefsteak an hour later."

"Negative thoughts," Paul replied. "Organic food can be as satisfying as your standard diet of beefsteak, Mike."

Connie snickered. "The only thing that bothers me about these health food places is the people who run them—they usually look like they're suffering from terminal anemia."

All of us instinctively looked toward the cash register where the manager was ringing up a bill. He was a wispy scarecrow of a man and just as we turned his way he happened to jerk his head down and cough loudly into his hand.

"You win," Paul said, throwing up his hands. "We'll go to a steak house."

152

"No, let's stay here," Connie insisted. She scanned the menu. "I see what I want." She put her hand over mine. "And I'm going to order for you, Mike. Okay?"

"Sure."

Once again Paul and I exchanged glances.

When the waitress came Paul ordered bean soup, a soyburger, and a glass of pineapple juice. For us, Connie ordered two servings of hot biscuits made from whole unbleached flour, a pot of raw honey, an artichoke with a melted butter sauce, and two cups of tea.

"Make that an extra large artichoke," Paul told the waitress. "I'll share it with you two. I dig those things."

"Me, too," Connie said.

"One of my cousins grows them down near Watsonville. They grow best right near the ocean."

"Paul. Are there any Chicanos in the west who aren't cousins of yours?"

He gave the question some serious thought. "Probably not," he finally answered.

One of the definite advantages to eating organic foods is that you don't have to wait long for your meal. It's either raw or quickly prepared. Two minutes later I was munching on a delicious biscuit covered with honey ten times as thick and rich as the kind you buy in supermarkets. The tea was red and hot. But the artichoke was the most fun to eat. It stood almost a foot high on its end. We all took turns pulling off leaves and dipping them in the cup of melted butter. When the leaf is properly saturated you put it in your mouth and then pull it back out again, letting it slide against your teeth in order

153

to strip all the juicy pulp from the bottom of the leaf. The taste is sharp and slightly bitter. One big artichoke has perhaps a hundred leaves, so it took us a while to finish our meal. When all the leaves were gone Connie took her knife and expertly sliced out the heart of the artichoke and we split that among us, too.

"That was delicious," I admitted. "But I'll be hungry again before midnight."

"Glutton," Connie chided.

"I'll ignore that. Paul, what about those nineteen people? Did you narrow down the field any for me?"

"I think so." He wiped his hands on a napkin and took out the list Hogan had given us.

"Connie knows these people pretty well," I said. "We can match her impressions of them with yours."

Paul's dark brown eyes skimmed the list. "You asked me to find out which of these people have been acting suspicious or irrational in any way. I got into the offices of all nineteen people on the list, talked to their secretaries . . ." he looked up and grinned . . . "and looked around and in their desks where I could get the chance. I've narrowed the field of possible sellouts to five people. Any one of them could be the person who's been feeding computer codes to Adam Franklin."

"Who are they?" Connie asked with a Dr. Watson frown.

"Herman Zimmerman, the corporate controller. Madeline Hassler, a senior systems designer. John Walden, manager of new product engineering. William Iverson, the national sales manager. And—this one's a surprise—Tom Hogan, George Hogan's son."

154

"Hogan's son? What have you got on him?"

"I had a long talk with his secretary. She has a thing for Tom Hogan and she's worried about him. When Tom came home from the Marines six months ago, Arthur Avery brought him into the company on the market research staff. Tom started out like a race horse. He reorganized the department . . . made an in-depth survey of the company's older products that resulted in two computer models being dropped from the product line . . . handled the market research for System/Sell. He was going great until about two months ago. Then he began coming in late and leaving early. Sloughing off his work on other people. His father hasn't noticed all this yet because Tom's friends have been covering for him, hoping he'll pull out of whatever malaise he's fallen into." Paul sipped at his pineapple juice. "I saw Tom twice today. The first time he was friendly. Said he hadn't seen me around before and introduced himself. The second time I saw him, in mid-afternoon, he went by me like a ghost. He was sweating and looked worried."

I turned to Connie. "Any ideas?"

"No. I'm afraid I can't tell you much about Tom. He came out of the service only a couple of weeks before I quit InterComp, and his father wasn't exactly in a rush to introduce us."

"Why not?" Paul asked.

"Don't push it!" I snapped, interrupting something Connie was about to say. She covered one of my hands with both of hers. It was an expression of affection I enjoyed more each time it was offered.

"It's all right," she said, smiling at me. "George Hogan and I . . ."

"Never mind," Paul interrupted. He looked sheepish. "Mike taught me his business too well. When I'm curious I go to work automatically, just to see what reactions I get. I heard about you and George Hogan, Connie. But when we met tonight I had the feeling you and Mike had known each other a long time. I wanted to find out how that could be. I'm sorry I embarrassed you."

"You didn't, Paul. Oh, maybe a little. But when you say Mike and I seem to have known each other a long time, that's worth a little embarrassment."

"Okay." Paul cleared his throat. "Let's talk about Madeline Hassler."

"Good!" Connie said, repeating her Dr. Watson frown. "I hope she's the sellout."

"Why do you say that?" I asked.

"Because she's a cruel sexless bitch."

"From what I learned she's certainly a bitch," Paul admitted, "but not sexless. She's been playing house with Tom Hogan."

"Tom Hogan and Madeline Hassler?" Connie shivered. "That's the oddest couple since Jackie and Ari. Madeline and I tangled several times when I was George's secretary. She's one of the *new women*. Chairman of ZPG and a leader in the fight to reform abortion laws. Naturally, she calls herself *Ms.* Hassler." Connie shrugged. "Nothing wrong with those things, but what I didn't like was her contempt for any girl who isn't a part of the women's movement. She has very nasty names for any girl who lets a man open a door for her."

"But what's Madeline Hassler done to make you think she might be leaking information to Adam Franklin?" I wanted to know. Connie's bitchy com-
156

ments were not exactly the kind of objective character examination I was looking for.

"Madeline is a very smart woman with lots of drive," Paul continued. "She's about thirty-five, single, attractive (Connie snorted), a mathematician who's been promoted over several men she once worked for. But the most interesting fact about her as far as you're concerned, Mike, is that for the past several weeks she's been taking home confidential documents about System/Sell."

"What kind of documents?"

"Tonight she took home a paper marked *Registered Confidential*. It was a list of all the engineering changes for their new computer. Isn't that the same kind of material you recovered for them yesterday?"

"Yes. Connie, what's a registered confidential document?"

"Let me think," Connie said, rearranging the long dark hair at the side of her face. "There were so many kinds of documents there. Let's see. Registered confidential papers are summaries of important technical work. They can only be checked out of the document control center for periods of twenty-four hours. Then they have to be checked back in again. It's part of InterComp's program to keep proprietary information from getting out of the plant."

"The program isn't working," I said. "They should require those papers to be checked back in at the end of the day, so people like Madeline Hassler couldn't take them out of the plant overnight. She could Xerox all that information very quickly. Would the summary of the engineering changes be as complete as the information on that subject that was stolen out of the computer?"

Connie shook her head. "The summary only tells what part of the system the changes apply to, and why they were made. There aren't any drawings or other details. And Madeline couldn't have Xeroxed the document; the pages are typed in blue specifically because copying machines can't reproduce that color."

"I'll still have to find out why she took that particular document home. Let's hear about the other three, Paul."

He squinted at the scribbling on his list of names. "Okay. Let's look at John Walden. He's in an important job and he's talking to several of Inter-Comp's competitors. I just happened to be looking through the appointment book on his desk this morning. I noticed he has a luncheon appointment tomorrow at the Blue Boar with a Mr. Logan of the Chalmers Company. Chalmers' product line is very similar to InterComp's. I went back through his appointment book. In the past three weeks he's talked with two other competitors besides Chalmers."

"Interesting. Did you see any references to a company called the Darby Corporation in Walden's book?"

"Not that I recall," Paul said. That meant there were no references to the Darby Corporation. Paul's memory is encyclopedic.

"What kind of guy is this Walden, Connie?"

"A very private man," she said. "All business. He seldom says anything not related to business. Drives his people like slaves. No one really likes Walden, but no one's ever gotten to know him well enough to have anything against him. I'm surprised Walden is talking to a competitor. He's always seemed too con-
158

cerned with his professional reputation to jeopardize it with something shady."

"People will sell off the best parts of themselves for money," I reminded her. "Arms. Legs. Reputations. Wives. Souls. Why should Walden be different?"

"Number four, William Iverson," Paul continued. "He took over Hogan's job as national sales manager when Hogan went upstairs as president. Before that he was sales manager for the western division. Iverson is a solid man, from everything I've been able to learn. But his salesmen are complaining that in the past few months he's started to slip. Their specific complaints are that he's changed from an interested, alert executive into a mooning daydreamer. That he doesn't answer his phone calls half the time. And that he's become a fancy dressing fop whose social life has become more important to him than his job."

"Fancy dressing fop," I repeated. "That's a strange phrase. What do they mean by that?"

"I don't know. One of his staff used that phrase when he was telling me that he thinks Iverson dresses too garishly for a businessman. This guy also says Iverson reads travel folders all day. He's seen Iverson slip them out of sight when he's gone into his office."

"Connie, give me your impression of Iverson."

"When I worked at InterComp he was known as a very industrious man. He's a good friend of George. He talks a little too loudly and laughs at jokes too quickly. He's like a lot of salesmen, I suppose. A hail-fellow-well-met on the outside and probably insecure on the inside."

"Okay. Give me number five, Paul."

"Number five. Herman Zimmerman. Another hard driver, but people seem to like him. The reason I'm putting him down as a suspect is this: yesterday when he came back from lunch his hands were shaking and he went right into Hogan's office and out of the blue requested a three-month leave of absence. The rumor is that he told Hogan he'd just been to his doctor and was ordered to take a rest immediately. But his assistant—who isn't too happy at having to assume all of Zimmerman's duties for three months along with his own—was grumbling today that Zimmerman had his annual checkup two months ago and his tests were all perfect. He's so healthy he could be an astronaut if he wanted to."

"So Zimmerman asked for a leave of absence right after lunch yesterday." That made him my number one suspect. "Franklin and I tangled just before lunch time yesterday. If Zimmerman is Franklin's connection he may have heard about that from Franklin and panicked. I'm going to see Zimmerman first."

"Tonight?" Connie pouted.

"Tonight," I told her. "Paul, I'd like you to take Connie home."

"I'll be happy to," he said admiringly.

"And keep your Latin instincts on a short leash," I warned him. "Stop at Connie's house first and pick up whatever things she might need, then take her to the apartment we've been staying at. Connie, keep the door locked and the phone close by. I don't think you're in danger from Franklin any longer, but let's not take chances. I'll be back there later tonight."

"You'd better be."

160

"Do you want me to go into InterComp tomorrow?" Paul asked.

"Yes. Give me your extension there and stay close to it. You did a good job today, Paul. One of these five people has to be Franklin's connection."

Paul wrote his extension number on the list of names and passed it over to me. He'd already added the home addresses of our five suspects next to their names. In a day of surprises there was one more: Tom Hogan and Madeline Hassler lived in the same apartment building.

CHAPTER
8

TWENTY MINUTES LATER I was at Herman Zimmerman's home in Redwood Shores, a little spit of land on the west side of San Francisco Bay that some developer had created by dumping enough fill into the bay to create high-priced real estate. The idea wasn't original with this particular developer. The fast-buck operators have been doing it for years, which is why the bay is only two-thirds as big as it was a hundred years ago. Some day the real estate crowd will run out of bay. I suppose then they'll come up with a way to fill in the sky. All that blank blue space must drive them crazy.

The Zimmermans' two-story home backed up against the bay. No one answered my persistent ringing, so I strolled around to the rear of the house where a small floating dock had been built out into the water. Each of the homes along Redwood Shores had its own similar dock and from the flutter of white sails out on the water it looked like they all used their boats. One of the skiffs was heading into the Zimmermans' dock. I walked out onto the rolling boards just in time to grab awkwardly at a line thrown to me by a man who was standing up in the narrow hull to bring in the sail. A woman sat at the tiller, and she brought the skiff—which looked like a fifteen-footer—expertly into its slip.

"Thanks," the man called, as I drew the boat in and put my foot against the hull to keep it from banging into the dock. He jumped smartly onto the rolling planks with me and completed the docking, then helped the woman out of the boat. They were both in their mid-forties, tanned from frequent sailing, and radiating the blustery good health that comes from lots of outdoor living. If this was Herman Zimmerman, he had lied to George Hogan about needing a rest.

"Good evening," I said. "My name is Michael Saxon."

"Oh!" He put an arm around the woman with him and drew her close to him. "The man in the red memo. What can I do for you?"

"Are you Herman Zimmerman?"

"I am. This is my wife, Ella."

Ella Zimmerman smiled warmly.

"George Hogan asked me to talk to you about a business matter. I hope you don't mind my coming to your home."

"You're perfectly welcome," Mrs. Zimmerman said graciously. "Do you like lemonade? We always have a glass when we come in off the bay." She led our way toward the house. "You can have something else, of course."

"I'd enjoy a lemonade."

"Ella doesn't use the canned stuff," Zimmerman said proudly. "Whole fresh lemons and plenty of shaved ice." Except for glancing at me once on the dock, Zimmerman's eyes never left his wife.

Zimmerman took me into a paneled study off his

164

living room and fiddled with a variety of pipes while I took a seat. His wife must have prepared the lemonade before they went out on the boat, because she returned with two frosted glasses full of pale green lemonade and yellow chunks of lemon and piles of ice before I could fit myself comfortably into the contours of a red leather easy chair.

"I'm going to do some sewing while you talk business," Ella Zimmerman said. "I hope you'll excuse me, Mr. Saxon."

"Of course." I struggled to rise, but the chair was too deep for me to stand up quickly. Zimmerman, however, dropped his pipes and scurried after her. He stood in the hallway while his wife went twenty feet or so to a sewing room tucked off the kitchen, acting as if she had to walk barefoot on hot coals to get there. It wasn't until a faint hum told him she'd begun sewing that Zimmerman came back into the study and sat down in another easy chair facing me. He picked up a pipe and a little pen knife and started cleaning the bowl absently. "What can I do for you, Mr. Saxon?"

"I understand you asked George Hogan for leave of absence yesterday."

"I did. He was good enough to give me a three-month leave. I went in this morning to clear up a few things and I don't expect to be back until October." He looked toward the sewing room again. "Or perhaps November. I can't be quite sure. I happened to see the red memo about you this morning, though. Something about a security audit."

"Why did you ask for a leave of absence?"

"My doctor told me I need a good rest," Zimmerman answered.

"I've heard that you had a checkup a couple of months ago and that your doctor said you're in fine condition."

Under his heavy tan, Zimmerman flushed a deep red. "My personal problems are no business of yours, Saxon. What did Hogan send you here for, anyway? Has he changed his mind about the leave? If that's it, then you can tell him to take his job and shove it!"

"Hogan hasn't changed his mind. I'll be frank with you. A highly placed person in your company has been leaking industrial secrets to someone outside. I'm trying to find out who that person is, and your request for a leave of absence comes at a time when I'm closing the circle. Now you look just too damned healthy to need a rest, Zimmerman. I want to know the real reason you're taking three months off."

"Looks can be very deceiving," Zimmerman said in a hushed voice. He put the pipe and pen knife aside again. I wondered if he actually smoked at all. "Are you interested in photography? I've got a dandy little darkroom set up in the garage. I'd like to show it to you."

I was about to refuse to see Zimmerman's "dandy little darkroom" and insist once again that he tell me why he was taking three months off the job, but there was a desperation in his voice that impelled me to stand up and follow him out to the garage.

One corner of the garage had been partitioned off and he opened the door to the darkroom and ushered me in ahead of him. The inside walls of the darkroom were lined with sound-proofing material and I fought back a sudden fear that Zimmerman had taken me in here to finish the job Franklin had started on me yesterday. My Walther was in the car again, so I backed as far away from Zimmerman as I could. He slid a latch closed and we faced each other in a dim red light that shadowed both our faces into evil masks. I had just about convinced myself Zimmerman was Franklin's silent partner when he quickly switched the red light off and turned on a glaring white light that showed me the anguish in his face.

"What's the matter?" I asked him.

He turned away from me and leaned both his hands on the flat expanse of table under his enlarging machine. The darkroom also contained a pair of sinks, some cabinets, and an outfit for drying prints. Strung along an overhead wire by little clips were negatives and developed pictures. As far as I could see at a quick glance, every piece of film in the darkroom portrayed the same subject—Ella Zimmerman.

"I started shooting pictures of her as soon as I got home from the plant this morning," Zimmerman said. "That was stupid. She told me to stop it. I have plenty of pictures of her already, taken over the years."

I gestured at the profusion of pictures. "What's the point of all this?"

"The point is that my wife has leukemia. We got the final word on that yesterday. She has perhaps three months to live. That's why I asked Hogan for the leave. I want to spend the time with her. And our kids are coming home from school; they're in that damn quarter system at UC Santa Cruz. We're going to do a little sailing . . . a little talk-

167

ing . . . a little living. I told George I wasn't well because I didn't want Ella taking a lot of sympathy calls from our friends at work."

"She knows?"

"Of course. I had to tell her, with the kids dropping out of school and me staying home from work."

The image of Ella Zimmerman offering me a glass of lemonade made my throat tighten. "I'm sorry, but I have to confirm this. We're dealing with the future of InterComp and . . ."

"I understand," he said quickly. "Our doctor is John Patrick. He's usually in his office about this time." There was a phone in the darkroom. Zimmerman used it. "John? This is Herman Zimmerman. Yes. She's fine tonight. Right, we'll be in Friday. The kids are coming home tonight. I know. I will." He lifted his eyes over the receiver. "John, there's a Mr. Saxon here. He wants to confirm Ella's illness with you. No no. This is a kind of strange business situation. Something to do with my taking a leave of absence. Would you speak to him? Thanks."

He handed me the phone. "Doctor. This is Michael Saxon. Would you tell me what Mrs. Zimmerman's condition is, please."

"Terminal leukemia," the doctor said shortly. "She may have a brief remission. But I doubt it. Is that all you wanted to know?"

"Yes."

"Then goodbye." He hung up.

"I'm sorry, Mr. Zimmerman."

He took the phone back and put it down. "Come back inside. She'll be hurt if you don't finish your lemonade."

We went back into the house and I drank my lemonade. Once in high school I joined a secret club. As part of the initiation I had to drink a glass of water filled with worms. Those worms weren't nearly as hard to get down as Ella Zimmerman's hand-squeezed lemonade.

She left her sewing to say goodbye to me.

"Please come again," she said. Now I could see the greyness in her face and the slight shaking of her hands. "We'd love to take you out on the boat."

"Thank you. It's been an honor meeting you."

As I was leaving a cab pulled up in front of the Zimmerman house. A boy and girl of college age, both bearing the vigorous stamp of the Zimmermans, jumped out. Ella Zimmerman ran down the front walk and threw her arms around them.

At the next gas station I stopped and went into the phone booth. There was a Dr. John Patrick in the phone book. His number was the same one I'd carefully committed to memory as Herman Zimmerman dialed it in his darkroom. I did so because he could have been calling a confederate who would then repeat a concocted story of leukemia to me as a cover story. I believed Zimmerman, but I had to check it out. That's what this business is all about: checking the details until you catch someone in an important lie. You have to do it, even when it makes you feel like a prize shit.

My next stop was Madeline Hassler's place. She lived in a sprawling complex of luxury garden apartments on Sand Hill Road within walking distance of the Stanford campus, the kind of place full professors and middle management people live. She was in apartment 306. Tom Hogan's address was apartment 141.

169

Madeline Hassler opened the door as I came up the narrow stairway to her landing. Apparently she was expecting someone and had heard my footsteps.

"Tom?" she said hesitantly. The sun had just gone behind the brown hills to the west and it was quite dark on the steps.

"No, Miss Hassler. My name is Michael Saxon. I'm . . ."

"Don't tell me. I've heard your name. Yes. You're the man the red memo was all about. What are you doing here?"

She closed the door partially as I came up even with her on the landing. Light from inside fell on both of us. She was a big woman. Not big in the way Connie was big—in a few select places—but big all over. She wore starched denim slacks, loafers, and a long-sleeved white shirt buttoned at the neck but with the shirt tails hanging out around her waist. Her face was hawkish but handsome and she had not closed the door because I scared her. I guessed that Madeline Hassler was just a solo lady who didn't like people peeking past her into her home.

"I'm here on a business matter. May I come in?"

"Can't we do this at the office tomorrow?"

"I'm afraid not."

"It better be important. Just a minute." She closed the door completely then and I heard her quick footsteps followed by the sound of rattling paper. When she opened the door wide there was a testy tilt to her head.

"I'm sorry to disturb you."

"That's all right. Just get on with it." She shook a cigarette from a package and paced the floor like a cat as she lit it. I sat down.

170

"As Hogan's red memo explained, I'm doing a security audit for InterComp. One of my concerns is the safety of registered confidential documents. As you know, those documents are not supposed to leave the plant. I have reason to believe you're taking such material out of InterComp and I'd like to know why."

"So that's it," she said. "George is worried that I'm passing on secrets to the competition."

"Are you?"

"Hell, no," she said mildly, looking me straight in the eye.

"Then what's your reason for taking confidential documents home at night?"

She cocked her head, making her bristly short brown hair tremble like a field of wheat in the wind. "Mr. Saxon, tell me what you see when you look at me."

The question made me uncomfortable. I don't like to have the advantage taken out of my hands when I'm questioning someone. I answered cautiously, "An attractive and apparently capable woman."

"Exactly!" Her answer came with a lashing invective. "A woman. And do you know what that means?"

I couldn't have come up with a sensible answer to that question, but she didn't wait for one.

"The fact that you see a woman first and an individual second means I have to work twice as hard at my job as any man. That means working nights, my friend. I bring work home with me every night, Mr. Saxon, and I don't much care whether that breaks a few rules."

She stopped talking but her eyes continued to

171

blaze. She was leaning forward with her elbows resting on her desk the way a lioness arches her legs before an attack. I had the feeling that if I said one wrong word I'd be leaving Madeline's apartment minus one or two of my cherished limbs.

I cleared my throat in an exploratory manner. "In that case, you'd better call me Mike and I'll call you Madeline. Or if that bothers you, just call me Madeline and I'll call you Mike. I didn't come here for a battle of the sexes."

Madeline raised an inch in her chair and her angry eyes widened. Then she threw back her head in a raucous laugh that shook the glass in the windows. She stood up and came around her desk, still laughing. "You fooled me, Saxon. I thought you were just one of those dusty little men who worry about initials on pieces of paper. But now that I take a better look at your very battered face I can see you don't work in anyone's office. You'd scare off the secretaries! You look like a cross-country freight driver that someone's dressed up in a two-hundred-dollar suit for a joke." She smiled more kindly this time. The change in attitude gave her whole appearance a softer and more feminine look, whether she liked that or not. "Since I'm a little larger than life myself," she went on, "I have a feeling we can get along. Now tell me what this is *really* about."

She plopped herself down on a huge cushion near my chair and gave me the kind of attention she probably reserved for her office: an intense, deeply penetrating focus of her whole personality on what I was about to say.

"Okay. Someone in a high position inside Inter-Comp has been stealing the plans for your new product, System/Sell. We've gotten some of that material back, and we'll ultimately recover all of it. But I'm not going to stop until I find the person inside the company. This may sound melodramatic, but people have been killed in this affair. If you know anything about it, you'd better tell me right now."

"Who's been killed?"

I told her about Ann Lane and Arthur Avery, leaning heavily on Lieutenant Pride's report to me in order to assure her the whole story didn't come out of my imagination.

"That's incredible!" she said when I finished. "But if you think I might have leaked information to this man Franklin, why are you telling me all this?"

"Why not? If you're the one who's working with Franklin, you already know these facts. If you aren't, then perhaps you can help me."

"Of course." Then, in a businesslike voice, "What exactly do you want from me?"

I took out my notebook. "Give me the titles of the documents you've been taking home during the past couple of months and the dates you checked them out. You probably won't be able to recall the exact dates; approximations will be all right."

"How will that information help you?"

"I want to know how much of the stuff you've been bringing home relates to System/Sell."

"I see. You want me to do a head dump. All right." She closed her eyes and began dictating, swiftly and without hesitation. I found it difficult to keep up with her. In the next five minutes she reeled off the titles of about three dozen technical documents. A few were related to System/Sell, but the bulk were support material for a computer labeled

173

the InterComp 500, a medium-sized machine that was the largest the company manufactured. She recalled most of the dates, too. Not approximately. Exactly. I wrote it all down, planning to check the information out later with the document control people at InterComp. Madeline Hassler's mind was impressive. It was certainly the kind of brain that could conceive and carry out the involved technical swindle I was faced with. A woman who believed she would never reach the pinnacle of the business world because of her sex might be just the person to break loose and form her own company.

"I think that about covers it," she said at last. "When you look into the records at the company you'll find I haven't checked out any System/Sell papers except the ones I've just mentioned."

"But why did you take the engineering change summary tonight?"

She glanced around uncomfortably. "I suppose you have to know. I've got my eye on John Walden's job. He's the chief design engineer for System/Sell. I happen to know that some of the engineering changes for System/Sell are going to cost a lot more than Walden has estimated. He knows that, too, of course. He's been stalling our product review board with low estimates while he tries to find ways to lick his costs. If I can prove that to the board, Walden will look pretty bad. You can't afford to play with figures at this stage of a product's development. They just might kick him out of the job, and I'm the logical person to move into his office." By the time she finished her explanation, Madeline Hassler's face was shining with delight at this prospect. I had no doubt she would get Walden's job—if not now, then the next time around. The business world is a game of musical chairs, and dumping your closest friend on his ass brings shouts of laughter and excitement from all the players.

"Do you think Walden can lick these cost problems?"

"Certainly. Given enough time. He's a brilliant man and his team is equally competent."

"Okay. Let's move to another subject. What kind of relationship do you have with Tom Hogan?"

Madeline Hassler jumped to her feet and threw her cigarette at me. I ducked and it flew over my head, landing on the cushions of a high-backed gold couch behind me.

"That's eight hundred dollars' worth of upholstery, you prying bastard!" She ran over and snatched up the butt before it did any damage.

"You threw it, Madeline."

She ground it out roughly in a large metal ash tray shaped like a hollowed-out elephant's foot. "Your inference was very insulting," she said. "Tom Hogan is ten years younger than me. Just a boy."

"An ex-Marine officer is not a boy," I pointed out.

"This one is," she said. "I didn't even know he lived in this apartment complex until a few months ago. He came to the door one evening and told me he had an apartment here, too. He said he'd lost his wallet at the beach and was wondering if I could loan him twenty dollars until he straightened things out. I did, and he left. Didn't even come in the apartment."

"And you've never gone out with him?"

"Never," she insisted.

"Then why are stories about the two of you floating all over InterComp?"

She found another cigarette and lit it. "I made the mistake of lending him more money," she said. "Several times."

"How much have you let him have altogether?"

"Right now he owes me fourteen hundred dollars."

"That's a hell of a big jump from a twenty-dollar bill. Did he get that from you in one big lump sum or in a series of smaller loans?"

"A bunch of little ones. Sixty dollars. A hundred. Ninety. Like that."

"How often?"

"Every Tuesday. Sometimes he comes to my office and closes the door behind him. He usually gives me some stupid story about misplacing his checkbook or some other patently obvious lie. I guess that's how the talk got started about us."

"What's he need the money for?"

"I don't know. Believe me, I've been trying to find out. His salary is close to twenty K a year. He shouldn't have to nickel and dime like this. I think others are loaning him money, too. I've seen him at the plant with people he doesn't really have any business reason to see. Some of them are very low level employees."

"I guess I don't have to ask why you've let Tom Hogan put the bite on you for such a hefty sum, Madeline. Having your boss's son in your debt will be quite an ace to hold when you make your move for John Walden's job. Especially if you can discover the reason he needs the money."

She gave me a wintry stare. "That's it exactly. Tom is hiding something. I'd like to know what it is, and I'd be willing to pay well for the information."

176

"I already have a client."

"Just keep it in mind." She gave me a jolly wink.

I changed the subject. "This is Tuesday night and when you heard me on the steps you called out Tom's name. Do you expect him to show up for another loan tonight?"

"Yes," she admitted. "He called about a half hour ago and said he needed a hundred dollars. I told him I wouldn't loan him any more unless he gives me the real reason for all this borrowing. He begged for just one more loan. I hung up on him."

"Then why do you think he'll show up?"

"He's counting on me."

The doorbell chimed. I suppose we'd been talking too loudly to hear Tom's footsteps. I hoped he, in turn, hadn't heard our voices.

"Give him the money and get rid of him," I whispered. "I want to follow him." I went into the kitchen.

"You're very free with my money," she whispered into the kitchen. But she took her purse out of her desk and set it on a small table in the entranceway.

"Hi, Madeline," Tom Hogan said when she opened the door. "Can I come in?"

"No."

"Look, I'm sorry I've had to borrow so much from you. It's a silly thing really. I've been having an addition built onto dad's cabin at Lake Tahoe as a surprise for him and the contractor is working faster than I expected. You know how those guys are about their money. They want it every week. That's why I've been short lately. If you can just let me have a hundred more I'll be squared away with him and next week I can start paying you back."

"I thought your father sold his cabin at Tahoe after your mother died."

Tom giggled. His raw nerves were exposed in the sound. "That's right. But . . . he bought another one. A smaller place. That's why I'm having a room added onto it."

Tom was about to come apart. I hoped Madeline would stop playing one-up and give him the hundred dollars.

"I didn't know that, Tom. All right. One more loan."

I heard her purse open.

"Thanks, Madeline. I'll see you tomorrow."

As soon as Tom left I came out of the kitchen. When I was sure he was all the way down the steps I turned and said, "Thanks, Madeline. I'll see you tomorrow, too."

"Super prick," she grunted back. "You owe me one hundred dollars."

CHAPTER 9

TOM HOGAN APPEARED and disappeared between the knee-high lights illuminating the walkway going in the direction of the carports. I headed toward the street where my rented car was parked. Two minutes later Tom's car emerged from the apartment complex and I began following him east. The car he was driving didn't match his salary or position. His elderly, puffing Volkswagen beetle was a peculiar automobile for a twenty-thousand-dollar executive. I suspected Tom's obvious financial difficulties had something to do with Adam Franklin. Franklin would certainly be making huge financial demands on whomever he was working with at InterComp.

I didn't play games with Tom. I stayed right on his tail as he wandered around town in a random pattern that gave me no clue to his destination. Finally I tumbled to the idea that he was just cruising until a particular time. I looked at my watch. Ten minutes to nine. It didn't take a Sherlock Holmes to deduce that Tom had a nine o'clock meeting with someone. The possibility that the someone was Adam Franklin both exhilarated and frightened me. Instinctively, I reached inside my coat and felt the cold grip of the Walther. I'd tucked it into my waistband after my scare in Zimmerman's darkroom.

Conflicting emotions were going on inside me. I wanted Tom to be going for a meeting with Franklin, and I didn't. I wanted to face Franklin myself, and I didn't. I wondered how I'd feel if Tom suddenly gunned his old VW through a traffic light and left me tied up in a blocked intersection. Would I be genuinely disappointed to lose him or would I rejoice at my salvation? I guess every man has frequent doubts about the depth of his own courage. I know I do. And driving alone in a rented car in a city that isn't your home is a very lonely place to discover how much backbone you really have. There's no one to remind you that you aren't the first person who's ever faced a wily killer. No one at all.

By nine o'clock we were on University Avenue, the long boulevard that stretches from the bay to the Stanford campus. As the street nears the campus it evolves from a tree-lined residential thoroughfare into the backbone of the city's downtown area: furniture stores selling the graceful artistry of Scandinavian countries, jewelry shops, restaurants, clothing stores, and theatres make up the bulk of the businesses. At eight-thirty most of them are still open and the street is alive with people.

Tom put his VW in a city lot on a side street. I watched him feed pennies to the meter. He dropped one and tried to scoop it up, missed, and bent lower to look for it. He was so nervous he hadn't noticed you don't need to pay for parking after 6:00 P.M. The little red flags were up on all the other meters in the lot.

After stuffing a half-dozen coins in the meter he

put his hands in his pockets and walked quickly toward University Avenue. I stayed with him. At the corner he turned right and continued walking. Tom Hogan was looking for someone. Every half block he'd step off the curb and peer both ways down the street. I knew when he spotted what he'd been looking for. He straightened and his pace quickened. It came as a shock when he left the sidewalk and stepped into—of all things—a bookmobile.

On the side of the bus was a sign advertising it as a mobile lending library offering *"All the newest best sellers . . . Art books and magazines . . . Biographies and travel . . . at new low-lending library rates!"* From the sidewalk I could see that it was a converted touring bus with the seats ripped out to make room for book cases and shelves. A few customers and shoppers were going in the two doors on the sidewalk side of the bus—one at the front and one near the rear. Tom had gone through the rear door. I went in the front.

"Evening," said a bearded man who was sitting at a tiny counter installed by the driver's seat. "Have you used our mobile library before?"

I told him I hadn't and he handed me a yellow sheet of mimeographed paper. "This is our schedule," he said.

"Thank you." I turned my back to Tom, who was browsing the rear stacks, and studied the sheet. According to the schedule this bookmobile was making a thirty-minute stop in downtown Palo Alto that was part of a regular weekly tour of bay area cities stretching from San Francisco to San José. Books on all subjects lent at small rates. A typical lending-library operation, except on wheels. The schedule in-

181

dicated this was the bookmobile's last stop of the day. It would be pulling out in fifteen minutes. Where was Adam Franklin?

I folded the sheet and slipped it in a pocket. It didn't matter anymore whether Tom spotted me. The time had come to push him. I let my fingers roll along the bindings of the books as I strolled down the narrow aisle. Tom and I were the only customers in the bookmobile at the moment. He was talking with a second clerk who was stationed at an even smaller counter near the rear door, a rat-faced character with buck teeth peeking out from between heavy lips. Tom was checking out a heavy volume as I approached him.

"That'll be $1.80, sir," the clerk said. "And the book is due next Wednesday."

Tom passed over the money. I caught a quick glimpse of the bills. They looked like hundred-dollar bills.

"Hello, Tom," I said, touching his arm just as he accepted the book.

"What? Oh. Hello there, Saxon." Tom's voice was hoarse. His eyes flicked from me to the clerk and back again. He didn't look much like an honored ex-Marine officer. "I was just . . ." He hefted the book in his hand. "Look, I'll see you tomorrow at the plant."

I took his arm as he tried to move away and felt it trembling under the expensive cloth of his business suit. It was a pitifully thin arm for an ex-Marine.

"What are you reading?" I took the book out of his hand. Despite its size, it wasn't heavy at all. Not nearly heavy enough, in fact.

"Sal! Roll it!" shouted the rat-faced clerk.

From the corner of my eye I saw the big bearded guy in the front jump behind the wheel of the bus. With a single fast movement of his right arm he pushed a lever that shut both doors and slammed the gear shift forward. The engine turned over and the bus jumped forward just as rat-face hit my back. I twisted and he went over my shoulder into a stack of books. The narrow band of wood meant to keep books from falling off the shelves when the bus is in motion snapped and a half ton of paper fell on the three of us.

By the time I struggled back to my feet the bus was hitting fifty miles an hour. Lights whirred past and car horns boomed angrily. I put my hand inside my coat but the Walther was lost down there among the books.

"Take the fucking wheel, Hogan!" rat-face yelled, and Tom pitched forward to the front of the bus. The book he'd been clutching fell. It was hollowed out. A package of white powder and multi-colored pills scattered from it.

I picked up the heaviest book in sight and heaved it at rat-face. The book sailed past his ear. He smiled, revealing the full horror of his dental work. A knife blade glistened between us. It was in his hand, of course. I snatched up another book and in a ridiculous moment of curiosity stared at the title. *Operating Manual for Space Ship Earth* by Buckminster Fuller. I'd already read it, so I threw it at rat-face, too. He dodged and came ahead, slowly and expertly, one hand against the shelving to keep his balance. We both lifted our feet high in the clutter of bindings and covers as we shifted position. The blade was perhaps seven inches long and had the sharpness that only hours of honing on an Arkansas whetstone will bring. I couldn't make any mistakes against rat-face.

Fortunately, the driver made the mistake. He was so eager to help his buddy that he slammed on the brakes to let Tom take the wheel. Rat-face and I pinwheeled forward as the bus shuddered to a jolting stop. More goddam books crashed into the aisle. We didn't fall this time. We were knee-deep in culture and struggling to pull our legs free.

"Get going, Hogan!" the beard yelled, surging toward me with his partner.

The bus started again with a lurch and moved crookedly ahead. Tom turned into a side street on an impulse and more books rained down. I jumped at rat-face and grabbed the hand holding the knife.

"You shitbird!" he squawked.

I got his wrist turned under and felt little bones give.

"YaaHHH!"

Rat-face's scream muffled the sound of his wrist cracking to pieces. I bent my knees and threw my whole body against his crippled arm to catapult him away from me. He was unconscious when he hit the counter at the rear of the bus.

For the first time I noticed lots of little bags of white powder and pills spilling out of many hollow books.

I turned to face the beard, who held a gun instead of a knife. A revolver with a two-inch barrel. The barrel wavered as he tried to get a straight bead on me. I writhed and kicked books and swore. The shot sounded like a cannon in the enclosed space of the bus. Glass broke behind me as I launched myself at
184

his legs. His second shot tore a hole in the roof and Tom swiveled around to see who had been killed. He was crying with terror and not watching the road. An instant later, just as I forced one hand around the beard's gun arm, the bus hurtled off the street onto the sidewalk for a sideswiping contest with a bank building. The bank won. The bus careened onto its right front and right rear tires and barreled along on just the sides of those two tires for about twenty yards.

"Help me!" the beard shouted, sliding to the right. He dropped the gun, clawing for something to hold onto. The grip I had on his arm loosened and he slipped farther to the right. He tried to keep from going through the window he'd broken with his shot, but the top half of his body popped through with a tinkle of broken glass. Just then Tom flew past me and the right side of the bus hit the pavement with a long screech and a spray of blue and red sparks. The beard gave a short brutish scream as the top of his body was mashed. A second later something shiny flashed at my head and everything went black.

I was only stunned. I managed to get to my feet a little later, before the police cars began to arrive. They weren't far behind us. I even found my Walther. The bus had finally come to a stop when it hit a lamp post, shearing it off at the base. The base caught the right side of the bus, snagging it like a fishing hook. The interior lights of the bus were still on, so that I could see the base of the post sticking up through the side of the bus. It was quite close to me. Another two or three feet and its sharp edges, broken at right angles, would have cut me to pieces. Or perhaps only severed a foot.

I found Tom under a pile of books and helped him up. He was able to stand. He even smiled at me gratefully. Rat-face was breathing and I left him where he was. Little remained of the beard but a pulpy mess.

The first two officers arrived with guns drawn. They put them away when they saw our condition and helped us out. Because the only two doors were on the side the bus had turned over on, I had to lift the emergency door upward on the opposite side. As soon as the officers pulled us through I told them, "One more alive in there. And a ton of narcotics."

The cops looked at each other and moved their hands close to their guns again, even as they helped us down and put us into the back of their car. They held a short conference with the next two officers who arrived, and one of them was detailed to watch us. I leaned out of the car. "It might help if you got Lieutenant Pride down here."

While the officer used his car radio the firetrucks arrived and the street was blocked off. One of the cops yelled at the firemen to keep water away from the bus if they could because it was loaded with junk.

I turned to Tom. "Can you tell me how you got into this before the police arrive? I might be able to explain it to your father a little better."

Tom sat like a stone statue, staring straight ahead. He had a slight scratch on his cheek. The blood had oozed down about an inch and clotted. "It was in Thailand," he said. "I was living with a girl named Mickey. A real sweet thing. She smoked something she called scag. I didn't know exactly what it was. I thought it was mostly marijuana.
186

Pretty soon we were smoking it every day. I didn't know it was mostly heroin till they sent me home and I started to get the screams from not having it. I found a contact and did all right for a while. I could work. I had a good salary. But pretty soon the salary wasn't enough. Then I met Sal, the guy with the beard, and he told me I could keep even with my habit if I did a little dealing." He closed his eyes and shuddered. "God! I've been buying heroin and amphetamines from Sal and selling it to about a dozen guys at the plant who are addicts, too. My old man will *kill* me for that. For a while I was able to buy a load for six hundred, sell three-quarters of it at street prices for the same amount, and have enough left for myself. But I started using more of the shit every week and pretty soon I wasn't taking in enough to make my buys. I've been borrowing to do that. Sold my Porsche. Whatever it took." He looked at me bleakly. "My father will never speak to me again."

"Sure he will."

Pride arrived a few minutes later. I got out of the police car after he had a quick conference with two men in plain clothes who were probably narcs. By now the bus was swarming with law.

Pride came up and looked me over. "Are you all right?"

"I guess so. I got the number of the bus that hit me, anyway."

"That's very funny." He bent and looked into the back seat of the car. "Who's that?"

"Tom Hogan. George Hogan's son. He's a dealer with a habit, like Ronald Cummings. And I'll bet you fifty that the guys who ran this 'bookmobile' are

187

the big operators who have been supplying Cummings and every other small dealer on the peninsula."

"No bet," Pride said. "The shit the narcotics boys have skimmed from that bus so far has a street value of about a hundred thousand. Hollowed out books! Can you beat that? How the hell did you get involved with these guys?"

I told him how I'd followed Tom and why. And what happened when I accidentally got hold of Tom's goods.

Pride laughed. "That must have been some ride. I wish I'd been along for the fun." He sobered. "I'm going to give you to one of the narcotics people. He'll take your statement and then you can go. We'll be taking Tom Hogan and that other creep downtown. Do you want to tell Hogan's father about this, or shall I?"

"I'll tell him."

"Okay. And by the way, as I was driving over here I remembered where I'd heard about the Darby Corporation."

"You did? Where?"

"I get a weekly list of every company that applies for a new business license. I'm sure the Darby Corporation was on one of those lists. Recently, too. I'll go back over them in the morning and call you. Get some rest, Saxon. You look like a plate of refried beans."

A very polite narc took my statement on the spot and had a uniformed officer drive me back to my car. Everyone inquired whether I felt well enough to drive. I did. In fact, I felt surprisingly well. When things start falling into place I usually gain energy

188

no matter how wild events become.

It was only nine-thirty when George Hogan answered his door, but he was dressed in pajamas covered by a long robe. He squinted petulantly into the darkness until he recognized me. "Oh. It's you, Saxon." He glanced back over his shoulder and expanded himself slightly in the doorway by squaring his shoulders and moving his feet apart. "What do you want?"

"I have to talk to you. Can I come in for a minute?"

"Now? It's late."

"Not really. This is important. What's the matter?"

"Nothing," he answered with a defensive smile. "Come in then."

As we went through the hallway into his living room he cast a furtive look upstairs that I wasn't supposed to notice. We sat down across from each other in stiff chairs. Hogan placed his fingers on his knees as if we were matched against each other in some obscure Oriental combat that called for a preliminary ritual.

"What is it? Have you found Franklin?"

"No. I have some bad news about your son, Tom." Hogan threw one of his hands up to the side of his face as if a dentist had just hit an exposed nerve. "Tom? What's happened to him? An accident?"

"He's under arrest. The Palo Alto police are holding him for possession of narcotics. I think he'll be charged with the sale of narcotics, too."

"But that can't be! Tom would never touch drugs. He's an adult. Not some hippie freak on a street corner." Hogan's legs straightened in a jerking reflex

189

action and he was suddenly standing above me continuing his catalog of Tom's good points. "He's a former Marine officer with an outstanding record. A graduate of Oregon State University. A well-paid executive with my own . . ."

"Shut up, Hogan!" I stood and faced him. The skin on his cheeks was stretched as thin as parchment. "You have to get this through your head right now or you won't be able to help Tom. He got hooked on heroin overseas and he hasn't been able to shake the habit. To support his habit he's been dealing in drugs in a small way. Some of his customers work in your plant. I don't know who they are, but by morning the police will. Does Karl Yoder handle your personal affairs as well as your corporate business?"

He shook his head no.

"Then call your family attorney and get him down to see Tom. It might be a good idea to bring your doctor into the case right now, too. What your son really needs is medical attention."

"Medical attention," Hogan repeated dumbly. With a great effort he pulled himself together and faced me with the same aggressive stance that had so impressed me when I first met him. "I can't buy this, Saxon," he said in his executive voice. "I know my son too well. I'm going to call police headquarters and get the facts." He marched to the phone and asked the operator to connect him with the police department.

I left him and went out into the hallway and up the stairs. At the top of the landing there were three doors. Two open, one closed. Bedrooms. A cut of light shone under the closed door. I turned the knob
190

and pushed it open.

Joy Simpson was sitting up naked in the big double bed reading a magazine. There was a single lamp on beside the bed, and she had the magazine tilted to one side to catch the light. When she saw me she gasped, dropped the magazine on the floor, and drew up the blankets around her shoulders.

"What are you doing here?"

"What are *you* doing here," I countered.

She opened her mouth to answer, but I said, "Never mind. That was a rhetorical question. May I come in?"

"No, you may *not*," she said with an impressive show of indignation. "Where's George?"

"Downstairs on the phone." I went into the bedroom anyway. But I didn't want to frighten her so I took a chair in the far corner and crossed my legs energetically. A man sitting with his legs crossed somehow looks too occupied to make a pass at a naked girl.

"I think it will be a while before George comes back," I told her. "His son Tom is in pretty serious trouble."

"What kind of trouble?"

"Drugs."

She bit her lip. I could see her little mind weighing the disadvantages to herself in this news.

"What's it got to do with you?" she said finally.

"Not much really. I happened to be there when Tom was arrested, so I came over to tell his father about it."

"You find yourself in a lot of funny places," she said sarcastically.

"I guess I do. Like this bedroom. Or like a gas sta-

191

tion on Camino Real about four o'clock this afternoon. Why were you following me today?"

"Me? I've never followed any man." But she slid a
little lower in bed.

"Yes, you did. I'm going to tell you a bedtime
story, Joy. And when I'm through you'll tell me exactly why you were following me today or I'll call a
very tough lieutenant down at police headquarters
who won't sit halfway across the room from you or
stop himself from looking at your delicious nipples
when he wants to." Then I gave her a sketchy rundown on why I was poking around InterComp, including a report on Adam Franklin's activities. It
had occurred to me when I saw Joy Simpson in
George Hogan's bed that Adam Franklin might have
gone after Hogan's present secretary and mistress as
well as one of his former playthings. It was a good
guess. Joy had been trying to ignore both me and my
story until I mentioned Franklin's name. Then she
sat up so quickly that she let the blanket and sheets
fall down in her lap. She sat that way while I finished my story, never taking her eyes from my face. I
didn't move my eyes much, either.

"Can I get dressed now?" was all she said when I
was done.

"Sure. I'll be downstairs."

I went down and found Hogan sitting next to the
phone, staring at a felt-covered board on which a variety of his son's medals had been mounted for display. He was touching them with the tips of his
fingers as if that were the way to get at the truth of
what really happened to his son in Asia.

He gave me a small, distracted piece of his attention when I joined him.

192

"I'm sorry. Everything you told me was accurate. I've called an attorney and our doctor." He put the medals aside reluctantly. "How do these things happen?"

"Two ways. Slowly and suddenly. You have to be ready for them in order to be able to stop them."

Hogan gave me the smile of a man who has just been told something he already knew. He rose heavily. "I'll be getting downtown now. Can you let yourself out?"

"Certainly. I'll see you tomorrow at your office."

"I can hardly wait." Hogan smiled sardonically this time, vaguely surprised at his own stab of humor. Being able to make a joke seemed to lift his spirits and he went upstairs at a trot. He met Joy coming down the stairs but didn't pause to speak to her or try to explain her to me. And she ignored him. They were like two experienced businessmen who had just seen a delicate deal blow up in their faces and had decided to forget each other's existence.

Joy was dressed in a slinky cocktail outfit and carried a blue overnight bag.

"Do you need a ride home?" I asked her.

"No," she said with a defiant shake of her head. "I don't have anything to say to you." But she stood rooted in one spot. Her defiance was hollow. I think she would have been genuinely surprised if I'd let her go.

"Sit down there until Hogan leaves."

She twitched her shoulders in a last pathetic gesture of anger and sat down. A moment later Hogan banged down the stairs and rushed out the front door. He didn't notice that we were still in his living room.

"Is the house empty?"

"Yes. Tell me what you want to know. I have to get home."

"I want to know about you and Franklin."

She groaned as if I'd been torturing her with hot irons. "All right. There isn't much to tell. I don't know Franklin nearly as well as that other girl, the one you say he killed." She gave me an appraising look. "Are you sure he killed her?"

"The police are."

"Okay. This Adam Franklin approached me about two weeks ago. He sat down at my table while I was having lunch at the Stanford Shopping Center. Just sat right down! I was startled, of course. He scared me. He's so big. His hands are so knotty and scarred. And those pale eyes." She shivered and scrunched her elbows against her sides. "I asked him what he wanted. He just smiled and pushed a big brown envelope across the table at me." Joy stopped talking and looked at her knees.

"Go on. What was in the envelope?"

"Pictures," she said softly.

"Of you?"

She didn't answer.

"Pornographic stuff? Something he'd taken of you when you thought you were alone? When you were with someone else? With Hogan? Answer me!"

"Not pictures of me. Pictures of my husband and children."

"What's your husband got to do with this?"

"He's black." She looked me straight in the eye with a fierce hatred.

"I see." I thought this over. "He wanted you to do something for him, so he blackmailed you with pic-

194

tures of your husband. Did he make you believe Hogan would have gotten rid of you if he'd known about your husband?"

"That's not quite it," she said.

At last her story got through to me. I looked more carefully at Joy's short dark hair, the palms of her hands, the dusky texture of her skin. "You're black, too."

She nodded. "Mostly."

"Well, so what? This is California, not Mississippi."

She laughed harshly. "Have you spent much time in the executive suites of big corporations?"

"I go in and out of them."

"Well let me tell you something, Mr. Saxon. Nine times out of ten when you walk into an executive suite you just crossed the state line into Mississippi."

"So you thought Hogan would dump you if he found out about you."

"I knew he would," she said forcefully. "I also knew that I needed the salary he pays and the little gifts he's been giving me from time to time." She looked wistfully around Hogan's living room. "Not that it's worked out, anyway. But I have two kids over in east Palo Alto to support, besides a husband who's sort of permanently out of work."

"So you did what Franklin asked. What was it?"

"Franklin told me to keep a close eye on George and to let him know if he got upset all of a sudden. I told Franklin that George gets upset all the time, but he said this would be about our new product System/Sell. Franklin just wanted to know if ever George 'got his wind up'—that was his expression—

over System/Sell."

"When was that?"

"A couple of weeks ago, like I said. Soon after Avery died and George got himself voted in by the board as president. Things were really hectic that week. They have been ever since. George has had so many things on his mind that he didn't pay much attention to System/Sell until yesterday."

"When he called me," I put in.

"That's right. Mickey Iwasaka went into George's office and all of a sudden I heard them both talking loudly about System/Sell. Then George asked me to find that story about you in *Fortune* and get your name and phone number."

"That was just before Hogan called me yesterday?"

"Yes," Joy agreed. "And I put through the call to you. Then a couple of hours later Franklin called and asked what had been happening at InterComp."

"What time did he call?"

"I don't remember exactly. Close to noon. I was about to leave the office for lunch."

"Has he ever given you a number where you could reach him?"

"Never. He said he'd keep in touch with me. But I've only heard from him three times since that day he sat down at my table."

"So you told Franklin that Hogan had sent me after him." I was thinking out loud. "He knew that already at noon yesterday. He must have called you for another reason. What else did he want?"

Joy tilted her head. "Oh yes. He wanted to know if someone named Chase had been talking with George."

196

"Chase? Gene Chase?"

"Yes. That was his first name, I'm sure of it. Gene Chase."

That threw me. What would Franklin's former brother-in-law, a freaky interior decorator from San Francisco, be doing talking to George Hogan?

"Has Hogan ever met Gene Chase?"

"Not that I know of. And that's what I told Franklin. At least this man Chase has never been to the office. Do you know Gene Chase?"

"I met him this morning. He gave me a drink with a slice of avocado in it."

"Avocado? He doesn't sound like one of George's friends."

"That would be my guess, too."

I let the conversation fall off while I thought over the possible connections between Hogan and Gene Chase. Joy took the opportunity to gather up her blue overnight case.

"I'll be going now," she said tentatively.

"Okay. I'll probably see you at the plant tomorrow. I'll want to know if Franklin contacts you again."

"Sure. Where can I reach you?"

I considered all the ways Franklin might get my phone number and address out of her and told her I'd be in touch.

"Fine. I'm on my way east."

East Palo Alto is the part of the city the university people and the big companies would rather forget. That's where the blacks are bottled up, bound in by the artificial barrier of the Bayshore freeway on the west and the natural boundary of the bay itself on the east. I wondered what circuitous route Joy took to avoid being seen going to and coming out of the ghetto.

The train of thought forced me to consider the women I'd met in the two short days I'd been on this case. They were all emotional cripples. Ann Lane, turning herself inside out to become whatever kind of woman her newest boy friend wanted. Irene Franklin, lying in her garden like a lazy spider waiting for a male meal to fall into her trap. Madeline Hassler, so embittered about being a woman that she was determined to destroy any man standing in the way of her ambition. Joy Simpson, denying her own race and cuckolding her husband to grab as many goodies as the affluent society had to offer. And finally Connie, pandering herself to earn promotions for her father and a horse ranch for herself. But Connie was at least working her way back to being a real woman. I hungered to be with her, helping her make it. A minute later I was back in my rented car, pushing it through the night to the apartment in Redwood City.

Chapter
10

I SLIPPED IN and out of sleep like a surfer catching and dodging a series of waves. A gusty wind off the bay rattled the aluminum awning over the front window of Sandy's apartment. I held my left wrist in front of my eyes in the darkness and tried to decode the pattern of green dots on my watch. It was either 2:15 or 3:10 in the morning.

I got up and went into the kitchen and poured a glass of milk. I didn't have any clothes on. My feet were pleasantly chilled by the tile floor. You never become completely accustomed to the way the temperature drops at night in California. I shivered, enjoying the creamy taste of the milk. My throat constricted from the coldness. I rinsed the empty glass quickly and hurried back to the foldout bed in the living room. Neither of us had wanted to use Sandy's bed tonight.

In the short time I'd been gone from the sofa-bed Connie had flung her arms and legs out. I had to push her over gently to make room for myself. She groaned and said, "Pfui." Her mass of black hair still covered the pillow. I laid my face in it and sniffed at hints of elm and oak leaves. She moved, drawing her warm legs up against me. I eased my left hand over one of her breasts and she trembled slowly out of her sleep.

"Ummm. Baby want another bottle?"

I touched my lips to her nipple.

"I was only kidding," she protested groggily. "Nuff's enough."

We had made love as soon as I returned to the apartment from Hogan's house. It had been totally different from the night before. Instead of a long slow experiment, it had happened unusually fast. We made love three times in machine gun bursts of energy, the way rabbits do it. *Bam bam bam* and then fall back exhausted. *Bam bam bam* and fall apart again. *Bam bam bam* and collapse in each other's arms.

Now Connie struggled up to a sitting position, waving her arms and making unintelligible sounds deep in her throat. Her hair slid down over her face. She parted it and peered out like an animal emerging from the shelter of a forest.

"Is it morning? Uggh!" She straightened her back experimentally. "You sadist. What have you done to my spine?"

"Don't worry about it. I'm a doctor of chiropracty. I took the full three-week course. Let me manipulate the muscles in your back." I put my arms around her in a medical fashion.

"My muscles have been sufficiently manipulated for one evening, thank you. Where did you learn to make love, anyway? At a contortionists' convention?"

"No. From reading Shakespeare. I was inspired by his image of *the beast with two backs*."

"Oh God! Is this what a girl has to put up with

when she makes love for free? Literary allusions?"

"I'm afraid so."

She sighed. "I guess I can put up with it." She looked around into the dark corners of the living room. "Your friend Sandy will be back tomorrow."

"Yes."

"I'm sorry about that. I've become kind of attached to this place."

"Maybe she'll sublet it to us."

Connie's body stiffened just slightly against me. "What are we going to do when your case is over? I mean, what are you and I going to do? About each other."

"Why don't you come down to Los Angeles with me for a while."

"For a while? What does that mean?"

"It just means I'm not trying to pin you down. We've known each other for about thirty hours. That isn't very long. If you come down to Los Angeles with me we can get to know each other."

"You mean we can shack up for a couple of months," she said in a biting whisper.

"No." I made a half turn in bed and faced her. "It might not be a couple of months. We might get tired of each other sooner than that. Or it might last longer than two months. Maybe forever."

"I like to know where I stand," she grumbled.

"You knew where you stood with your father's commanding officers. You knew where you stood with your husband and George Hogan and Len Compton. What good did it do you?"

She nuzzled down against my chest. "Sorry, Mike. You're right about that. What's the use of knowing where you stand if it's a rotten place to

201

stand? Let's just wing it and see what happens, like we've been doing. I can close up my house as soon as you finish your case and put everything I need into two suitcases. When do you think you'll be through here? Are you close to catching up with Franklin?"

"Yes. I have a feeling everything will be wrapped up tomorrow."

"Good!" Connie gave me a quick fierce hug. "I'm anxious to get moving. Where do you live exactly?"

"I have a small house on the Pacific Coast Highway between Malibu and Ventura. It's not right on the beach; I'm on the other side of the highway. But I have a great view of the sea from the front of my house and I can walk down to the beach in five minutes."

"Sounds grand. I'm going to like it there."

"Pack all your sweaters. It gets cold at night."

"You'll keep me warm."

We fell silent, each imagining the future in our own way. I burrowed down into the blankets, dragging Connie with me. We slept the rest of the night away gripping each other tightly.

The next morning we rose early because Connie wanted to show me she could scramble an egg. It was fortunate that we did, because at just after eight I heard a key slip into the front door lock and Sandy came into the apartment. I hadn't expected her so early. She appeared suddenly in the kitchen doorway, holding a bright orange suitcase in one hand and a nylon garment bag over her other arm. Her purse was tucked under her chin and a key case dangled from between her teeth.

When she saw us her mouth opened and the keys and purse fell to the floor with a clatter. "My God, you're still here!"

"Let me help you, Sandy." I jumped up and took the garment bag and overnight case. "Sandy, this is Connie Morgan. Connie, Sandy Rawlings."

They lowered their heads to each other like experienced diplomats entering a series of difficult negotiations.

"I'll put these away for you," I said, fleeing the kitchen. As I was hanging the garment bag in Sandy's closet the phone rang. "I think that's for me, Sandy," I called out.

The phone was for me. It was Lieutenant Pride.

"I've located the Darby Corporation," he said. "They have an office not more than six miles from InterComp. I was right about the name being on that list of new business licenses. The Darby Corporation took out a license a month ago. The name on the license is Adam Franklin, vice president."

"What's the address?"

Pride gave it to me and I wrote it down. "That's out toward the Lockheed space systems plant," he added. "By the way. It wouldn't have mattered if I hadn't remembered where I saw the Darby Corporation's name. Your friend Roger Max called me just as I came into the office to give me the same information. It seems the phone company installed teleprocessing lines at the Darby Corporation the same week they took out their business license. Max is sending the phone company's security chief for the northern California district down here. We're going to rendezvous at eight-thirty at the Darby Corporation. I don't suppose you'd care to join us."

A glance at my watch told me it was now five after eight. "I'll be there."

Pride chuckled. "I thought you might."

I placed a quick call to Irene Franklin's home in San Francisco as soon as Pride hung up. A very young voice answered. It was Mark Franklin.

"Mark? This is Michael Saxon calling. I'd like to speak to your mother, if it's not too early for her."

"Oh, it's not too early," he said. "But she isn't here."

"She's gone out already? Do you know where?"

"No, sir. And she didn't go out. She just hasn't come home yet."

"Who's with you?"

"No one." He went on quickly, "But don't worry about me. I'm used to taking care of myself."

"I see. Well, do you know where your Uncle Gene might be?"

"I'm sorry, sir. I don't. He left soon after you did yesterday morning. Your visit upset Uncle Gene." Mark seemed rather pleased about that.

"Thanks, Mark. Do you have a close neighbor you can turn to if you have any real problems?"

"Mrs. Cantolli next door is very nice. I'm okay, Mr. Saxon. Really." He hesitated. "Have you seen my father yet?"

"No, I haven't."

"If you do, you won't forget what I wanted you to tell him for me."

"I won't forget," I promised.

"Thanks."

I went back to the kitchen after talking to Mark and found Connie and Sandy chattering across the table like old neighbors. The smiles they gave me were genuine. I heaved a sigh of relief.

"I'm afraid I have to leave right away," I told them. "The police have a solid lead on Franklin and I want to be there when they move in."

"He's the one who killed Connie's friend," Sandy said. "Connie was just telling me what's happened. And about the two of you." She laughed at my discomfort. "Don't look so squirmy, Mike. I understand everything except what this girl sees in a weird character like you."

"You're a good friend, Sandy. And I'm really sorry I have to rush away. If I finish this case today, perhaps we can all go out for dinner."

"No chance. I'm working flight 645 between San Francisco and L.A. tonight. I leave San Francisco at 5:00 P.M."

"Mike," Connie said, "maybe you'll be through by then and we can fly down to L.A. on Sandy's flight."

"Could be. But don't count on it." I left them gabbing and drove south on the Bayshore. It was a little past eight-thirty when I found the address Pride had given me. It was a ten-story office building surrounded by a three-tier parking garage. Pride's unmarked car was in one corner of the ground tier. I stopped next to it and Pride and another man got out to meet me. I recognized the man with Pride as Chester Horn, a former police chief of a large midwestern city who lost his job because he refused to play politics with his city's machine. He's now chief of security for the northern California district of the phone company.

Pride introduced me to Horn, who appraised me as if I were a racehorse he was considering betting on. "Are you Terry Saxon's son?" he asked.

I said I was.

"Terry was a fine man and an exceptional police officer," Horn said. "I took a course with him at the FBI Academy about twenty years ago. I was sorry when I heard about his death."

"Thank you."

Horn rubbed his hands together and let his bright inquisitive eyes dart around. "This is a very complicated case you fellas have developed. Ma Bell doesn't like to have her lines used for stealing. I've got a crew standing by to disconnect the Darby Corporation." He pointed to a pair of phone trucks parked across the street. "I'm keeping them out of the way until we find out just who's up in that office."

"Let's go find out," Pride suggested.

As we approached the lobby of the building six other men strolled casually toward us from other directions. Pride wasn't taking chances with Adam Franklin. We all converged on the lobby at the same time. Pride detailed one man to come up to the third floor with us and posted the other five at ground floor exits. He introduced the officer who came with us as Detective Fisher.

The lobby directory listed the Darby Corporation in Suite 305. The elevators were built exactly in the middle of the building. When we took one of them and stepped off at the third floor we found ourselves in a hallway that appeared to run completely around the inner core of the building. We followed the corridor all the way around, returning to the exact spot in front of the elevators that we had started from. It took us about a minute to make the circuit. During that time we passed Suite 305 and took note of the gold lettering on the dark walnut door of the suite. It said:

THE DARBY CORP.
Adam Franklin
Executive VP & Gen. Mgr.

Suite 305 appeared to be a single large office rather than a complex of offices. An insurance agency had a similar suite next to the Darby Corporation. On the other side was a smaller corner office occupied by Joseph Lane, Christian Science practitioner. A larger suite of offices next to that one had no tenants.

"Okay, we've seen the setup," Pride said in a low voice. He lifted a packet of papers part way out of his inside coat pocket. "I have a warrant here for the arrest of Adam Franklin and a court order allowing me to search the Darby Corporation premises for material stolen from the InterComp Corporation. I want you, Chet, and you, Saxon, to stay clear. I'll go in first and Detective Fisher will follow me. You two will remain in the hallway unless I call on you to identify stolen property or disconnect telephone equipment being used for illegal purposes. Is that understood?"

Horn and I muttered affirmations and Pride pushed the papers back in his pocket. "Let's go then."

Horn and I followed Pride and Detective Fisher along the corridor. Pride had us stop about ten yards from the Darby Corporation entrance. He went up and tried the door, standing well off to the side. It didn't budge. Pride then rapped his knuckles on the door. Not hard. Just the way you'd knock if you were delivering a telegram or calling on a friend. No one called out or opened the door from inside.

When it was obvious no one was going to answer, Pride motioned to Fisher. I understood then why Pride had selected him to come with us. Fisher took a thin leather case out of his hip pocket and knelt down beside the door, taking care just as Pride had not to expose himself. He put the flat leather case down on the floor by his knee and opened it. The case was about the size of a large wallet. It contained a number of slender lock-picking tools. Fisher selected one, holding it up and examining it briefly the way a surgeon might look at his instruments, and bent his head to the lock. I couldn't see what he did. But a moment later I heard a muffled click and Fisher withdrew the tool from the lock and gathered up his case and stepped back.

Pride drew his gun with one hand and turned the door handle with his other. Horn drew his breath when Pride entered the office.

Fisher had his gun out, too, and Horn and I instinctively put our hands inside our coats. But a few seconds later Pride stuck his head out and said in a normal enough voice, "Come on in."

We went in gingerly just the same, but the office was empty. Not empty, really. But Adam Franklin wasn't there. I felt let down. My nerves were getting a little strung out from just missing Franklin all the time. The office did contain a desk and chair, a telephone, a large steel storage cabinet, and a computer terminal similar to the one I'd seen in the back room on Century Boulevard in Los Angeles.

There was a connecting door to the Christian Science practitioner's office, but it was locked. Pride tried the desk drawers and the storage cabinet. Both locked. He told Fisher to do his thing. Fisher had

208

them open before you could clear your throat.

When Pride opened the storage cabinet he had to put his hands up fast to stop the huge pile of computer printout paper stacked inside from falling out on the floor. The pile was about six feet high, just as George Hogan had said it would be. We all leaned in to help him, balancing ourselves against at least four hundred pounds of paper.

"I guess we found the stuff you've been searching for, Saxon," Pride grunted.

"Let me take a closer look." I reached up and edged a section of paper off the top of the stack. Holding it awkwardly in my arms, I leafed through the pages looking for key words that would identify this as the property of InterComp. I found several references to System/Sell as well as a dozen Inter-Comp headings. I pointed them out to Pride.

"That's good enough for me," he said.

"And for me," Horn added. "Can I bring my men up here to disconnect this equipment now?"

"Go ahead," Pride agreed.

I put the stack of paper back in the cabinet and was helping Pride close the door when the computer terminal in the corner started working. The sudden clatter of the machine startled all of us. We stood rooted in our places watching the terminal do its mysterious business. We could see the typewriter ball in the carriage race along churning out words. The noise was enormous in the small office. Like several automatic weapons firing at once. Then it stopped as suddenly as it had started, the whole operation taking only a few seconds.

We approached the terminal cautiously, the way people in science fiction movies walk up to flying saucers. The printout in the terminal had been raised several lines above the carriage. There were typewritten lines on the previously blank paper.

I reached out and pulled the paper farther out and ripped off the sheet. After all, there's always one brave man in a science fiction movie who just has to touch the flying saucer. I held it up where we could all see it. The message said:

FOTO CAMP

SAXON GETTING TOO CLOSE. IMPORTANT YOU DIS-POSE OF HIM IMMEDIATELY. WE WILL PROCEED WITH-OUT ENGINEERING CHANGES. FURTHER INSTRUC-TIONS COMING THIS AFTERNOON.

A tingling sensation charged the tips of my fingers. It isn't every day a man gets to hold his own death warrant in his hands.

Pride laughed nervously. "That's the first time I've ever seen a computer put out a contract for a killing. You might say Franklin's been programmed to kill you."

"The damned machines are into everything," Fisher glowered. It was the first time he'd spoken since we came up together in the elevator.

"What's FOTO CAMP mean?" Horn wondered.

I counted the letters in the phrase. Eight. "I'd say it's a computer code phrase. Whoever sent this message uses the code phrase to route his messages into this terminal and to keep them from being chan-neled into someone else's computer."

"Well, who sent it?" Pride demanded to know.

"Maybe I can find out," I said. I went to Frank-lin's phone and called InterComp. I asked for Mick-ey Iwasaka. When his harried voice came on the line I identified myself and said, "Mickey, I need to find out if a person there at InterComp could use one of your terminals to send a message to another computer terminal a few miles away."

"Over teleprocessing lines?"

"Right."

"Sure he could," Mickey answered. "As long as he has whatever security code he needs to get into the other party's computer system."

"And could you tell me which terminal at Inter-Comp was used to send the message?"

Mickey groaned. "That would be almost impossible. You see, the terminals here are all hooked into a multiplexer that takes in all the messages and feeds them through the computer. The way our system is programmed, we'd have a record of a message going from InterComp and being received at the other location, but we couldn't tell exactly which terminal here sent the message."

He began an even more technical explanation but I cut him off and asked instead, "Could you transfer me to Karl Yoder's office?"

When Mickey did that I told Yoder what we'd found and where we were and asked him to come over and make a formal identification of Inter-Comp's property.

"That's just great!" Yoder boomed. "You've done a terrific job, Saxon. Jesus, I can hardly wait to tell George you recovered our plans! He won't be able to thank you enough. I'll be right there. Give me the address again."

I repeated the address but added one cautionary note. "Don't mention this to anyone except Hogan. We still have to find the person at InterComp who's behind all this, and so far he doesn't know we've got our hands on his loot. I want to keep him from finding that out as long as possible."

"You can trust me," Yoder said.

While I'd been talking on the phone, Pride and Fisher had been examining the contents of the desk and Horn had been bringing his crew up to the office. The desk drawers were packed full of oversized Polaroid prints of engineering drawings. They were of surprisingly good quality, considering the fact you get rather poor contrast on a cathode ray tube. I suspected Franklin had used some kind of customized camera.

The two phone technicians had disconnected all the teleprocessing lines by the time Yoder arrived. He identified the InterComp material with repetitious sighs of relief.

"I went right to Hogan and told him you'd found the rest of the plans to System/Sell," Yoder said. There was a question mark in his voice. "He surprised me. Didn't seem particularly pleased about the news. In fact, George is a positive zombie this morning." Yoder studied me carefully. "Also, our plant is teeming with narcotics detectives looking for dope users among our employees and a friend at city hall tells me young Tom Hogan has been arrested for selling the damn stuff. Do you know anything about that?"

"I do. But I don't have Hogan's permission to pass on my information to you. It's largely personal. I think you should ask Hogan yourself. This narcotics business has nothing to do with the theft of the System/Sell plans, but InterComp could be affected by it anyway."

"I will ask him," Yoder said, continuing to watch

me keenly. Lawyers like to do that. They think they can make people crack under their penetrating scrutiny. When I didn't come apart and tell him everything I knew, Yoder said with an annoyed shrug, "I'll go back to the plant right now and find out what's happening from Hogan."

"You can tell him I'll be in to see him later."

Yoder left and a pair of uniformed officers arrived, each pushing a hand truck. Within a couple of minutes they broke the tall pile of computer printouts into two stacks and put the photos in cardboard boxes and trucked the whole mess away to police headquarters to be held as evidence.

"What happens now?" I asked Pride.

"Now we wait," he answered, looking out the window and down into the parking spaces around the building.

"I don't suppose you could count me in on your stakeout," Horn said. His gruff plea had the tone of an old firehorse begging to get back in his harness. "After all," he argued, "this man Franklin has been stealing from us, too, in a way. He's used our lines illegally."

"Sorry, Chet. You know the rules. You aren't a member of a law enforcement agency."

"I know," Horn said.

"There's no one I'd rather have with me," Pride continued. He should have dropped it. Horn was becoming embarrassed. "But my hands are tied."

"I said I understand," Horn snapped. He looked around the office quickly as if searching for some legal excuse to stay. Finally he sighed away his melancholy. "Good luck then, Joe. Saxon, see you around." He stalked out.

"You'd better be on your way, too," Pride said to me when Horn had gone.

"I'm going. If I never see Adam Franklin again I'll be a happy man. How are you setting up your stakeout?"

"I'll wait for him in here," Pride said, moving around the room with deliberate steps. He was showing me his plans the way a stage director would assign specific movements to all the actors in a play. "Fisher will be on the stairway landing at the end of this hall. The other plainclothesmen will be in their cars near the two main exits from the building. When they spot Franklin downstairs they'll let him come up here, calling me on a car phone to warn me." He stopped and put a hand on the one phone he had asked Horn to leave connected. "The office door will be locked. Franklin won't suspect anything until he's inside." He reached to his belt and touched the brown handgrip of his pistol. "By then I'll have him covered."

He noticed my dubious expression.

"What the hell's wrong with that plan?"

"I don't like the idea of you bracing Franklin by yourself. You haven't seen him move. I have. He may be the most dangerous man you've ever faced."

Pride snorted, flaring his nostrils. "You've been off the force too long, Saxon. We meet tough guys every day of the week."

"Not like Franklin," I repeated. "He's a psycho, and you know how irrationally they react."

"Don't worry about me." His expression clouded. "I'm only afraid that Franklin won't show up until tomorrow or even later in the week."

"No. He'll be here today. That message we just

intercepted indicates he comes in at least once a day to receive instructions. At least that's the way I read it."

"Let's hope so," Pride said.

I left him giving final instructions to his men and drove back to InterComp. A cluster of police cars, both black-and-whites and unmarked vehicles, were parked at awkward angles in the visitors lot near the entrance. The receptionist hardly noticed me. She was talking excitedly on her color-coordinated phone.

A noticeable extra buzz of conversation ran through the entire plant. Down every aisle groups of three and four workers from adjoining departments were huddled to pass on the latest rumor. I caught sight of little knots of policemen questioning people behind the glassed-in cubicles that served as offices for production floor managers. Some were uniformed and others were in plain clothes. The narc who had taken my statement the night before was looming over a pale young man who looked like he needed a paper of heroin very badly.

I had talked to Tom Hogan, Herman Zimmerman, and Madeline Hassler. The fourth suspect on Paul's list was William Iverson, InterComp's top marketing man. His secretary told me I'd find him in the computer center. I made my way there and located Mickey Iwasaka hunched over a flow chart. He was drawing in computer symbols and talking to himself in a singsong torrent of technical phrases.

"How are you, Mickey? Looks like you're making progress on that security system Hogan wants."

Mickey's head snapped up. "Hello there, Mr. Saxon. Yes, I'm getting there. What can I do for you?"

"I'm looking for William Iverson. His secretary said he might be in the computer center."

"Bill?" Mickey looked at his watch. "He probably is. He sometimes comes in when the computer operators are on their breaks, about ten in the morning and two-thirty in the afternoon. He likes to use our terminal because it has a few more features than the one in his office. Come on, I'll show you where he is."

Mickey slipped off his wrist an expensive-looking bracelet that was a combination watch and compass and left it on his desk before leading me around a corner and into the main machine room. A florid and rather heavy-set man with long hair and sideburns was sitting at the console, pecking away with two fingers at the terminal keys. He couldn't hear us coming up to him because of the steady whirring sound from the computer. Mickey touched his shoulder.

"Yes?" Iverson said. He looked up and dropped his hands in his lap. I wondered why people had told Paul that Iverson had suddenly begun overdressing. He was wearing what I considered to be a conservatively cut olive suit and matching lime shirt and tie.

"Mr. Iverson, this is Mike Saxon," Mickey said in a voice raised a few decibels above the whine of the computers. "He'd like to talk to you."

Iverson smiled. "Sure. Just one minute." He made a few more pecks at the terminal and then stood. Mickey left us and Iverson waved me toward another enclosed glass capsule office. We went into it. The background noise ceased entirely when Iverson shut the door.

216

"There," he said. "No one seems to be using this office at the moment. What can I do for you, Mr. Saxon?" Iverson sat down behind the desk with a proprietary air, giving the impression of being very much the man in charge of this interview.

"You may have seen the memo George Hogan sent around about . . ."

"I did," Iverson said. "And I'll be happy to help you in any way I can."

He took a peek at the wall clock. The gesture was designed to tell me he was a busy man. I decided to go for the gut with him.

"Then perhaps you'll explain why quite a few of your colleagues are saying you've lost your grip on your job. They say you don't know what's going on in the sales offices around the country anymore. That you sit around reading travel folders instead of answering your calls."

Iverson's eyebrows raised and he leaned back in his chair with a look of total surprise, as if I had just told him a shocking story about a close friend.

"So that's what they're saying about me." He pursed his lips and a gradual deflation of his ego began. Sliding deeper into the borrowed chair, he hunched his shoulders and let out his stomach. In a few moments he turned himself from a strapping executive into a cowering little neurotic. His hands moved with fluttering motions on the top of the desk. His eyes darted everywhere. Finally he let them lock onto mine. The effort seemed to bolster him. He pushed himself back up in the chair.

"I'm afraid those charges are true. I have been upset lately and my troubles have interfered with my work. But I've gotten a good grip on myself this

217

week. And I've made an important decision about my personal life. Now I can get back to selling computers!"

He spoke that last line with the professional confidence of a salesman. But there was still a lot of hollowness in his voice.

"What is this decision you've made?"

He frowned. His florid face reddened more deeply. "I don't see what that's got to do with you. Or George. That memo said you were conducting a security audit."

"I am. There's a security leak in InterComp and I'm trying to plug it. That's why I have to find out what's bothering you, Iverson. Is it really a personal matter or are you nervous about a deal you're cooking up with a rival firm? That's what I have to know."

He looked relieved. "So that's it. I thought George was getting ready to give me the axe or something." He laughed. "I should have known better. George and I have been together too long. We started with InterComp as salesmen on the same day, you know."

I ignored his reminiscences and waited for an answer to my question.

"You see," he stumbled on, "I've been having problems with my wife." He bit his lower lip, apparently regretting his phrasing. "Not with my wife, really. She's a fine person. But there's another woman . . . I've been seeing her for the last year or so. Finally I decided to ask my wife for a divorce so I can remarry. It's taken me two months to get up the nerve to do that . . . we've been married eighteen years . . . and I'm afraid my work has been sliding

218

as a result. But Monday I asked her for the divorce and so it's done." He gave a long, expansive sigh.

"Who is the woman?"

"Do you have to know that?" Iverson groaned. "She works here at InterComp."

"I have to know," I insisted.

He groaned again and sat very still for several seconds with the unspoken words hanging between us. At last he wet his lips, as if to lubricate the name. "Madeline Hassler."

"Madeline Hassler!"

He jumped in alarm. "Do you know her?"

"We've met," I said, just barely biting back the question of what Madeline wanted out of him.

"She's a charming woman," Iverson said, leaning forward to receive the compliment he had just solicited.

"Charming," I agreed.

Iverson grinned. "The travel folders were for her. When I get my divorce we're going to take a cruise. After we're married, of course. We've been planning it for months."

I recalled seeing some travel folders at Madeline's the night before. Everything Iverson said was plausible, except for the fact of Madeline Hassler. What was the bitch mother of the women's movement doing planning a honeymoon with this blustery, red-faced salesman?

"I'll have to confirm this with her."

"Must you?"

"Yes."

Iverson leaned across the desk and put his face close to mine. It was a stock salesman's bid for intimacy and I resented the maneuver. He said in a low voice that invited my confidence, "I'd appreciate it if you didn't tell Madeline that your information about us came from me. We've been keeping our relationship quiet because of my wife and the fact we both work here. Madeline has kind of sworn me to secrecy about us."

I replied in a voice just as low, "I can't promise that."

He pulled himself away from me and stared into my face in surprise. "That's very callous of you, Saxon. You could do terrible damage to my relationship with Madeline by plunging in like a bull in a china shop and asking a lot of intimate questions of her."

"I'll try to avoid breaking any china, Iverson. But I have to get at the facts no matter how that inconveniences you."

He stood and went to the door. Before he opened it he turned and said, "In that case I feel no obligation to help you. You can tell George that if you wish."

"That won't be necessary."

Iverson snorted with satisfaction, finding some obscure ration of compromise in my words. Then he stalked out and went back to work at the computer console.

I still had one suspect to interview: John Walden, manager of new product design. I hadn't forgotten that he had a luncheon appointment today with one of InterComp's competitors. My plan was to catch him off guard just before that meeting. It was a fine plan, except that John Walden proved to be a hard man to catch off guard.

His office was in the same walnut-paneled corri-

dor that led to Hogan's suite. A meeting was just
breaking up. Half a dozen men in shirt sleeves
pushed past me. They were scowling and talking in
whispers. Evidently Madeline's information about
the problems Walden was having in keeping the
costs down on System/Sell was quite accurate. Walden's secretary didn't even notice me standing at her
desk. She had her back turned to me as she bent
over her typewriter with feverish concentration. I
started into Walden's office but saw that he had two
men still with him.

Hanging back from their view I could hear Walden
haranguing them. "I don't care how fast your vendors are! If they can't give us those parts at the price
we've quoted to the product review committee none
of us will last very long around here. Get out of your
goddamned offices and find some new suppliers."

"But we won't get the quality we need from anyone else," one of the men argued.

"Quality, balls!" Walden shot back. He had a
voice reflecting perpetual disappointment in his fellow man. "Get the costs down first, then worry
about quality. Besides, we may not even need new
vendors. Once the word gets around that we're shopping for new suppliers the people we're dealing with
now will cut their prices fast enough. You just have
to put some pressure on them."

"But what if they don't cut their prices?"

"They will," Walden replied. "They have to. It's
up to you to see that they do."

The two men left Walden's office with their jaws
set to hold back their anger. I wandered into Walden's office to fill the void their absence had created.
Walden was keying some data into the terminal next

to his desk. He stopped when he saw me and frowned.

"Do you have an appointment with me?"

"No. My name is Saxon."

"Saxon? The man in the red memo?"

"That's me. Tell me something, Mr. Walden. Were you using that terminal much this morning?"

"Why?"

"Were you using it at about a quarter to nine?"

"I don't believe so. Why do you want to know?"

Before I could answer, Walden said, "Never mind. I don't have time to talk to you right now anyway. See my secretary for an appointment." He came around his desk and took my arm. I started to tell him I'd only take a minute of his time, but he literally shoved me out the door and shut it behind him. He hadn't acted mad or annoyed. And I hadn't seen any fear in his cold eyes that might have reflected some guilt in him. It was more the act of a rude, self-involved man who didn't care what people thought of him.

I considered barging back in on him, but only briefly. It would be more fun breaking up Walden's little luncheon with his friends from the Chalmers Company.

The receptionist in the lobby gave me Paul's office number. I found him in the small cubicle reading a technical manual with a relish most men reserve for *Playboy* magazine.

"Racy stuff?"

Paul flashed one of his sunburst smiles. "These are interesting little machines." He pointed at a diagram that he mistakenly assumed meant something to me. "I'd like to build one sometime."

"I'm glad you're staying close to your phone. The police found Franklin's office and they've got it staked out. We should have some action here today, too."

"Did you find out which of those five people we talked about last night is the sellout?"

"Not yet. But that was quite a group you gave me. Herman Zimmerman. Tom Hogan. Madeline Hassler. William Iverson. John Walden. They each have something to hide. One of them is our sellout."

Paul looked troubled. "There's one other possibility, Mike. I could have blown my assignment. The person you're looking for might be someone I haven't spotted. One of the other fourteen people on the list, for instance."

"No. I'm convinced our insider is one of those five."

Paul changed the subject. "Rumors about Tom Hogan are flying around here. They say he's a junkie and that he turned on twenty people here at the plant. Two men from quality control have been taken in already and George Hogan hasn't stuck his head out of his office all day."

"It wasn't twenty. More like six."

"That's about what I guessed."

"Well, hang loose here, Paul. Something has to pop today."

I made one more tour through the plant and back to John Walden's office. His secretary whimpered that Walden had left for lunch early. The fear in her voice told me all I wanted to know about Walden. She had the look of a slave waiting to be whipped. I could hardly wait to see Walden again.

A few minutes later I was slightly surprised to

pass Herman Zimmerman hurrying down one of the aisles on the manufacturing floor. He was in a deep conversation with another man and almost didn't notice me.

"Mr. Zimmerman? Mike Saxon."

"What?"

"We met last night at your home."

He seemed ill at ease and neglected to introduce the man with him. His colleague was about ten years younger than Zimmerman. I guessed he was the assistant controller Paul had mentioned.

"Certainly," Zimmerman said. "Good to see you again."

"How is Mrs. Zimmerman today?"

"Better," he replied cryptically, looking even more uncomfortable. "I just came in to tie up a few last details before beginning my leave of absence. I'm in a bit of a hurry now, in fact. So if you'll excuse me . . ."

"Sure. Just one question first. Did you happen to be in your office and using your terminal at about eight forty-five this morning?"

"Eight forty-five?" Zimmerman repeated. He made something of a show of cocking his head and thinking back about it. "No. I was in a meeting with some of my staff then."

Zimmerman's colleague spoke up for the first time. "No, sir. The meeting started at nine."

Zimmerman glared at him and said, "That's right. It did. I stand corrected."

"And you were on the terminal just before the meeting. I started into your office about a quarter to nine to ask a question and saw you were busy." The younger man was transparently pleased at being able to contradict his boss. Paul was right. He was quite bitter about having to take up the slack during Zimmerman's leave.

"All right. All right. Does it matter?" Zimmerman demanded.

"It might," I said.

Zimmerman told me again that he was in a rush and hurried away.

Last night I had put his name at the bottom of my list of suspects. I shouldn't have done that, I now realized. I'd let myself become sympathetic to him because of his wife's illness. What I should have been thinking about was the tremendous costs involved in dying. A woman slowly wasting away with leukemia needs special treatments, periodic tests, constant medication, and finally a long lingering terminal stay in a hospital. That can cost thousands, even if you're decently insured. And most companies don't carry your hospitalization when you're on a leave of absence. I couldn't help speculating that Zimmerman might have sold out InterComp to get cash to take care of his wife.

I had plenty of time to make John Walden's luncheon meeting at the Blue Boar, so I dropped by Madeline's office. She was standing in the doorway talking to a man who had a roll of blueprints under one arm and a sheaf of drawings in his other hand. This seemed to be my day for eavesdropping. I stopped a few feet away and listened to their conversation. She was giving him instructions about preparing for a meeting. She rattled off names of people to call and items for the agenda with a dizzying speed. When the fellow broke in to ask her to repeat one of the agenda items she cut him off with a sarcastic remark about his memory.

He left a moment later with a hangdog look. I caught a brief flash of malicious delight on Madeline's face. Then she saw me standing there and switched to a more businesslike expression. "Saxon. I didn't expect to see you this morning. Come into my office."

I followed her into a bare, windowless room. The grey walls were unadorned with artwork and there were no personal objects on her steel desk, like flower vases or family pictures or empty coffee cups. I've seen prison cells that looked more homey. The warmest thing in the room was her computer terminal.

"When do they send in the cask of Amontillado?" I asked, sitting down in a narrow chair that was twice as uncomfortable as it looked.

She glanced around disinterestedly. "It's functional." But her eyes lit up as she said, "Tell me what happened to Tom Hogan last night. It's all over the plant that he's been arrested for selling drugs."

I didn't like Madeline's insatiable appetite for bad news, but I still needed her cooperation. So I said, "That's true. The people he was selling to work here at InterComp."

"Who are they?" Her lips smacked obscenely as she asked the question.

"I have no idea. But the police are here so I'm sure you'll know before the end of the day."

"Christ, what a mess," she said with delight. "The board of directors will crucify George for this."

"Not if System/Sell works out," I suggested.

"Have you seen John Walden this morning," she asked with a sly look.

226

"Yes. I'd say you're right. He's having problems."

"*Big* problems. He'll never make his cost estimates now. A general rise in plastics prices was announced this morning."

"That sounds very promising for you, Madeline. But I didn't come in to gloat with you over Walden's plight. I want to know about you and Bill Iverson. Is it true that you two are going to be married when he gets his divorce?"

I certainly accomplished my goal of dampening Madeline's ghoulish glee. She rocked back as if I'd slapped her.

"Who told you Iverson is divorcing his wife?"

"He did. He says he's doing it so he can marry you."

Madeline reached for her phone and dialed an inter-plant number. "Bill? This is Madeline. Come to my office right now. *I don't care who's with you.* Get over here!"

She slammed down the receiver and gave me a poisonous stare. "What else did that fat-mouthed fool tell you?"

"That the two of you are planning a honeymoon trip together as soon as he gets the divorce. I seem to recall seeing a stack of travel folders in your apartment last night, Madeline."

"We talked about a trip," she admitted, shifting her large body impatiently. "But I never told him I'd marry him. I don't know where he got such an idea."

"Have you been sleeping with him?"

"Yes," she answered in a rush, "but that couldn't be the reason he asked his wife for a divorce. I don't think Bill even enjoyed it. Behind all that sales-

227

man's bluster he's too passive. If I wanted to marry a man I'd pick one who could at least give me a good screwing."

"Why have you been seeing Iverson if you don't care for him?"

Madeline stood up and paced in a tight circle behind her desk. "Bill is George Hogan's closest friend. They joined the company at the same time and George has always pushed Bill into better jobs. That's the only reason Bill has made it as far in the company as he has. He's really a very weak man. But George tells Bill everything, and it's been obvious for a long time that George would someday step into Arthur Avery's job. I've been seeing Bill mainly as a way to keep tuned in to George's thinking."

"What's the matter? Couldn't you get George himself into bed with you?"

She almost got mad about that, but changed her mind. Instead she opted for pure honesty. "No, I couldn't. Though I sure as hell tried. But George likes them a little younger than me, and a little less hefty." She said this with contempt, her bared teeth showing behind her lips.

Iverson appeared in the doorway. "What's wrong, Madeline?"

"Come in and close that damned door," she snapped. For the first time we both realized that Madeline's secretary might have heard our conversation. I hoped she had. If Madeline's maneuvers became more widely known she'd have a much tougher time completing her climb to the top of the company.

"Where the hell did you get the idea I was going to marry you?" she demanded of Iverson as soon as he

228

closed the door.

Iverson looked at her with an uncomprehending frown. "Madeline, we've been talking about it for months."

"I haven't even been *out* with you for the last two months."

"But I told you we'd have to stop seeing each other until the divorce. Or at least until Pam and I separated. And she's going to Nevada tomorrow." Iverson turned to me with a pleading noise, begging me to confirm his wife's imminent departure.

"But we never talked about *marriage*," Madeline insisted.

"Of course we did," Iverson answered just as insistently. "We even planned our honeymoon trip." Like an insurance salesman following through on a canned pitch, Iverson drew a travel folder from his coat pocket.

"A *trip*," Madeline said, painstakingly emphasizing the second word with a kind of crazy desperation. "Not a *honeymoon* trip."

"This is the love scene I came in on," I told them. "If you need a best man, don't look me up." I went out, leaving them arguing in louder and louder tones.

CHAPTER
11

THE BLUE BOAR is one of those dark expensive restaurants where businessmen love to have lunch. The food is awful but it has exposed beams running across the ceiling, padded booths, and the light is so bad you don't have to keep up a facade of smiling interest in your companions. The restaurant is divided into three large main rooms all served by the same roaring fireplace set in big flagstones in the center of the building. Along the side of one of the big rooms are several smaller dining rooms reserved for private luncheons.

I found John Walden in one of the private rooms, sipping martinis with three other men. Their table was set at one end of the room, but they were standing together at the opposite end chatting and blowing cigarette smoke. The men with Walden were like him—tall and sleek, with cat eyes that gleamed in the subdued light. A younger executive hovered nearby to freshen drinks and light cigarettes and he tried to block my way as I approached the group. I pushed him aside and went up to Walden.

"Hello again, Walden. I'd like that little chat with you now, if it's convenient."

He stared at me as if I'd just exposed myself.

"Not now, Saxon," he said with a quiet throb of anger. "I told you to see my secretary for an appointment." He turned away from me with the arrogance of a man accustomed to having unwanted visitors slink away nursing their wounds.

I heard one of the men standing with Walden say behind his hand, "One of John's vendors, I imagine. These fellows get pretty hungry."

"When I get hungry I eat vice presidents," I said rather loudly. Their heads snapped and they looked alternately at me and Walden. They weren't used to being spoken to loudly and they expected Walden to handle me. If he couldn't handle me, they wanted to know that, too. That would mean he didn't belong in their league.

I'd have liked to stand there like a tree taking root and see just what Walden would do about me, but unfortunately I needed his conversation more than his blood. So instead I said in a quieter voice, "I'll wait in the bar, Walden. Sorry to intrude, gentlemen."

I went to the bar and ordered a Jack Daniel's and water. A moment later Walden slid onto the neighboring stool.

"What the hell are you doing here?" he swore. "This is a private business meeting, Saxon. You have no right barging in. I've told you twice now to see my secretary for an appointment. If I have to tell you that again you'll be looking for a job with the rest of the bums down on Third Street."

"I don't look for work, Walden. People work for me. About fifteen hundred people, in fact. And if you don't begin cooperating with me right now I'll see that *you* never work in the data processing industry again. It would take me about a month to ruin your reputation, plus five or ten thousand dollars spread around among the right people. But it just might be worth that to me."

He looked me over carefully and realized I wasn't bluffing. He'd underestimated me and he knew it.

"I'll have a vodka martini on the rocks," he said to the bartender. "Okay, Saxon. What do you want?"

"Why are you having lunch with those fat cats from the Chalmers Company?"

He began a lie, then changed his mind. "They're considering me for a job. Quite a big job, in fact. Vice president in charge of systems design."

"And what are you supposed to give them in return?"

"Come again?"

"Don't bullshit me, Walden. They're giving you a big job and you're turning over to them the plans for System/Sell."

Walden looked astonished. "That's not true!"

"Prove it."

He rolled his head on his long neck and sighed heavily. "How am I supposed to prove I'm *not* selling out InterComp. Hell, I could have peddled designs a dozen times in the four years I've worked there and I haven't. Why would I do that now?"

"System/Sell promises to be a big money maker. And Chalmers manufactures a similar product."

"Sure they do. So do twenty other manufacturers." Walden snapped his fingers and pulled out his wallet. "Maybe this will convince you." He took out a white card. The card had dates and figures typed on it and had been sealed with clear plastic in

233

one of those seal-it-yourself machines. The card looked quite old. It might have been in Walden's wallet for years.

"I typed up this card fifteen years ago when I graduated from college," Walden said. "It's a blueprint for my career. A list of my personal goals in life. Take a look."

He passed it over as he might handle a family relic that couldn't be replaced. I looked at some of the dates. They were bracketed in three-year periods starting fifteen years ago with sums of money listed next to each period of years . . . "1966-$30,000 . . . 1969-$35,000 . . . 1972-$42,000 . . ." and so on into the future. The list stopped at 1982 and $100,000.

"When I got out of college I drew up these goals. I wanted to project exactly how much money I could make during my career. I was right on schedule until the bear market hit everyone two years ago, and the only way I can make it up now is to jump from Inter-Comp to another company. I switch companies about every three years anyway. That's the only way to get ahead in this business. You can look that up in my personnel record. I've been with InterComp almost four years now and I've *got* to make my move. That's why I'm seeing the Chalmers people today. Don't you understand? I have to change companies this year or I'll fall hopelessly behind in my schedule!"

Walden was leaning toward me, speaking with an evangelic urgency. "I'm only making $40,000 a year. I should be making $42,000, just to stay on schedule. Chalmers is my chance to jump ahead of my schedule in one big leap. Don't you see?" His earnest
234

voice was cracking. "I can't afford to double-cross InterComp. I've spent too much of my life developing my professional reputation. If I pulled something unethical now the word would get around and I'd have a tougher time changing companies three or four years from now. My schedule would be shot to hell!"

I handed him back his card. He took it and put it gently into its grooved space in his wallet. I wanted no part of his card or his schedule. I've met plenty of people obsessed with their careers, but never anyone with such a tunnel vision of life as this man.

"That's a convincing story."

He looked genuinely relieved.

"But I'm just wondering if your desire to change jobs right now might have something to do with the fact that you can't make your costs for System/Sell."

"Who told you that?"

I saw no reason not to tell him. "Madeline Hassler."

"That bitch just wants my job," he laughed. "And she can have it as soon as I go over to Chalmers. With my compliments. She'll have her hands full, believe me."

"Then it's true you can't hold down those costs?"

"Oh, we'll get them down," he promised. "We'll get them down." But I thought he needed to convince himself more than me.

He finished his martini in a gulp. "Are we all through now? I have to get back to them."

"Sure. We're done."

As he slid from the barstool I thought of one more question.

"Walden, what happens when you start making a

hundred thousand a year?"

"What do you mean *what happens*?"

"I mean, what will you feel? How will your life change? What will the whole long climb to the hundred K plateau have meant to you?"

He stared at me blankly. "I have to get back to them."

I let him go.

Our conversation had depressed me so much that I couldn't eat lunch anyway, so I decided to drive over to Pride's stakeout and see if Adam Franklin had turned up.

On the way I reviewed my progress in finding the insider at InterComp. Tom Hogan: probably too busy supporting his habit to work with Franklin. Herman Zimmerman: possibly in need of big money to cope with his wife's illness. Madeline Hassler: desperate to reach the top and ruthless enough to do anything to attain her goal. William Iverson: also in need of big money to divorce his wife and start a new life. John Walden: another career maniac with a frenzied need to succeed.

And the link between Adam Franklin and one of those five people appeared to be Gene Chase. When Joy Simpson told me that Franklin called her to find out if Chase had made contact at InterComp, I couldn't understand his connection with the case. Gradually the idea had occurred to me that Chase could be the man who brought Franklin together with the insider at InterComp. Chase knew Franklin well enough to see his potential for violence and his need for money and power. The question I should have been asking each of my five suspects was: Do you know a man named Gene Chase?

I was disappointed in myself for not coming up with that key question sooner. I'd have to go back to Walden, Iverson, Madeline Hassler, Zimmerman, and Tom Hogan to ask that question and look for a reaction.

But first: Adam Franklin

The unmarked police cars in the parking structure were tough to find. They were tucked next to supporting posts with only their hoods and windshields showing. There were two cars, one holding three men and the other holding two. Each had an unobstructed view of the building lobby.

The two men in the closer car recognized me and let me climb in the back seat. We introduced ourselves and I asked if there'd been any action.

"There sure has," said the bigger of the two, a quietly steady cop named Dykes. "Pride asked me to tell you. This girl involved in the case . . . Connie Morgan . . . was kidnapped by Franklin about an hour ago."

"What!?"

Dykes nodded. "Took her out of an apartment up in Redwood City. The place you've been staying. The other girl who was in the apartment, a stewardess, said Franklin was looking for you. He belted the stewardess a couple of times, and when the Morgan girl began making a lot of noise he twisted her arm behind her back and pulled her out of the apartment."

"Sandy . . . the stewardess . . . is she all right?"

"She's okay. Mad, mostly, the Redwood City police said." Dykes pondered a question and then asked it. "How did Franklin know where you've been staying?"

"I'm not sure." But I had a nasty suspicion Joy Simpson had conned me. She must have been even more afraid of Franklin than I had realized. When I let her leave Hogan's house before me she must have taken her little Mustang out on the street and parked somewhere, then followed me to Sandy's apartment. I had been thinking too many lecherous thoughts as I drove to Redwood City to pay attention to the cars behind me. Franklin must have called Joy just this morning. If he had gotten in touch with her sooner than that I would have had a caller during the night. The thought was not too pleasant.

"Why did he take the girl?" Dykes's partner wondered. He was a much younger man, his greenness still showing.

"He's going to try to use her to get to me," I said.

I don't like sitting still and feeling helpless. My natural tendency to move . . . to look for action . . . was hard to put down. I knew this was the logical place to nail Franklin, but I couldn't stop thinking of all the other places Franklin might have taken Connie to work her over. An empty field in the foothills. A duck blind on the edge of the bay. He wanted me now; I'd become too much trouble for him and he thought Connie could lead him to me.

It was twelve-thirty. I decided to stay put until one o'clock. If nothing happened by then, I'd go back to InterComp and start really leaning on people.

But something did happen.

At twelve-forty-five Dykes glanced up at the glossy photo of Franklin clipped to the sun visor, then back down again. "There he is," he said, pointing the tip of a gnarled finger toward a parking space about a hundred yards away.

Adam Franklin was emerging from a blue Buick. He had Connie with him. She looked pale even from a distance, except for red blotches on her throat and arms where Franklin had apparently manhandled her. Franklin looked just as he had when I saw him Monday. That surprised me. Somehow I'd expected him to be changed by the last two days of running and killing. He strode confidently toward the lobby, a briefcase in his left hand and Connie's arm gripped tightly by his other hand. She moved reluctantly, as if being helped through an invisible crowd of people. Her eyes were darting around looking for a friendly face. Or a cop. Franklin whispered something to her as they walked that made her stop looking as if she was being dragged along. I imagine he threatened to kill anyone she tried to signal for help. He looked every inch the gentleman, escorting his lady in the old-fashioned way. His mouth was clamped as puritanically tight as before and his expensive clothes were immaculate.

Dykes was on his car radio before Franklin took a dozen steps. "Call Pride now," he said to the dispatcher at police headquarters. "Tell him Franklin is on his way up and he has Connie Morgan with him." Dykes hadn't used any code number to reach the dispatcher, so I assumed he'd been sitting with his radio open. I relaxed a little. The stakeout looked well enough organized so that Franklin wouldn't get away or have the chance to hurt Connie.

As soon as Franklin went into the lobby and took an elevator upstairs, we were out of the police car and running for the lobby. The three men from the other car were running, too.

"You cover Franklin's car," Dykes called over his shoulder to his young partner, but the other cop either didn't hear him or chose to ignore Dykes and stayed with him.

The six of us reached the lobby together. A door slid open on an empty elevator. Dykes said, "You three go on up. I'll cover the lobby." He suddenly realized that his partner was still with him. "Jerry, I told you to watch Franklin's car. Get out there!"

Dyke's partner scowled but went out of the building.

A scant second after the elevator door closed on the three cops, the muffled sound of a shot echoed down from the third floor. Dykes and I looked at each other. He drew his gun and I took my Walther out of my belt. Two men in business suits came into the lobby, saw the guns, backed out. We heard two more shots. Louder. They appeared to come from the stairwell to the right of the elevators.

Dykes charged through the door to the stairwell and started up the steps. I fell in behind him. He took about two leaps and came face to face with Franklin, who was rushing down the stairs still dragging Connie with him. He let go of Connie and vaulted over the rail at the second floor landing, his long legs slamming into Dykes's chest. Dykes let out a big "ufff" and catapulted backward into me, both of us crashing to the cement landing on the first floor. I blacked out for perhaps a second as the air was knocked out of my lungs.

"You little bitch!" was the next thing I heard. My eyes cleared. I felt Dykes trying to push himself up off me. Saw Franklin waving his gun, unable to aim it because Connie had landed on his back like a cat and was clawing over his shoulder at his face and arms. He did manage to stagger down to Dykes and strike him hard on the head with the barrel of the long automatic. Dykes groaned and became dead weight on me.

"Killer! You bastard! You can't do this!" Connie was still yelling and clawing, kicking her long legs and digging sharp heels into Franklin's legs. He finally stopped her by pivoting and throwing himself against the wall of the stairwell, knocking Connie off him. She flew into the stairs with a sharp cry of pain.

I groped the cement floor for my gun as Franklin rushed past me and jerked back the door to the lobby. It hit my right shoulder and stopped. He couldn't get through. We looked at each other in dim light, the recognition in his eyes turning me cold.

"You! I should have finished you Monday. You're spoiling everything . . ." He aimed the automatic point-blank into my face and pulled the trigger. I was twisting and heaving at Dykes when the *pow* of the big gun rang in my ears. A bullet ricocheted off the concrete walls and metal steps. I'd moved myself and Dykes far enough from the door so that Franklin could get through it at last. He saw that and I watched him use a split second to choose between taking a second shot at me or escaping through the door. He chose escape.

With a final heave I moved Dykes off me and patted the floor around me. My fingers closed on the butt of Dykes's .38 police special.

By the time I reached the lobby Franklin was running to his car. Dykes's partner stepped in front of the car with his gun raised and called something to Franklin. Franklin shot him without breaking stride and the policeman crumpled like a cast-off puppet.

I steadied myself against a mailbox and took careful aim at Franklin as he slid behind the wheel of his Buick. I had a couple of seconds while he got his ignition key in and started the engine. I cocked the piece and lined up Franklin's head in the sights. But just then an old Dodge appeared, driven by an elderly lady who had no idea that bullets were flying around her. She eased the Dodge into a spot directly between me and Franklin, ignoring the white lines marked out for her and creating her own parking place out of three conventional spaces.

I lifted the gun and swore. Franklin's car surged forward and I locked onto it again and took one shot as he careened away.

A burst of white dust exploded from the right rear tire of Franklin's car. He hit the brake and the Buick skidded out into the street. It collided with the side of a soft drink truck rumbling slowly past the entrance to the parking structure. The collision made the biggest noise I've ever heard. Both sides of the truck were stacked with heavy cases of Dr. Pepper that jolted off in rolling waves and hit the street like bombs, some of the cases collapsing onto the hood and windshield of the Buick. I ran toward this incredible scene as the driver of the truck staggered down from his cab and sank to his knees in the street.

The car and the street were covered with shining slivers of broken glass and rivers of Dr. Pepper boiling up into dirty, caramel-colored rapids of foam. I reached Franklin with Dykes's gun still drawn, but I didn't need it. Franklin was mostly dead. A dozen cases of soda pop had crashed directly through the windshield, pinning his crushed body to his seat. I didn't try to untangle him. It would have made the last minutes of his life even more painful. There was still a frenzied anger in his eyes, though.

He moistened the thin bluish lips with his tongue and said, "Who was it?" His voice had a death rattle.

"What do you mean?"

"Who was that man in the key? . . . The sell-out . . . at InterComp . . . I never knew."

"I haven't found out yet myself. Gene Chase knows."

"Gene . . . wouldn't tell me."

"Where is Chase now?"

But I was asking a dead man by that time. I turned away, then recalled my promise to Mark. I leaned back in the shattered window of the car and told Franklin's lifeless face, "Your son wanted you to know that he still loves you." It was a useless gesture, but I felt curiously relieved that I'd remembered to deliver Mark's message. Walking away I discovered something dark and sticky on my hand and pulled out my handkerchief to wipe it away. I couldn't tell whether it was blood or Dr. Pepper.

I went back to look at Dykes's partner. He was dead. Two of the three cops who had gone up in the elevator came thundering out of the lobby and took in what they'd missed at a glance.

I grabbed an arm and asked, "What happened to Pride?"

"He's hurt," was the quick answer.

Dykes came out of the stairwell, his stride shaky and uncoordinated. Connie was with him. They were sort of leaning into one another. I gave Dykes his gun back and put my arm around Connie. "You all right?"

She nodded. "I think so. Did Franklin get away?"

"No. But he shot your partner," I told Dykes.

Dykes went outside and knelt by his partner, who was dead. He draped his coat over the young man's body. There was nothing I could do there so I turned back to Connie.

"What did Franklin want from you?"

"He wanted to know everything you'd found out about him. He didn't seem to realize the police were closing in on him, too." She pushed back the long hair and gave me a handkerchief to dab on a small cut at the corner of her mouth. "He was taking me to an office here. To ask me questions, he said. I don't think I would have survived his questions."

One of the detectives appeared at Connie's side. "You'd better let me take you to the emergency hospital, miss. Just to check those cuts."

"All right." Connie squeezed my hand. "Come with me."

"I can't. I still have to find the man behind this."

She looked troubled. "I'll meet you at Sandy's apartment, then. Is she okay, too? Have you heard?"

"She's fine."

Connie went with the detective to the hospital and I stepped back in the stairwell to find my Walther.

When I came out the building was swarming with uniformed cops. I took the elevator to the third floor where heads were sticking out of doorways but no one wanted to come out in the hallway where Detective Fisher sat on the floor. One of his shoulders was matted with blood.

I squatted down next to him. "The ambulance should be here in a minute."

"Great," he said without enthusiasm.

"How did Franklin get to the stairs?"

"Through there." He raised his good arm and pointed to the Christian Science practitioner's office. "The empty office was a phony. Franklin must have rented it himself and put that Christian Science stuff on the door. It was his escape route. When he took the girl into the Darby Corporation office I moved up by the door and waited. I heard someone hit the floor inside and then another door open and close. I went in. Franklin had gone out through the door connecting to the Christian Science office. Pride was on the floor. I followed Franklin and came out around the corner here in the main corridor. Franklin shot me as he was going through the door into the stairwell. I couldn't shoot. He had the girl between us."

Two men in white jackets arrived with a stretcher. One of them went to work on Fisher. I followed the other to the Darby Corporation.

Pride was sitting in the one chair in the office, holding his hand to his head. He took it away so the doctor who came in behind me could see what he had to work with. There was a big gash above Pride's eye. "Did you get him?" he asked immediately.

"Yes."

"You were right," Pride said to me. "Franklin was

different."

I peered at the cut. "How did he manage to do that?"

"He came into the office nice and easy, pushing the girl in front of him. I braced him and told the girl to step aside. I had my gun on him and I told him to put the attaché case on the floor and turn around. Instead he slammed me in the head with it." The stuff the doctor was putting on the cut obviously hurt him, but he managed to keep from wincing too much. "Franklin sent his attaché case flying at my head so fast I didn't even see it. He must have thrown it the way he used to pass basketballs. I seem to remember his elbows going out at his sides and snapping in, but everything else is a blank."

"You were lucky he was in too much of a hurry to kill you. He shot Fisher in the shoulder and killed Dykes's partner."

That news hurt Pride a lot more than the medicine on the cut. His whole body sagged. But he gradually drew himself back up. "The girl's safe, though?"

"Yeah."

"That's something," Pride said. Then, crisply, "The man I want now is the one who's been giving Franklin his orders. He's still in town and will be until he hears what happened to Franklin."

"He might even stick around after that," I suggested. "He won't be afraid that Franklin talked before he died because Franklin never knew who was running him. I'm sure of that now."

"How could that work?"

"Just the way it did this morning."

I went over to the unplugged terminal.

"Franklin got his orders over this machine. I think the person who steered Franklin into this setup was his former brother-in-law, Gene Chase. Chase is the man who knows the identity of the insider at Inter-Comp. He should be picked up right away."

"I will," Pride promised. "And right now I'm going over to InterComp and rattle George Hogan's cage. Have you narrowed down the field over there?"

"Yes. I've got four suspects for you." I told him about Herman Zimmerman, Madeline Hassler, William Iverson, and John Walden. "For a while I thought Tom Hogan might be our man. He certainly had a need for money and access to InterComp's computer codes. But he's out of it now."

"Why?"

"Well, he was in jail this morning. He couldn't have sent that message to Franklin over the terminal. The one about eliminating me."

"He wasn't in jail at a quarter to nine this morning," Pride said. "His family doctor and lawyer got him out before dawn. They found a judge who agreed to release him for medical care."

"I wonder where he was when that message was sent."

"That's what I'm going to ask his old man."

The doctor finished working on Pride's cut and helped him to his feet. Pride tested his balance. "I guess I'll make it, doctor. Thanks."

"Sure. I'm sorry about your man in the parking lot."

I went downstairs with Pride. Most of the commotion had died down but an officer with a legal notebook wanted Pride's account of what happened while it was fresh in his mind.

"I'll see you at InterComp," I told him.

To return there I cut over to Camino Real again. The luncheon traffic was moving in spasms and I soon found myself stopped in a tangled jam of cars near the California Street intersection. A sign across the street caught my eye:

Gumper Bros. Hardware
Est. 1904

The name was familiar enough to bother me. Then I recalled Gene Chase's anger when Mark Franklin relayed a phone message from Gumper Brothers about a package arriving for him. The coincidence was too great to resist. I worked my way to the right lane and parked and went across the street.

In a world that's moving at an insane rate, Gumper Brothers Hardware was an oasis of sanity. The old wood floor creaked under my steps as I went to the rear of the store where the counter and cash register were located. I passed bins of carefully separated pipe joints, nails, screws, bolts, electric cords, wrenches, washers, sockets, rubber tubing, rope. Pungent aromas of sawdust and epoxy and cement and metal shavings mingled in my nostrils. Prices had been marked in pencil by a careful hand on white tags attached to each bin. A man who looked to be in his eighties was stacking heavy bags of fertilizer with a slow ease. He stopped his work and came up to the counter to greet me.

"Well, sir, what can I do for ya?" He placed both hands palms down on the counter and gave me his complete attention.

"Good afternoon. My name is Michael Saxon . . ."

248

"John Gumper."

We shook hands solemnly.

"I'm a private investigator, Mr. Gumper. I'd like to know . . ."

"You don't say!" Gumper's jaws worked with amusement. "Ever been on the television?"

"I'm afraid not. I wonder if you could tell me something about an order . . ."

"On the television the private detective always carries a little card in his wallet that proves he's a detective. I've always kinda wanted to see one of them cards."

"Certainly." I took out my wallet and passed it over to him, opening it to the flap that holds a copy of my license.

"That's it," Gumper agreed. "Just like on the television. Michael Saxon. Well, well. And who's this?" He turned my wallet around and showed it to me. "Betcha I can guess. Your father, right? You look just like him. Fine-looking man."

"Yes, that's my father. It's an old picture."

"Best kind," Gumper said promptly. He returned my wallet. "Sorry to ask you for that. But a man came in here once back in 1948. Said he was a private detective. Looking for a customer of mine. I give him the customer's address but he wasn't no private detective. No sir! He was just one of them car repossessors. Sure felt bad about giving him a customer's address when I found *that* out." Gumper's large pitted face clouded with fresh anger over the old betrayal.

"The man I'm looking for is a customer of yours, too. But I assure you he's involved in something a lot more unpleasant than missing a few car pay-

249

ments. His name is Gene Chase. You called him in San Francisco yesterday about an order he placed with you. Can you tell me what the order was?"

"Gene Chase? Sure. Very colorful fella. Dressed all in green. He came in about two weeks ago and ordered a gross of magnets." Gumper threw back his head and laughed out loud. "A *gross* of magnets. I was bustin' to ask how he was gonna use all them magnets. But I don't like to pry at a customer." Gumper lowered his voice. "Fella came in once and asked me what to use to bind a rubber to the tip of a two-foot length of three-quarter-inch copper pipe. By God, I didn't bat an eye! Just told him what he wanted to know. But I didn't sleep good for a week wondering about it."

"So Gene Chase's order came in yesterday," I continued. If I didn't watch myself I'd spend the rest of the afternoon enjoying Gumper's conversation. "Has he picked up the order yet?"

"Didn't pick it up. Had it delivered."

"Delivered where? Here in Palo Alto?"

"That's right. Called back yesterday afternoon and said he was staying at one of the motels. I had the boy take it over."

"Do you remember which motel?"

Gumper wrinkled his brow. "Nope. I sure don't. But the boy probably does. Let me ask him." Gumper turned. "Gordon. Come on out here a minute."

The "boy" came to the door of the back room. He was a man of about sixty.

"Where'd ya deliver all those magnets yesterday, Gordon?"

"Sunflower Motel," Gordon answered.

250

"Thanks." Gumper turned back to me. "Sunflower Motel," he said, making every vowel stand out.

I felt obliged to repeat the name, too. "Sunflower Motel." I'm not sure how he did it, but Gumper had me acting like a dim student retaking a test I'd failed. I cleared my throat. "And Chase didn't say why he needed 144 magnets? They must have been pretty heavy."

"They're special magnets. I call them nickel magnets cause that's about how big they are. They're powerful for their size, though."

"Where's the Sunflower Motel?"

"Ten blocks south, one block east."

I thanked Gumper and went looking for Gene Chase.

The Sunflower Motel is not Palo Alto's finest. The manager took his time answering the little bell that I dinged on his desk. When he came to the desk he was sloppy, unshaven, and uninterested in me. He handed me a pen and registration card without looking at my face.

"I'm not registering. I'm looking for a friend who's staying here. Gene Chase."

The clerk put down the pen and went through his cards. "Room 260."

When I left the motel office he still hadn't looked at my face. Chase had picked the right motel. I started up the steps to the second floor. A balcony ran around the U-shaped wings of the motel and I could see the door to Room 260 from the top of the steps. It was slightly ajar. I pushed it open with my foot and went in as cautiously as a skier testing fresh snow.

Gene Chase lay sprawled on the floor, a green

lump splashed with red. I knelt by him and tried to find a pulse. There was none. Franklin had worked him over with his knuckle sap glove sometime before he had showed up at the Darby Corporation. Evidently he had been unable to make Gene talk. The decorator's face still registered a resolute defiance.

I picked up an overturned chair and sat down. All the pieces to this puzzle were in my head. Somehow I had to put them together. My eyes closed as I gave up thinking about it and let all the pieces go past me in a series of visual images. It was like watching a slide show with the projector running the slides out of sequence. I saw flashes of Adam Franklin jumping at me with his gloved fist . . . Connie falling from her horse . . . Ann Lane furtively catching her plane . . . Mickey Iwasaka sliding off his bracelet before going into the computer room . . . George Hogan burying his head in his hands . . . Tom Hogan careening the bus through the night . . . Madeline Hassler with a foul word on her lips . . . William Iverson in his neat green shirt . . . John Walden arguing with his employees . . . Karl Yoder looking through a stack of printouts . . . Cecil Mock sipping his wine . . . Irene Franklin stretched out on her chaise lounge . . . Mark Franklin opening a door with sad eyes . . . Herman Zimmerman looking at photos of his wife . . . Gene Chase lying dead at my feet . . . Adam Franklin running fast away from me.

I must watch too much football on television, because my brain suddenly gave me an instant replay on two of those slides: Mickey Iwasaka taking off his bracelet before entering the computer room and William Iverson in his neat green shirt. I looked at my watch and jumped for the phone. I called Paul Avilla at InterComp. He came on the line quickly.

"Paul, this is Mike. Our sellout is William Iverson. It's two-thirty now and that's the time he usually goes into the computer room to use their terminal. He's got a box of magnets with him. Get him and those magnets out of the computer room fast! Lock him in Hogan's office. Pride should be somewhere in the building by now and I'm coming right over."

Paul said, "Got it," and hung up.

Downstairs in the manager's office I rang the desk bell again. He sauntered out after a minute and examined my belt buckle, handing me a pen and registration card.

"I'm still not registering. I just stopped in to tell you that one of your rooms is a real mess."

"Yeah?" The news was no surprise to him. "What's the matter with it?"

"There's a murdered man on the floor and blood all over the walls."

I had the satisfaction of seeing him snap his eyes up to mine before I headed again for InterComp.

At George Hogan's outer office a clutch of executives and secretaries were standing around Joy Simpson's desk pretending they weren't eavesdropping on the loud noises coming from Hogan's private office. I pushed past them and went inside.

". . . my attorney and sue each of you for every cent you've got." Iverson was speaking. He turned on George Hogan, who sat befuddled behind his desk. "I'm especially disappointed in you, George. We've been friends too long for you to treat me this way."

"You counted on that, didn't you, Iverson," I said.

He turned and came at me with a fist raised. "I knew you caused this!" he shouted. Paul Avilla, Pride, and Mickey Iwasaka, who had been standing in a half circle around Iverson, grabbed him and forced him down into a chair.

"I'm glad you're finally here," Hogan said to me. "Bill is right. You'd better have a good reason for telling Mr. Avilla to drag Bill out of the computer center like a criminal."

I turned to Paul. "Did he have the magnets?"

"Yes. Mickey has them now."

Mickey handed me a briefcase with Iverson's initials on it. "He had them in this," Mickey said. "He was scattering them in our tape library when we found him."

I opened the case and dumped the contents on Hogan's desk. The small magnets spilled everywhere. I picked one up and put it about two inches from a metal letter opener on Hogan's desk. The opener jumped and clamped itself to the magnet.

"I don't understand," Pride said impatiently. "What have magnets got to do with this case?"

"Computers store information magnetically," Hogan said. "A few magnets placed strategically among our tapes and disk packs could wipe out a lot of information." His voice was rising as he spoke, like the volume being slowly turned up on a radio. "If the tapes and disks holding the System/Sell plans were wiped clean by magnets, it would take us months to reassemble all the data. If it could be reassembled. Bill, you know better than to take magnets into a computer room! You must have been deliberately trying to destroy data!"

254

"I demand to see my attorney," Iverson said stiffly.

Pride stepped forward then and made his policeman's speech about rights. Iverson tried to ignore him.

When Pride was finished, Mickey said to Hogan, "The tapes and disks he was trying to wipe clean were the System/Sell files. He only ruined a couple of them before Mr. Avilla stopped him. Another fifteen minutes, though, and we'd have been in trouble." He asked me, "How did you know that magnets could destroy computerized information, Mr. Saxon?"

"I saw you take off that combination watch and compass you wear before going into the computer room this morning, Mickey. It occurred to me a few minutes ago that you probably take it off whenever you go into the computer room because a highly magnetic object like a compass might affect a computer."

"Why did you do this?" Hogan asked Iverson plaintively.

Iverson again demanded to see his attorney.

"You will," Pride promised, giving me a look that said he hoped I had some more substantial evidence against Iverson.

"You can't hold me for anything except destruction of private property," Iverson said, catching Pride's look.

"I think you can be held for much more than that," I said. "If not, we can always turn Adam Franklin loose on you."

"Who?" Iverson asked too quickly. He should have ignored the remark.

"Adam Franklin," I repeated. "You know him better by the code name you gave him. FOTO CAMP. Do you want to see how his code name is used?" I went behind Hogan's desk. "How do you get this damn thing going?"

Hogan, puzzled, fingered a few keys on the terminal. I bent down and typed the words FOTO CAMP, followed by the phone number at the Darby Corporation. Nothing came on the screen because the terminal had been disconnected by the phone people at the office. But Iverson couldn't see the screen from where he sat.

"Okay. We're on line," I said. "Now I'll send a message to FOTO CAMP. I think I'll say: DISPOSE OF WILLIAM IVERSON IMMEDIATELY."

Before I could finish typing out those words Iverson leaped up, screaming, "Don't! Franklin is an animal! He'll kill me!"

"You said you didn't know the man," Pride reminded him.

Iverson's green shirt was becoming patched with dark stains of sweat. He slumped down.

"It doesn't matter," I explained. "The terminal at the Darby office was disconnected right after you sent your last message this morning. The one ordering Franklin to kill me. I couldn't turn Franklin loose on you anyway. He's dead. This was just my way of getting even with you for that. I had quite a scare watching my own death warrant being delivered by a computer."

"I don't know what you're talking about," Iverson countered.

"We also found all the plans to System/Sell that you and Franklin stole," Pride said. "Your scheme failed."

"What scheme?" Iverson said, persisting in his role as an innocent man.

"Getting Gene Chase to recruit Franklin to do the dirty work—like seducing Ann Lane into working the terminals to pull System/Sell plans out of Inter-Comp's computer and then killing her when the police started closing in. Like killing Arthur Avery. Why did you kill Avery, by the way?"

Iverson sat stonelike, staring straight ahead past Hogan.

At last, with a tired sigh, Pride moved to Iverson's side. "We'll finish this after you're booked, Iverson."

"Give me one more minute," I said.

Pride looked skeptical.

"Iverson," I went on. "There's been one more development you don't know about. Neither do you, lieutenant. Gene Chase was murdered by Franklin earlier today. I just found his body in a motel room."

Iverson looked up in complete horror. With a long moaning sound he threw himself to the floor like a wounded animal and began rolling and twisting and crying. The animal image was so strong Hogan jumped up and stepped into a corner as though he feared being bitten on the ankle.

"I have some work . . ." Mickey began, and fled.

"I'll be going, too," Paul said. "This isn't my kind of job. I'll see you in L.A., Mike."

When they had left, Pride and I hauled Iverson into his chair. His muscles were as tight as shotgun triggers. Hogan felt safe enough to go back to his executive chair and we all gazed in different directions while Iverson finished his crying jag. It took a while.

At last, with a trying effort, Iverson straightened himself and gripped the arms of his chair. "I'm sorry, George," he began. "You've been a good friend for so long . . . But this was something I couldn't control."

Hogan again repeated his earlier question. "Why, Bill?"

Producing a bright green handkerchief, Iverson mopped his face. "It started about three months ago. Pam called in an interior decorator to have the living room done over. It was Gene Chase. When we met, something magical occurred. I'd never had a homosexual experience in my life, but Gene showed me just how beautiful it could be. We fell in love." He paused. "I've always had problems about sex. A psychiatrist once told me that's why I became a salesman; the act of closing a sale is my substitute for seducing a woman. Anyway, I felt fulfilled with Gene. I asked Pam for a divorce without telling her why. Just that I was fed up. She's been fed up with me for quite a few years anyway, so the divorce was all right with her."

"But why all the killing, Bill?" Hogan broke in. "And why did you try to steal the System/Sell plans?"

"I was forced into that," Iverson argued. "One night Arthur Avery saw me coming out of a motel with Gene. He found out what was going on and asked for my resignation. You know what a goddam puritan he was! Arthur told me to take three months to find another job. Another job!" Iverson's voice grew bitter. "I couldn't start all over at some other company. Especially with alimony payments on my back. Besides, Gene and I wanted to get away. To
258

Greece. Just lie on a beach together and enjoy life."
He sighed at what might have been. "So between us
Gene and I dreamed up a way to steal the plans to
System/Sell. We set up a dummy company called
the Darby Corporation and used it to peddle the
plans to one of InterComp's competitors, the Chalmers Company. They're putting together a production team to build System/sell right now. They
offered us two million dollars in cash for the complete plans—drawings, specifications, names of vendors, the works. It would be a tax-free deal because
they didn't want any connection with the Darby
Corporation. But they'd only agree to the deal if I
guaranteed them a year's headstart on InterComp.
That's why I had to bring the magnets in to destroy
the System/Sell data. The disruption would have
slowed you down at least that long.

"Gene got Adam Franklin to handle the details,
including killing Arthur to stop him from firing me
before we could carry out our plan. Franklin would
have gotten a full third of the profits. But our only
mistake was bringing him into the deal. He was insane!"

Iverson suddenly stopped talking and lapsed into
a depressed silence. Pride looked satisfied with the
statement and itching to get Iverson downtown, but
I wanted a few more answers to satisfy my curiosity
on a few points.

"What about your affair with Madeline Hassler?"

"That was going on when I met Gene. I told you
I've always had hangups. She was one of them. She
likes to play the man in bed. We never talked about
marriage. I invented that this morning to throw you
off the track."

259

"It did," I admitted. "But you shouldn't have dressed in green, like Gene did. That's how I finally made the connection between you two."

"Bill! You and Madeline were having an affair?" Hogan was incredulous. It was the final straw for him.

Iverson burst out with a childish giggle as a pair of uniformed officers came in. One of them whispered something to Pride, who said, "I just heard about that."

"Let's go, Iverson," Pride said. "I want to get all this on the record." The uniformed cops led Iverson away.

"Saxon, after you left Dykes told me that you handled Franklin while the rest of us were stumbling around with our thumbs in our mouths. Thanks."

"I'm glad you got him," Hogan said. "He sounds like a monster."

"He was all of that," Pride agreed. He turned to me. "Going back to L.A. tonight?"

"As fast as I can."

"Well, you aren't the worst private cop I've ever met," he mumbled. "Take care of yourself." He said goodbye to Hogan and left.

"Coming from a policeman like Pride, that sounded like rare praise," Hogan remarked.

"I suppose so."

"You've done a good job, Saxon. You're all *Fortune* magazine said, and more. Send me your bill and you'll get a check by return mail. There's just one thing I must tell you: I hope that on your next case someone kills you."

Hogan meant it. He was exhausted from spending all night getting his son out of jail, from fending off policemen searching his plant for junkies, from dealing with betrayal in his own organization. Right now he was taking out his disappointments on me, because I was the catalyst for all his trouble. In an obscure way, he probably blamed me for his son's addiction and Iverson's betrayal. I wasn't surprised. In my business there are few truly satisfied customers.

Later that afternoon Connie and I were browsing through the shops at San Francisco International Airport while we waited to board Sandy's L.A. flight. Connie found a tie clip in the shape of a horse and insisted on buying it for me.

"This looks just like Daisy," she said, taking off the plain tie clip I was wearing and dropping it in the trash bin. She paid for the clip and fastened it to my tie and shirt, looking very pleased with herself.

I thanked her with a kiss and we strolled on. The exchange happened so fast that I couldn't bring myself to tell Connie she was throwing away a solid gold tie clasp worth about a hundred dollars. She would have been curious to know where I'd gotten it and I would have had to tell her it was given to me by a very lovely girl one rainy, thundering night in Seattle. So the hell with it.